Sebastian's v(
"Ladies and gentl   ...ve and a half
years, you have had the opportunity to experience The
Witches of Vegas four nights and three afternoons a
week right here at the Sapphire Resort and Casino's
main theater. But today, you will be the very first
audience to witness something truly spectacular!"

Isis' shoulders tensed. A knot formed in the pit of
her stomach. She had levitated many times, but never in
front of more than four people. This time, it would be in
front of over four thousand strangers. Wow,
goosebumps popped out all over her arms and legs. She
took deep breaths, just as they taught her, in through the
nose and out through the mouth. It always helped calm
her nerves. Right now, they really needed calming.

"We are about to bring out a new, young witch to
the stage," Sebastian explained. "She will have you
believing that a young girl can become lighter than air!"

"Lighter than air." Isis closed her eyes and chanted
under her breath. "Lighter than air." Her hands and feet
tingled with each step toward the stage. The magic
flowed through her veins like a steady leak from a
faucet.

"Ladies and gentlemen, put your hands together for
the future goddess of magic, *Isis*!"

The Witches of Vegas

by

Mark Rosendorf

The Witches of Vegas Series

Thanks,
Mark Rosendorf

The Witches of Vegas

COPYRIGHT © 2020 by Mark Rosendorf

Cover Art by *Jennifer Greeff*

The Wild Rose Press, Inc.
PO Box 708
Adams Basin, NY 14410-0708
Visit us at www.thewildrosepress.com

Publishing History
First Young Adult Fantasy Rose Edition, 2020
Trade Paperback ISBN 978-1-5092-3211-6
Digital ISBN 978-1-5092-3212-3

The Witches of Vegas Series
Published in the United States of America

Dedication

To my lovely wife, Sue,
the magic in my life

Acknowledgments

There are a few who deserve to be acknowledged for their influence in my creating this work. For starters, my wife, Sue Rosendorf, who is the greatest support system a writer could ever need. Besides being a fountain of encouragement during the writing process, she provides the first round of proofreading and editing. She is also an amazing wife in more ways than I can count.

I give special thanks to my parents, Beverly and Martin Rosendorf, who have been in my corner since the day I was born. Once learning of the idea for this book, they immediately planned a family vacation to Las Vegas so I could experience the atmosphere firsthand and bring it into the pages of this book. The trip helped enormously, and I also had a great time that week.

Sometimes an idea popped into my head and it needed to get put on paper immediately before it could disappear. My ideas have always been like lightning, one bright flash, then it's gone. Therefore, I would like to thank my mother-in-law, Norma Garfinkel and my sister-in-law, brother-in-law, and niece, Amy, Ted, and Emily Sharkis for their support and understanding, especially when I missed family gatherings in order to write.

Let me also mention fellow Guidance Counselor, Steven Fox. Although we are both part of the same organization, we only get to work together during the summer months. However, many back and forth discussions on Carl Jung's Synchronicity Theory and its conjectural connection to Quantum Mechanics had an influence on how the witches' power works in this book. To think, most people at their job discuss TV shows and sports.

I want to acknowledge the long-gone Hicksville Magic Shop. It was many years ago that I walked through those doors as a shy high school student with an upcoming presentation in a speech class on an interest or hobby weighing heavily on my chest. The idea of speaking in front of a class of thirty students stressed me out, and I didn't have any hobbies that wouldn't come off as "geeky." The man behind the counter showed me a few easy but amazing magic tricks I could perform in front of my class.

The reaction I received from students who never even knew I existed prior to that day was exhilarating. It sparked my interest in magic, an interest that I pursued for many years and with many visits to that magic shop. In fact, there were many aspiring and established magicians who frequented the Hicksville Magic Shop, one of which was the amazing Chris Angel. Performing magic built my self-confidence, and it is a talent I now teach my students as part of the school's performing arts program in order to build their teamwork skills and self-confidence.

Finally, I wish to thank Isis Rivera, Zack Galloway, and The Witches of Vegas for coming to me in the middle of the night and telling me their story. The idea for *The Witches of Vegas* jumped into my head as if the characters were speaking directly to me, telling me about their lives and this specific adventure. It is my pleasure to bring their story to the world.

Is this story a work of fiction? Or, could it be a historic event from another reality which somehow channeled itself through me? If it's the latter, I hope to hear more about this world and bring even more of their tales to you in the near future. For now, I hope you enjoy reading *The Witches of Vegas* as much as I enjoyed writing it.

Sincerely,
Mark Rosendorf
Author of *The Witches of Vegas*

Prologue

~ Based on a true story from a different reality... ~

Six years ago

Isis ran as fast as her body would allow, despite the aches in her legs. Her heaving breath echoed through her ears. It sounded like a car engine about to explode. The large rows of apartment buildings on either side of the street passed at a rapid rate, but not fast enough as she could hear the screams of determination behind her. Soon, they'd catch up and probably kill her in a most brutal way. Maybe if she stayed, they'd have granted her some mercy and killed her quickly.

The bruise on her face still stung. Worse yet, the swelling blocked the vision on her left side. The beating was supposed to cure her, at least that's what they said, but it didn't. Neither did holding her head under water. And neither did locking her in a dark basement without food or drink. "*Matarlo de hambre*, starve it out," they shouted through the door. They meant it, too. No one fed her. No one even brought her something to drink. The only liquid she had in her system came from the condensation she licked off a rusty pipe.

Three, or maybe four days, had passed before Isis could will the deadbolt to slide. She had to work on it at

1

night, and for most of that time, it barely budged. During the day, people were around the door. If any of them had caught the deadbolt moving, they'd have opened the door and done who knows what to her. The hunger and pain made it a taxing endeavor, but whispers of setting her on fire were motivation enough.

The whispers had come from her foster parents, a fact that made Isis' brain want to explode. Who the hell would set a nine-year-old on fire, and one they had raised for the last eight months? Then again, they didn't really raise her. For the most part, they never treated her like their kid, only as the reason they got their monthly check. Still, she tried to make it work; it was slightly better than the last place, a tiny bedroom she had to share with four older girls who kept getting into fist fights with each other. Well, at least this was better until her new foster family discovered what she could do. A temper-driven scream had caused that picnic table to fly across the park and crash into a four-year-old. It wasn't what Isis wanted to happen, and it definitely was not how she wanted everyone in the neighborhood to find out.

Her skinny legs screamed in pain with each lunge. So did her stomach, which growled for anything edible. The vision in her right eye blurred. With that went her balance. Isis hit the pavement…hard. The only thing that came between her body and the solid ground was her right arm. The crunch sound upon impact hurt, but she didn't have it in her to scream.

Despite her best efforts, Isis only made it half a block. The chase was about over.

"I see her. She's over there!" the adult female voice shouted over the sound of feet scampering against the street. The voice belonged to her foster mother, Nikki. Not the friendliest of ladies, but Isis had thought their relationship was growing. She'd thought Nikki was warming up to her. Guess not.

Isis' huffing increased as nine adults—five men and four women—surrounded her. Some held baseball bats; one had a steak knife. Her foster dad, George, kept a pistol pointed her way. Although his hands shook, the narrow eyes and furrowed forehead told Isis that he had every intention of shooting if she tried anything. Nikki held a rolled-up newspaper with a flame at the top.

"I'm going to die," Isis muttered. "I'm really going to die."

"I told you all," one of the women shouted, "and then you saw it for yourselves! This girl is filled with *maligno*!" Isis' Spanish wasn't good at all, but she knew from the tone that "maligno" didn't mean sugar and spice. This woman was their sweet old next-door neighbor and the only one Isis had felt close enough to trust with her secret. It freaked the lady out. Then, she told everyone. No one believed her, until that moment in the park when Isis proved her right.

Nikki's eyes were opened wide. She stepped forward and pointed the homemade torch at Isis. Isis flinched from the heat licking at her face. "Mom, please!" she cried, using the name she had called her for the last few months. It never got much of a reaction, but she hoped it would now.

"Don't you call me that, don't you dare!" So much for the sympathetic plea. "If I knew the devil was inside you, I'd never—"

"Just do it, Nikki, you have to!" George shouted. "We all saw what it can do to us!"

Everyone in the circle shouted at once. Although Isis couldn't make out every word, they all seemed to want Nikki to do the unthinkable. These were people who knew Isis, her neighbors for the last eight months. Now, they were screaming for Isis to die. They actually wanted her to get set on fire while she was on her knees, helpless in the middle of the street. For Isis, the worst part was hearing George refer to her as "it." She wasn't an "it," she was a person, a little girl who right now was scared out of her mind.

The shouting turned into a deafening roar. The flame at the end of Nikki's rolled up newspaper grew, engulfing half of the makeshift torch. She was really going to do it.

"No, I don't want to die, I don't," Isis mumbled. She narrowed her eyes as rage filled her head. The vein in the back of Isis' neck throbbed. It matched the pain that traveled through her right arm.

"LEAVE ME ALONE!" It was the loudest Isis had ever screamed. She pounded her left fist against the ground.

The street vibrated. Then, it outright quaked. The adults lost their balance. One woman fell, while the others scurried a few steps back. Isis darted her head in all directions. The shaking, somehow, was caused by her. It created a little more room, but not enough to escape even if she could stand up. A slight crack in the pavement formed. The ground made a tearing sound, like paper ripping. The crack enlarged. It grew into a circle around her—like an island. Screams and gasps filled the crowd.

The shaking stopped. Screams turned into frantic murmurs. They were shouting words that shouldn't be said by adults. Her display may have startled everyone, but not enough to make them scatter. It also scared the hell out of Isis. She didn't want to hurt any of them. Hell, she'd never in her life even stepped on a bug. The thought of killing anything filled her with guilt. Not that any of these people cared about how she felt at the moment.

The circle of people started to close in. Isis had no more fight left. Her head and right arm screamed in agony. It was time to accept her fate, burned to death in the middle of a dark street. She hoped it would happen quickly. She didn't like pain…

A loud roar filled the sky. It sounded like a lion, but amplified about a hundred times. The pistol dropped from George's hand, as did everyone else's weapons. George let out a loud shriek, then ran as if he were the one about to be set on fire. Panicked screams filled the air as footsteps stampeded in the opposite direction. The fire from the newspaper torch burned out the moment it hit the ground.

Isis wiped away the brown matted hair that covered most of her face. She gawked through wide eyes. What she saw made no sense. A red dragon with a long nose, wings, and a forked tail trotted her way. This thing was nearly as tall as the surrounding buildings. She could probably climb the scales that ran across its legs. "This can't be real," she said to herself, blinking her eyes several times to bring it into focus.

Isis took a deep breath and struggled to her knees. The dragon's red eyes locked onto her. At first she thought it was her imagination, but the others had seen it, too. Isis had accepted that she would die today, but from starvation, beaten to death, or the most likely scenario, getting set on fire. She never expected she'd meet her end getting eaten or crushed by a large red dragon. Maybe this was the better way. At least her death would be different.

As the dragon approached, its body turned to a red smoke, a smoke that grew lighter with each step toward Isis. Soon, it evaporated completely, leaving only a Caucasian man in tight blue jeans and a plain black T-shirt. Isis figured him in his early thirties, just like her foster parents...well, her former foster parents. That relationship was probably finished the moment they decided she was the devil.

"Wow, conjuring one of those is harder than you'd think," the man said in a tone filled with pride. "It looked pretty good, though, didn't it?"

She'd never seen such a thick head of hair on a man before except on television. It was dark brown, wavy, combed upward, and spiked in the front. She was sure he had more gel product in his hair than Nikki had on her bathroom counter. Isis had a ton of questions she wanted to ask him. The first was whether or not he was here to kill her. Right now, her throat was so dry, she'd gladly give her life for a cold glass of water.

The man walked up to Isis and leaned down on one knee. He wasn't fat, but based on his gut, it was clear he ate well. "*Hola.*" He smiled, sporting pearly white teeth. "*Como estas?*"

"I-I don't know too much Spanish." Her lower jaw trembled.

"Oh. That's good, because I just exhausted all the Spanish I know." He chuckled and patted her right shoulder.

Isis winced.

"What's your name?" he asked.

"I'm…Isis."

"Isis, like the ancient Egyptian goddess of magic. But you're not from that part of the world, are you?"

"No." Her voice croaked through heavy breaths.

"What is your last name, Isis?"

Isis clutched her forehead. With the striking pain going through her skull, she actually had to think to remember the answer. "It's, um…Rivera. Isis Flores Rivera."

"Isis Flores Rivera. That's a pretty name. I'm thinking you're from somewhere in Central America? Maybe farther south, like Colombia?"

"I'm from the Bronx."

He chuckled. "Fair enough. My name is Sebastian. Sebastian Santell." He rubbed a finger along the crack in the pavement. "How long have you been able to do this, Isis?"

"I don't know. A few months? It started happening after my birthday."

"After your birthday." His eyebrows rose. "How old are you?"

"I-I'm nine." Isis caught her eyelids closing. She forced them open. This wasn't the time to fall asleep, even if her body demanded it. Right now, she wanted to know more about this strange man who just saved her life.

"Holy cow, nine years old," Sebastian responded. "It's rare that it happens so young."

"I can also move things with my mind. I don't know how I do it." She also couldn't make it happen all the time by choice.

"I know how you do it." Sebastian's grin widened.

"You are connected to a great power that surrounds us every single day. It's the universal energy that gives our planet life. It's in the air. It's in the ground, in the space we occupy at any given time. The energy is everywhere around us. It makes up everything we know."

Sebastian brought a fist toward Isis' face. She flinched back. Her heart beat so fast she expected it to rip out of her chest.

"Stay still," he demanded.

Sebastian opened his hand a few inches from her ear. Her forehead tingled where she had the gash. It felt like many tiny insects scurrying around the bruise. The throbbing stopped.

Sebastian closed his hand and pulled it away. He stared at her, admiring his work. "Okay, that looks much better." He gave her a smile. "I'll bet you feel better, too."

Isis placed her fingers against her forehead. She couldn't feel the raw, open skin. Somehow, the gash was healed. The bruise that had swollen her left eye shut was gone. For the first time in three days, she didn't feel like she could throw up at any moment. "How did you…?"

"People tap into this energy all the time," Sebastian explained. "When a mother lifts a car off her child, or when someone has a dream that comes true, they are connecting with the planet, but unconsciously. Psychics and hypnotists are tapping in at a low level as well. We happen to be among the lucky few who have a far stronger relationship with our planet. We can manipulate the energy around us. Many centuries ago, people with that gift were called witches. I've heard that the term was originally meant to be derogatory.

Over time, though, the meaning changed and the name stuck."

Sebastian put a finger under Isis' chin and brought her head up. "Right now, you tap into this energy through instinct. But once you learn to control it, you will be able to do more than you ever dreamed possible."

"How...how do you know me?" Isis asked.

"You ask a lot of questions. I like that. A curious mind is a good thing." Sebastian held out his hand and made circular motions. A tiny rainbow appeared inside the imaginary circle. Isis reached with her left hand for the rainbow. Her fingers went straight through as if it wasn't there.

"My wife and her sister sensed you. They're far more connected to the energy than I am. But maybe not as connected as you. We'll have to see." Sebastian's rainbow suddenly spread wings and morphed into a butterfly. Isis watched it fly into the night sky. Wow. Isis had to admit, she was impressed with this witch guy. As easily as he created a big scary dragon, he could also make something as beautiful as a butterfly.

"We haven't sensed another witch in years, not since we were teenagers. Curiosity took over and we came looking. We wanted to find out who you are. It seems we got here at just the right time. Wouldn't you agree?"

She did, although a few days ago would have been better.

"Those people may come back. We should probably get out of here as soon as possible."

Isis tensed at his words. Were they coming back to finish the job? Isis swung her head back. No, they were alone, at least for now.

Sebastian stood and stretched his hand toward Isis. "The others are waiting. They'd really like to meet you. I think you will fit in well with us, even with Luther. He can be a bit standoffish, but he's basically a big teddy bear. Sometimes."

Isis stared at his right hand reaching for her to take. "I'm sorry, I can't…I can't feel my arm."

"Hmm, it looks dislocated," Sebastian said. "I'm sorry I didn't notice right away. Let's fix that." A light flickered inside his pupils. He chanted, "Heal the arm, heal the arm, heal the arm."

The tingling returned, now against her shoulder and down her arm. Once again, the sensation felt like dozens of little feet scurrying over her flesh. This time, it didn't freak her out, especially when she was able to wiggle her fingers. "My arm…" She held her hand in front of her face. "I can feel it."

"It's healed," he replied. "We should go. Now."

Isis took Sebastian's hand. She didn't know anything about this man except what he told her…and that he could create a huge red dragon. That part was really cool. So was the butterfly. Besides, where else could she go? Whatever he wanted of her, wherever he wanted to take her, it had to be better than staying where she clearly wasn't wanted.

Sebastian pulled Isis to her feet. With a wave of his hand, he motioned her to come with him. She stepped forward, although her right ankle throbbed, and when it touched the crack on the ground she almost fell over. Sebastian grabbed her by the arm, keeping her upright.

"Take it easy. The others are nearby," he said. "I'd teleport us to them, but twenty-foot illusions take a lot out of me."

"I'm a witch?" Isis asked more to herself than to Sebastian. "Like, with magic spells?" She thought back to all the movies she'd seen about witches. They were usually real ugly and real evil.

"Essentially, yes, although the spells are just how we define them. They're more like chants. Their sole purpose is to help us focus on a single thought. The last thing we want is for our minds to wander onto other ideas while in the middle of manipulating the planet's energy. If that happens, we'd lose the effect. Even worse, we could lose control. That could lead to terrible repercussions. Do you understand?"

Isis shrugged. She'd think this man was playing her for a fool, if not for the dragon that chased away her would-be killers. Well, and the fact he just healed her face and arm with his mind.

"I promise, soon enough this will all make sense. Right now, are you hungry?" Sebastian peeked at her midsection. "I'm guessing the answer is yes. You look like you haven't eaten in years."

Isis looked down at her stomach, or what was left of it. Everything he said sounded nice. It also went against everything she'd been taught about trusting strangers. Of course, that advice came from a social worker who kept leaving her with strangers.

"Wh-what are you going to do to me?" she asked.

"Short-term, I plan to get you cleaned up and fed. Based on that limp, I'm betting you have a few more wounds in need of healing." Sebastian put his arm across Isis' back, hooking his hand under her shoulder for support. "Long-term, I want to teach you the full extent of what you can do. I want to teach you how to move things with your mind…on purpose."

Yeah, she liked how that sounded.

"I want to bring you into my coven, Isis," he continued.

"What's a…coven?"

"Normally, they're a gathering of witches. With mine, however, they're my family." Sebastian grinned. "We will combine our powers to create a new path in this world. I have a plan that ensures we can live freely and flaunt our powers without fear of being hunted or persecuted." Sebastian once again threw a glance at Isis. He giggled. "I can't wait to see their faces when they find out you're nine."

Isis lifted her head. "Are we going to hurt people?"

"No, not at all. We don't do that."

"Are we going to help people?"

"Well…" Sebastian paused in thought. "I guess, in a way. We will be providing amusement in their lives, if that counts as help. I think it does count, don't you?"

Isis nodded, although she really didn't have a clue what he was talking about. She couldn't remember the last time her life had "amusement" in it. Most people just treated her like an annoyance. This definitely sounded better, or so she hoped.

Sebastian walked forward, letting Isis lean against him. "You don't need to be scared anymore, Isis. No one is ever again going to hurt you. Trust me."

Although they just met, she did.

Chapter One

Now

The large indoor theater had a capacity of over four thousand people on two levels. It was a sold-out crowd this afternoon, and everyone was at the edge of their seats. The audience murmured as a casket-sized wooden box levitated three feet from the stage's vinyl floor and hovered in place. After a few moments, the box came apart. The four sides and top fell to the floor, leaving only the bottom levitating. It revealed nothing inside. The crowd gasped, then applauded. So did Isis from backstage.

The Sapphire Resort's theater was huge in both size and capacity. In fact, it was the largest theater in the largest hotel along the entire Las Vegas strip. Part of their popularity was because the seats weren't expensive by Las Vegas standards. Seats cost between thirty and seventy-five dollars depending on how close they were to the stage. Isis always had the best seat in the house, offstage to the right. She leaned on one knee while peeking through the red curtain. Watching Sebastian command the stage never got old. Sebastian, decked out in a black tuxedo, waved a hand toward the separated box.

"Ladies and gentlemen, the beautiful Selena Quinn

has teleported out of that very box," he announced through the microphone. "It is an impossible task for a mere mortal, but it is accomplished through a spell only a true witch should ever attempt."

Isis held her hand in front of her face. It was visibly shaking, not from fear, but anticipation. For years, she had seen the show from the side. Today, it was different. This show was special. Instead of hanging back in her T-shirt and jeans, she sported a beautiful mint green blouse and black slacks. In a few minutes, for the first time ever, Isis would step onto that stage in front of an actual audience and do something amazing. All the training and practice would finally pay off. Tonight, some of those cheers would be for her. This was so exciting.

They even let her wear make-up for the first time in her life, a little bit of blush and eye shadow, for the performance. Isis did ask about putting on some cute pink nail polish. She received the same answer as always—"When you stop biting your fingernails so they can grow, then we can talk about polishing them." Maybe they had a point. She really needed to break that habit.

To Isis' left, Selena sat Indian-style while her sister, Sacha, younger by four years, stood behind her. Sacha laid her hands on Selena's shoulders. The two sisters wore matching tight tan blouses and short green skirts. They looked nearly identical right down to the freckles and button noses. The only real difference in their appearances was Selena's red hair—it was two shades lighter than Sacha's. Selena's hazel-colored eyes were also wider.

The two sisters flashed smiles at Isis. Selena's was

filled with concern, but confidence. It was a promise that she'd be there for Isis no matter what happened on that stage. Sacha's grin simply said "go have fun up there."

"And now," Sebastian shouted from the stage, "Selena will reverse the spell and return from whence she came." With another wave of Sebastian's hand, the pieces of the wooden box rose, and, like a puzzle, came together.

"Get ready, Isis. You're up next." Selena gave her a wink. Isis returned the gesture with a smile.

"Kiddo will be fine out there. She's ready," Sacha said. "But first, it's all you, big sis. And don't forget to smile to the audience."

"I never forget to smile." Selena rolled her eyes.

"You did during last night's performance."

"Last night I was agitated. I asked Sebastian if our new outfits made me look fat. His answer struck me as noncommittal."

"You know the two of you make me sick, right?" Sacha turned to Isis. "Don't they make you sick sometimes?"

Isis just offered Sacha a slight shrug. There were certain family squabbles where she felt it best to play it neutral. Sacha did have a point. Selena and Sebastian flirted with each other a lot. Isis found it sweet.

Selena stood up and closed her eyes. "Teleport to box." She disappeared.

The box lowered to the ground while Sebastian continued his patter. "…no doors on any side of the box, not above, not below. No way in, no way out. And yet…"

The front wall of the box fell onto the stage

revealing Selena behind it.

Sebastian took her hand and led her out. "With magic and witchcraft, we don't need doors."

The crowd roared with applause. Selena curtsied, then trotted off the stage. She exchanged a thumbs-up with Sacha. Their magic proved flawless as always.

"How did she do that?" someone shouted from the front row.

Isis giggled. She'd witnessed at least a few hundred sold-out shows in the last few years. Both tourists and Vegas natives loved watching The Witches of Vegas flaunt their power on this stage. "How did they do that?" was the most commonly asked question throughout the theater every few minutes. In all this time, not a single person figured out that Sebastian was outright telling them their secrets. Well, almost all their secrets. He never mentioned the *charisma* spell he placed on himself prior to each performance.

A deep, monotone voice boomed from behind. "You are nervous, young one. It is useless and unnecessary."

Isis peeked over her shoulder at the tall egg-headed albino man glaring down at her. When Sebastian first introduced her to his coven, the sight of Luther scared the hell out of her. She couldn't stop gawking at his fingernails, which were longer and dirtier than anyone's she'd ever known. Sacha's fake nails weren't even as long as Luther's real ones. His blackened teeth weren't easy to look at either.

Years later, her throat still went dry whenever he spoke through those abnormally thin lips. It took a long time to get comfortable around him. His constant cold stare during her training sessions didn't make that task any easier. To this day, she jumped out of her shoes whenever he barked a command, or a criticism. Still, the idea of having a 500-year-old vampire hanging around was kind of cool, even if he did usually act like a dick. Maybe all vampires acted like that, not like Isis knew anyone else who was actually dead...or undead, or whatever.

"I'm not nervous," Isis said to him. "I'm not nervous at all."

"You are. I can smell it." Luther's cape swung as he spun away. "Concentrate on your power and you will have no reason to be afraid. I know concentration is not your strong suit, but give it your best shot."

Man, even when he gave advice, it sounded like chastising. Of course, he was right—fear was never a good emotion to have when practicing witchcraft. Actually, most emotions made her power erratic, but fear was the worst. Not that Isis was scared, she was just nervous. Despite Luther's insistence, they were not the same thing.

Sebastian's voice boomed through the theater. "Ladies and gentlemen, for the last five and a half years, you have had the opportunity to experience The Witches of Vegas four nights and three afternoons a week right here at the Sapphire Resort and Casino's main theater. But today, you will be the very first audience to witness something truly spectacular!"

Isis' shoulders tensed. A knot formed in the pit of her stomach. She had levitated many times, but never in front of more than four people. This time, it would be in front of over four thousand strangers. Wow, goosebumps popped out all over her arms and legs. She took deep breaths, just as they taught her, in through the nose and out through the mouth. It always helped calm her nerves. Right now, they really needed calming.

"We are about to bring out a new, young witch to the stage," Sebastian explained. "She will have you believing that a young girl can become lighter than air!"

"Lighter than air." Isis closed her eyes and chanted under her breath. "Lighter than air." Her hands and feet tingled with each step toward the stage. The magic flowed through her veins like a steady leak from a faucet.

"Ladies and gentlemen, put your hands together for the future goddess of magic, *Isis*!"

The crowd applauded. A slow, soothing music played through the speakers. Isis took a deep breath, then stepped out from behind the curtain. She could hear the audience but couldn't see them behind the blinding spotlights. "Lighter than air," she whispered a few more times.

Isis raised her right foot as if resting it on the first step of a long staircase. She placed her left foot next to the right. A few inches separated the soles of her bare feet from the stage floor. The crowd let out an "ooh."

Time to make them "ahh."

Isis reached up with both hands, then, like a swimmer at the bottom of a pool, pulled her body straight up. She floated until her hands touched the ceiling. Way too high. Isis pushed against the ceiling so she'd float down ever so slightly. She let her body go horizontal, then breast-stroked past the spotlights and directly over the audience. Astonished faces pointed her way.

"Lighter than air," she said once again as a reminder to herself not to lose concentration.

Several feet ahead, a metal hoop hung from a rope attached to the ceiling. It had been placed there specifically for Isis' benefit. Isis swam through the air until she passed through the hoop.

The crowd applauded.

This was the moment Isis was supposed to return to the stage. But from the sound of chaotic murmurs, this sold-out crowd was digging her. She wanted to give them more. Isis brought her knees to her chest and performed a somersault.

The applause brought her a sense of glee.

Isis straightened her body and executed a backflip, which she paused while completely upside down. From this angle, she could see every single mesmerized face. They all had widened eyes and open mouths. Couples were holding hands tight, as if it was their daughter up here and they feared for her life. Mothers and fathers held their young children while pointing up as if they didn't know where to look.

She took notice of one boy about her age who didn't blend in with the rest. It wasn't his golden-blond hair or his worn-out leather vest that may have been jet black a long time ago. It's not like he looked bad in the vest. She just didn't think boys her age wore vests, not that she hung around a lot of people her age. Maybe vests were a thing. She really didn't know.

What stood out to Isis was his lack of awe. While everyone had their eyes planted on her, this boy was scratching his chin, glancing at every part of the ceiling except where she hovered. Whatever the reason, something about him seemed familiar. Isis was sure she'd seen him before, maybe in passing on the Vegas strip. She rarely forgot a face, especially one so cute with such green eyes…

OH CRAP!

The spell broke. The air rushed past Isis as she went down. The audience gasped. So did Isis. The floor approached at a rapid speed…

She stopped mid-air and hung face-to-upside-down-face with the boy. He looked panicked, which probably mirrored the expression on her face. "Um, hi," she said.

She was suddenly yanked through the air and to the stage as if a hook had snatched her around the midsection. Isis managed to turn her body right side up on the way. She dropped and landed on all fours in the middle of the stage. Dizziness forced her eyes shut. She could barely hear cheers and applause that boomed through the theater.

"Are you okay?" Sebastian called, but not through the mic.

"I'm good." Isis opened her eyes, stood, and stretched her arms to the roaring ovation.

"Ladies and gentlemen," Sebastian's voice boomed through the speakers, "the young witch who defies gravity, *Isis*!"

Isis shook off the lightheadedness so she could take a hearty bow and exit through the side curtain. She stepped aside while Sacha rolled a clear glass coffin onto the stage. She stepped away from the curtain where Selena wrapped her arms around Isis and gave her a tight hug. "Wow, that was a close call," she said in Isis' ear.

"I'm okay," Isis said.

Selena placed a hand under Isis' sweat-covered chin. "Good. It's over now. You did well up there except for that little gaff. We'll work on it. For now, go catch your breath."

The applause fizzled out. Anticipation for the next trick grew. Sebastian introduced Luther to the stage. It was time for the finale where Luther would get locked inside that glass coffin. The coffin would fill with water, submerging the vampire, all while Sebastian provided dramatic commentary. After that came Isis' favorite part, when the coffin would levitate in the air and float through the theater rows, passing each seat. Luther always made eye contact with the audience members. He did this while gasping for air he didn't need.

After giving everyone a chance to see it up close— and even touch the glass as it passed—the coffin floated high above the audience. It then exploded into an amazing multi-colored fireworks display. From the explosion, confetti fell and covered the crowd.

After the amazing display, smoke from a machine they controlled off-stage would cover the stage. Once the smoke cleared, the audience would cheer from seeing Luther standing in the middle of the stage, soaking wet. Of course, he never bowed. It just wasn't his style. The only reason he begrudgingly participated in the grand finale was because it involved the witches' use of illusion, teleportation, and transmorphing. It also forced them to work together on one cohesive project. He called it good practice for their teamwork.

Everyone always left the theater commenting on that amazing explosion. For Isis, she had seen that effect more times than she could recall. She always enjoyed it, but with a slight disappointment that she couldn't be out there soaking in the moment. Today, not only was she part of the show, but the act before the grand finale. Wow, all that anxiety coursing through her veins, and now it was over.

Isis leaned against the wall and let out a deep exhale. She felt a bit wobbly, but proud. It wasn't entirely the debut performance she anticipated, but it wasn't all bad. Sure, she almost cracked her head open on the floor and splattered brain tissue on the audience, but she didn't, and it worked out. She survived, and the crowd loved it. Overall, she gave herself a B. Well, maybe a B-minus. Nah, definitely a B.

Chapter Two

Twenty minutes had passed since Zack Galloway started his walk along Vegas Boulevard from The Sapphire Resort to the Felicity Hotel and Spa, the place he called home for more than half his life. Zack had walked the entire Vegas strip so many times that he knew most of the street performers and the Three Card Monte hustlers by face. He even knew a few by name. A twenty-minute stroll shouldn't have tired him out. Of course, that's if it wasn't eighty-eight degrees and he wasn't wearing his leather vest, which, under the Vegas sun felt like being wrapped in layers of aluminum foil.

What fifteen-year-old wears a vest, anyway? He'd asked himself that question a number of times, and so did a few of his schoolmates. But it was a fourteenth birthday gift from his uncle, and it had become part of Zack's trademark on stage. The better question to ask himself—how many fifteen-year-olds got to perform magic in one of Las Vegas' premiere theaters? Well, that girl he saw earlier did, and she was totally amazing.

How had he not seen this girl around Las Vegas before? Did she go to his school and he never noticed her? Zack didn't associate much with his schoolmates, but he did notice faces when walking through the Las Vegas High School hallways. He was pretty sure he'd have remembered her brown eyes and dimpled cheeks.

Maybe she went to private school or something?

Outside the front of the hotel, Zack's rectangular table was set up, waiting for him. He was supposed to be performing card tricks for by-passers and piquing their interest in The Amazing Herb Galloway Show in the hotel's Galloway Theater. He skipped today's time there to see The Witches of Vegas. His curiosity about the number one magic show got the best of him. Besides, it wasn't like they were competitive rivals. That hadn't been the case in years. There were still plenty of seats available for tonight's Amazing Herb Galloway Show, but to see The Witches of Vegas, Zack had to buy his ticket three weeks ago.

Zack made his way through the Felicity lobby to the theater. It was an old auditorium in desperate need of renovation. Hell, it still had wooden seats and a blue curtain that had to be opened and closed manually by a set of strings in the back. Despite all that, Zack liked the timeworn ambiance. For him, it was home since the age of six.

The echo of tapping grabbed Zack's attention. It came from long-heeled shoes against the floor. Bambi, their sexy magician's assistant—emphasis on sexy— strolled up the aisle. Her skin-tight white half-shirt sure didn't leave her cup size to the imagination. Working the show with her helped Zack connect with his manhood.

"Hey, Sweetie," Bambi said as she passed. "Your dad's behind the curtain setting up for tomorrow's show. He's asking for you."

"Thanks, Bambi," Zack replied. "But he's my uncle, not my dad." Jeeze, how many times had he called him "Uncle Herb" in front of her?

Bambi spun around and threw him a confused shrug. "I'm new here. I'm still learning all the relationships. Anyway, he's looking for you back there." She waved a hand toward the curtain. "I'm off for my pre-show mani-pedi so I can look cute for the crowd."

Bambi had been their assistant for the last six months. Not the sharpest pencil in the case, that was for damn sure. More than once she'd forgotten the schedule and not shown up for a show. But besides working cheap, she had great stage presence and learned her parts fast. She also wasn't bad looking for a twenty-seven-year old.

Zack's left pocket vibrated. He pulled out his phone. After a quick glance at the name on the screen, he brought the phone to the side of his face. "I'm in the theater, Uncle Herb."

"Great," his uncle said. "Come onto the stage. I have something new to show you."

"On my way." If only his uncle would learn to text. It was almost embarrassing for Zack whenever his phone rang.

Zack trotted down the aisle. A larger-than-life landscape poster hung in front of the curtain. The picture featured his uncle as a younger man with a vibrant smile, wearing a red vest. His salt and pepper hair was short and wavy, which contrasted with the gray messy mop he sported now. The face had far less wrinkles. On the poster, large bubble letters read, "The Amazing Herb Galloway, Las Vegas' Top Magician." He used to sell out all twelve hundred seats at each and every performance in this theater. Back then, there were several employees working on the show including stagehands in the back and rotating assistants in the front. That was long before, well, before The Witches of Vegas debuted.

Zack leaped from the floor onto the stage and stepped through where the two halves of the back curtains met. It was like a small warehouse back there with various magic props either on shelves or on the floor. The once-great Herb Galloway was in the middle of the area wiping a hankie across a wooden table. "Zack, I'm glad you're here. I have something new for a grand finale."

Zack eyed the mirror that now stood under the table; it leaned just enough to reflect the floor. "We've done the disappearing act with Bambi before, but never as a finale. I thought you said it wasn't powerful enough to end the show."

"It's different now. I've made some modifications." Herb ran across the stage and grabbed a thick green oversized sheet. He laid it across the floor in front of the table. "We lift the sheet, Bambi disappears. We lift it again, she comes back. But then, we lift it a third time!" Herb's shaky hand motioned to a thin wooden latch across the table's bottom. "Remove this latch and the legs pull in, and the entire table collapses. Now, check this out…"

Herb opened the sheet. Once in his hands, the sheet looked as if it covered something solid. It ran the length of the table. "I set up a wire from metal hangers so the tablecloth would hold the shape of the table. That'll give Bambi cover as she collapses the table, tips over the mirror, and rolls under the back curtain. Both the assistant *and* the table disappear. We drop this sheet across the table. It's thick enough that no one will realize. Then, we have Bambi reappear in the audience."

This was the first time in years Zack had seen his uncle excited over a new magic trick. How he wished the feeling was mutual. "We could also use it as a modified metamorphosis trick, but we'll need to think that one through."

Zack took a deep breath. He could tell from his uncle's sudden accusatory glance that the next question would start an uncomfortable conversation.

"So, Zack, did we make some decent tips with the card tricks out there?"

Yup, that was the question.

"I...I didn't work my table today." The lack of surprise on Uncle Herb's face revealed that he already knew this. Uncle Herb was always one step ahead of him. "I know we need the money and everything but—"

"It's not just the tips," Herb cut him off. "It's also the publicity. You impress them with those fast hands of yours, it sells tickets and fills seats."

"I know. That's why I'm out there every day after school and weekends."

"You weren't in school today, Zack," Herb shouted. "You know they call me each time you don't show up. What's your excuse this time?"

Zack did know this—Herb let him know incessantly every single time they called. It wasn't that Zack was a bad student, his grades were decent, but the social aspect of school didn't make a lot of sense to him. Even though so many of his schoolmates watched him perform, Zack still didn't fit in with a single social clique. It was like he was two different people—Zack the magician on the Las Vegas strip, and Zack the invisible in school. Even after hanging around his table and calling his magic amazing, back at school, a few still made fun of him for being a magician.

It was time to fess up. He knew his uncle wouldn't like it. "I went to see the other show."

"The other…you went to see the witches' show?"

Zack nodded.

"You understand our budget is tight."

"The ticket was only forty bucks," Zac replied. "I wanted to know what all the hype was about. I was curious what we've been up against all these years."

"Okay, I can understand that. So, what did you think?"

"I think we have nothing that can compete with them." Damn, should have considered his wording before just blurting it out. "I'm sorry, Uncle Herb. It's just that you've been training me in the world of magic since I was six years old. Even with all that knowledge, I couldn't guess at most of what they did."

The words hurt. Zack knew it, and the slumped shoulders confirmed it. But they also seemed to intrigue him on a professional level. Uncle Herb was a big believer in studying the works of other magicians.

"Give me an example," Herb said.

"They introduced a new magician—a girl I think was around my age. She was actually kind of cute, in a girl-next-door sort of way. She looked nervous up there, but man…"

"Zack, focus," Herb snapped.

"Right, sorry. The girl flew through the theater. She even did backflips up there. It was impressive."

"We know how that works, Zack. We've known magicians who have done the flying routine."

"This was different. She flew through a stationary ring. Even if they spun it, it wasn't wide enough to bypass any wires that may have been attached to her."

"Stationary." Herb's gray eyebrows rose. "It couldn't have been solid. There would have had to be a way for a wire to get through. It's an expensive illusion, but it is doable."

"But then, it seemed like the wire snapped. The girl fell…until she just stopped falling. She hovered in mid-air for a moment, then flew back to the stage. It looked like a pulley yanked her back."

Herb stared straight up, smacking his lips. "A wire couldn't yank her sideways. Up, sure, but the harness would have had to be attached to something heavy."

"I didn't notice a harness anywhere on her, although it could have been hidden well. They do seem to have a lot of resources at their disposal. That wasn't even their most impressive act. Some of our most expensive stuff, they did as throwaways in between these huge illusions. Even those came off smooth."

"Wow. I can't begin to imagine what the overhead on their show must be." Herb shook his head. "A levitation effect is thousands of dollars alone with wires and set-up, plus the manpower needed to pull all that off…"

"I didn't notice any stagehands in the background, and I was looking for them."

"It just doesn't compute in my head." Herb began pacing back and forth. "Even if they sold that place out every single show, their ticket prices wouldn't nearly cover the expenses for such a high-end performance. Hell, it would barely cover the hotel's share."

A strong female voice made Zack nearly jump out

of his skin. "Then perhaps we could find out the real story together," the woman said through what sounded like a deep accent, which Zack couldn't place. It wasn't quite British, but close to it. Zack knew that voice, too. He'd heard it before, but he couldn't place where.

The woman stood at the end of their stage wearing a long black dress that looked more appropriate on a mannequin at a museum depicting ancient history. She was tall, a few inches taller than Herb, but it could have been the black leather boots that gave her an extra inch or two. Tons of purple powder across her cheeks did little to hide her seriously pale skin. The dark brown hair that hung to her waist looked like long, thin strands of dead grass. She stared them both down through unusually purple irises. Zack could tell right away this wasn't just another crazy fan who snuck in and wanted to meet The Amazing Herb Galloway.

"I'm sorry ma'am"—Herb took a step forward in her direction—"but you can't be backstage. I have to ask you to leave."

"I am not here as a fan." The woman placed her hand and long manicured nails against her chest. "I was hoping we could speak. My name is Victoria Hunter and I am a reporter—"

"Victoria Hunter!" The name rang a bell in Zack's head. He realized where he had heard that distinct voice. "I've seen your videos online, and you're no reporter. Uncle Herb, she exposes magicians' secrets."

"You're a debunker?" Herb asked.

"You could say that is the basis of my work, yes." Her tone offered no apology.

"She's fairly new, and without much of a following," Zack said. "Her videos have absolutely no comments or reviews attached. It's by chance I stumbled across them. She's never seen on them, but she narrates." One look at her and Zack understood why.

"Be assured," she said, "I am not a threat to you. In fact, I believe we can be of assistance to one another."

"I don't know you," Herb roared, "but I know your kind. You're all just a bunch of failed magicians trying to scrounge a living by ruining the rest of us who have achieved success. I won't let you come in here and destroy my reputation." Herb took her by the arm and attempted to move her.

Victoria's body didn't budge. "Your reputation isn't all that meaningful anymore, Mister Galloway," she said with a demeaning brashness. "Exposing you would not accomplish a thing for me. Needless to say, I am not here for you or your show. In fact, my reason for being here in Las Vegas could be to your benefit."

"We can't trust her," Zack whispered.

"Miss Hunter," Herb replied. "Whatever it is you're selling to benefit us, I seriously doubt we'd be interested."

"Oh, I believe you would be quite interested. I wouldn't be here on your stage otherwise."

Victoria's statement didn't make much sense to Zack. How could someone who makes a living ruining magicians be a benefit to them? It suddenly hit him. "You're here to expose The Witches of Vegas, aren't you?"

Victoria smiled. "I am here to expose The Witches of Vegas."

Herb took a step back. He eyed her cautiously, but curiously.

Zack had seen that look in his uncle's face many times, whenever he was contemplating a new idea. "You're not seriously considering working with her, are you?" Zack asked.

"It wouldn't hurt to hear her out." Herb looked toward Victoria. "What do you have in mind?"

Chapter Three

Once the dizziness subsided, Isis strutted around the backstage dressing room filled with pride. She had spent years watching the others flaunt their magic in front of a roaring audience, then celebrating their performances while she could only use her own magic in practice behind closed doors. All she kept hearing was how she wasn't ready. Being honest with herself, they were probably right. But for this afternoon's show, they decided she was ready. Isis was officially part of The Witches of Vegas. The adrenalin made her body shake. It was like being on the world's greatest sugar high.

Isis caught Sacha at the make-up table spying on her through her vanity mirror and paused.

"Have fun up there?" Sacha asked.

"Oh my God. It was such a rush!" Isis squeezed her hands together.

"Except for that one scary moment at the end, I thought you did well." Sacha's eyes darted across the room, along with her sarcastic smirk. "Wouldn't you agree, Luther?"

Luther, seated in an old-lady rocking chair, rolled his eyes and let out a loud grunt. His fingernails tapped the wooden armrests. From him, that was as much of a compliment as Isis could have hoped for.

She never got why he hung out in the dressing room. It's not like he needed any sort of creepy make-up to look the part of a vampire on stage. In fact, he needed the hat and scarf offstage to cover his pale white skin from onlookers. Well, that and to protect himself from the blistering Vegas sun.

The mirror didn't do him much good either. One of the biggest misconceptions was that vampires didn't cast reflections. Luther sure did, but his skin in the reflection was gray, peeled, and decaying. Sebastian and Selena explained that the reflection was what Luther would really look like if he weren't undead. When Isis first saw his reflection, it creeped her out to the point she threw up her breakfast. Of course, she was only nine at the time. Now, his reflection still creeped her out, but at least breakfast stayed inside her stomach.

The dressing room door swung open. Sebastian walked in with purpose, followed by Selena. This was usually the moment he offered everyone compliments and congratulations for another great show.

Isis stepped forward, ready to receive those accolades for the first time.

"Are you all right, Isis?" Sebastian asked.

"Yeah, I'm good."

"Glad to hear it. In that case, what the hell were you thinking out there?" He stared her down with narrowed eyes.

Isis' jaw dropped. "What do you mean? The spell worked. I did it." This was not the congratulations Isis was hoping to get.

"I'm talking about those little flips you pulled up there. We didn't practice any of that. It wasn't part of your act. Why did you stray from the routine? Did you plan that all along without first running it by us?"

Isis stepped back. She dropped her head. "I-I just wanted a good ending. It felt right so I—"

"You got cocky and it broke your concentration." Sebastian stepped forward and closed the gap between them. His breath blew against her hair. "You lost control of the spell in mid-air. That could have cost you your life. Your *life*, Isis!"

Damn, she hadn't seen him this angry at her since that time she was ten and practiced with her powers in the suite's living room unsupervised. In her attempts to make a pencil float from the coffee table, she ended up sending the couch through the suite's picture window. The couch fell forty floors to the street.

The situation only got worse from there. Isis' panicked attempts to make the couch disappear from the crowd that formed ended up setting it on fire. Somehow, it also caused every single picture frame to fly off the living room walls. Then the chandelier crashed from the ceiling, leaving shards of glass everywhere. The pencil on the coffee table never budged.

"What the hell were you thinking?" Sebastian screamed at her multiple times once he and Selena returned home. Isis didn't have a good answer except to drop to the floor and cry. It worked in that the yelling stopped, but only because Isis was ten.

The incident happened mere months after their show's debut and left a lot of people freaked out. Luckily, no one got hurt, but it caused a hell of a ruckus. The hotel's general manager wanted to cancel the show and evict them over the dangerous couch-falling spectacle. Sebastian talked him into a second chance, claiming it was a practice session gone wrong. He probably used an influence spell to make the manager a bit more accepting of his excuse. Two years had passed before Isis was allowed to be alone anywhere except in her own bed.

"We are very lucky the sisters pulled off a retrieval spell in time," Sebastian continued the verbal berating. "Otherwise, you would have landed head-first. From that height it could have killed you. No healing spell would help at that point, Isis. There is nothing we could have done to save you."

"Couldn't Luther just turn me into a vampire?" she replied with a slight grin.

Sacha's laugh filled the room. "That's why I love this kid," she crowed.

"It's not funny," Sebastian shot her way. "It's not funny at all."

In an attempt to break the tension, Selena stepped in front of Sebastian and threw her arms around his neck. "Sebastian, honey, I think she gets the message. Now, why don't we cut the girl just a little slack this one time?" she said in her sweet melodic tone. "It all worked out, and those moves did look good up there. The audience responded positively."

Selena ran her fingers through the hair on the back of his head. The romantic gesture didn't faze him. "I know we are powerful witches, and we use those powers for entertainment, but there is still an element of risk on that stage. I am not looking to cut her slack. I am looking to keep her safe."

"I'm sure she gets the point," Selena said. "She's a smart girl, she'll learn from this—"

"I'm sorry, okay?" Isis said as genuinely as she

could. "I promise I won't do it again." The last thing she wanted was an ugly spousal argument over her.

Sebastian exhaled. "Okay, if you want to do the fancy air stuff, then you need to practice. When we see you can do them consistently without losing your concentration, then you can take it out on the stage. But only then, and not without our say-so. Do you understand?"

"Yes, sir," Isis said with her head down. Better he thought her concentration broke due to an ill-advised back flip and not over some random boy in the audience. If he knew, it would probably be another five years before she was allowed back on the stage.

"Stop with the 'sir' crap, Isis. I'm being serious right now. I want to hear you say you understand," he demanded.

"I understand," she parroted with a sniffle.

Selena took Sebastian's hand and gave it a tight squeeze. "Well, if that's settled, I think we should take advantage of it being Monday night. Since we don't have an evening performance, who's up for a nice family dinner?" She spun toward her sister. "Sacha?"

"Sorry, Sis," Sacha said, while wiping her face with a make-up removal pad. "I have a date tonight. A local man I met on the strip. I believe he is a casino blackjack dealer."

"I hope not from this hotel," Sebastian said.

"No, Sebastian, he works at another hotel," she replied.

"Where is he taking you?" Selena asked.

Sacha smirked. "His place."

Isis didn't think there were any local men left that Sacha hadn't dated, then ended up at his place. In fact, there were a few women in that number as well.

"Have fun," Selena said. "I'm sure I don't have to warn you to be careful with a man you barely know?"

Sacha smacked her lips. "I'm a powerful witch, Selena, and a semi-celebrity in this town. I'm sure I'll be fine."

"How about it, Luther, any chance you'd like to join us?"

His silence was answer enough. He'd never dined with the group before. No doubt he wouldn't tonight. In fact, Isis had never seen him actually eat food. Luther had his own set of plans every evening that he did on his own. Luther needed a good amount of live blood every twenty-four hours to survive. He spent his nights hunting wild animals in the surrounding desert. If ever he ran out of time and couldn't find an appropriate animal…well, no one ever discussed that. Isis did see a recent headline on a local newspaper in the gift shop. It mentioned a rash of homeless people around the strip who disappeared without a trace.

Selena turned back to Sebastian. "I guess it's just us tonight. I'll make a reservation." She placed a hand under Isis' chin so she'd look up from the floor. "Go get ready. We'll eat in an hour."

Isis nodded, then watched the two leave the room. A tear rolled down her cheek. "Damn, he's still pissed," she muttered once the door shut.

"Why didn't you run those flips by them during practice?" Sacha asked, looking at Isis' reflection through the vanity mirror.

"I knew they'd say no."

"Ah, better to ask for forgiveness than permission." Sacha chuckled. "I used that philosophy a lot when I was your age." She spun in her chair from the mirror to face Isis. "For whatever it's worth, I've had a number of reckless near-miss catastrophes on that stage, especially toward the beginning. I don't recall Sebastian batting an eyelash over any of those close calls. Big Sis, on the other hand—believe me, kiddo, you've never seen her vicious side. She can make a stink that puts Sebastian's to shame."

"What's my next move?" Isis asked.

"Go to dinner. Flash that dimply smile of yours. If it comes up, reassure them of your commitment to work on your craft." Sacha turned back to the mirror. Her reflection eyed Isis while wiping a moist pad across her lips. "It always worked for me, and I've done a hell of a lot worse growing up with the two of them looking over my shoulder."

"That is true," Luther said, interjecting himself into the conversation. "Frankly, it is a miracle you are still alive, today."

Sacha gave him a teasing eye roll.

"I'll promise to practice," Isis said. "And then what?"

Luther stood up. "Make sure you do." He headed for the door.

Chapter Four

Zack placed three chairs around the old wooden table on the stage. He stood by as his uncle Herb took a seat. Victoria sat in the chair across from Herb. She crossed her legs, keeping her back perfectly stiff. To say this lady looked like a reject from an underground horror flick was a huge understatement. Then again, with all the magicians and performers Zack had seen in his life, Victoria certainly wasn't the weirdest looking person he had ever met. She waved at Zack to take the third seat. He declined, preferring to stand.

Victoria turned her attention back to Herb. "May I ask you a question?" Without waiting for approval, she went on, "Given the success of The Witches of Vegas, so many magicians have left, choosing to resume their careers in other parts of the country. In fact, of all the Las Vegas magicians, only you have remained, despite losing much of your audience and fame. Why have you not sought out greener pastures?"

Zack threw a raised eyebrow toward his uncle. It was clear this woman had been keeping tabs on them and their declining audience. He wondered how long they'd been under her scrutinizing microscope. How long had they been like fish in her aquarium—swimming around for her amusement?

"Vegas is our home, and I'm not ready to abandon

her," Herb answered. "I realized a long time ago I can't compete with the witches. We're doing magic while they're presenting huge illusions. Their show is powerful, especially for the prices they charge. In fact, it's far too powerful to remain in one theater in Las Vegas. Sooner or later, they will realize there are more lucrative opportunities for an act like theirs and move on. They'll go national, international, or whatever is the next step for them. When it happens, this will be the only magic show in a town that loves its magic."

Victoria let out a high-pitched cackle that bounced off the walls of the empty auditorium. "So, your master plan is to wait them out and hope they choose to leave?"

"Nothing else has worked," Zack muttered.

"It is a naive plan." Victoria glared at Herb.

"I suppose you have a better one?" Herb asked.

Victoria leaned across the table. "What if I were to tell you there is a reason they will remain here and not look for national exposure?"

"What reason would any magic group not want to go big-time?" Zack asked.

"I have a theory on how they manage their performances." Victoria leaned in. Her breath must have been vile as Herb quickly leaned back. "Their act is more honest than all presume, and it gives them the advantage over other magicians, an advantage they abuse."

"I'm not following," Herb said. "What exactly are you trying to say?"

"I think she's saying they are actually witches." Zack chuckled. It was a bad joke, but one meant to lighten the tense mood. He suddenly realized Victoria

41

wasn't laughing. And not because she took offense. "Oh my God, you *are* actually saying that, aren't you?"

"You were at the show today, weren't you, young man?"

Zack's jaw dropped. Before he could ask, she held a hand up. "I was seated just a few rows behind you and I never forget a face. Now, did any of their magic strike you as common to your industry? I'm guessing not."

"I'm familiar with their show as well," Herb said. "What they do is unbelievable, but anything is possible in magic with the right knowledge and budget."

"I see." Victoria looked toward Zack. "Tell me, young magician, did you find their magic easy to debunk?"

Zack answered, "Of course it wasn't, but you're saying the only possible answer to tricks another magician can't figure out is actual magic? You're not a very good debunker."

"Please pardon my nephew's brashness. We're working on that." Herb threw Zack a sideways glance. "But he does make a valid point. I have been a professional magician for a long time. I've worked with some of the best. One thing I can tell you is that, no matter how amazing or unexplainable a stage illusion may seem, there is always a simple concept behind it. We know it is never supernatural because there is no such thing as the supernatural."

Victoria flashed her brown-stained teeth. "Perhaps you are right. Perhaps I am a fool. But your nephew has seen my videos, and he can attest that I find out the truth, no matter how tightly magicians guard their secrets."

The ugly smile faded. "You and I have a mutual

goal—to find out the truth behind the curtain and expose it for the world to see. Once their secrets are public, The Witches of Vegas will lose their mystique and fade away."

"At which point," Herb replied, "we'll be the only magic show in Las Vegas."

Zack eyed his uncle carefully. Herb leaned his chin against his palms. He was clearly considering the option in front of him. Zack tapped him on the shoulder. "Um, Uncle Herbert, can we talk in private?"

"Absolutely." Herb hoisted himself from the chair. "Would you please excuse us for a moment, Ms. Hunter?"

"Of course." Victoria folded her hands on the table. "By all means, take your time."

Herb followed Zack through the curtain and down the steps. They stopped and faced one another between the stage and the front row.

"Uncle Herb, please tell me you're not really considering this," Zack whispered, realizing only a curtain separated them from Victoria's earshot.

"This woman represents everything I hate," Herb responded in an equally low tone. "She makes a living and a reputation out of purposely ruining our industry."

"Then tell her to take a hike!" Oops, forgot to whisper.

Herb stepped away from Zack and faced the twelve hundred empty seats. The sadness in his eyes didn't escape Zack's notice. "Remember some years back when The Amazing Herb Galloway show filled this entire theater?"

Zack wasn't sure if Herb's comments were directed at him or at the seats.

"It's been a while. Now, as their show's reputation grows, our audiences become smaller and smaller, as are our profits."

Herb refocused his attention on Zack. "I've been pulled into three meetings in the last two weeks, two with the general manager and one with the hotel board of directors. They are considering following suit with all the other theaters and bringing in a Broadway-type musical. If that happens…I don't know what becomes of us."

"If that happens, we have options," Zack insisted. "We can take the show on the road or relocate. I hear magic is getting huge on the east coast. A number of the magicians from the strip are making it there. We could follow them, or even go somewhere else, bring magic to another part of the country."

Herb lowered his head and shook it. "Even if someone out there wanted to invest in an old, washed-up magician like me, we couldn't afford to go."

"What about the savings from our shows over the years? Couldn't we use that to relocate?"

"Most of that went to upgrading our props during the years we tried to compete." Herb rubbed his temples with his right thumb and fingers. "Frankly, if the hotel wasn't giving us room and board, we'd be sleeping in the streets right now."

"I don't understand. You said we had enough to weather the storm."

"That was years ago, Zack! I never thought they'd still be here after all this time." Herb's shoulders slumped. "I guessed wrong. Now, we're practically broke."

Zack blinked his eyes rapidly. He tried to respond,

but all he could muster was a dry heave. He felt like someone had just punched him square in the gut. He'd suspected things weren't going well for them, but he had no idea just how bad it had become. Perhaps he should have. The writing was certainly on the wall. They hadn't eaten a single meal off the property in several months.

"I didn't know," Zack said once he could will himself to speak. "Why didn't you tell me before now?"

"Because you're fifteen! You shouldn't be worried about where our next meal is coming from. That's *my* job."

"So…" Victoria stepped from behind the curtain before Zack could respond. "Have you finished your discussion?"

Herb eyed Zack, who nodded. The idea of working with this clearly unscrupulous woman in order to destroy another magic show sickened him. On the other hand, Zack didn't want his convictions costing them everything. He knew his uncle shared the same principles. If he was willing to compromise them, it had to be necessary.

"What would I have to do?" Herb asked.

"There is nothing you can do," Victoria answered. "You are not the key to my plan."

Victoria sauntered past Herb, and toward Zack. The lump in Zack's throat threatened to explode through the back of his neck. Her smugness and five-inch advantage intimidated the hell out of him. "I'm the key to your plan?" he asked.

"You are, and the plan is simple. Befriend the girl, Isis. Develop a trust. Through that relationship, we gain access to her secrets."

Herb raised a finger to object. "Ms. Hunter, there's an unwritten rule that says 'magicians never reveal their secrets.' This Isis may be a kid, but she is still a magician."

The corner of Victoria's eyes crinkled. "Adults keep their secrets. Children, however, look for someone they feel they can trust to spill all they know." She eyed Zack with a sarcastic smirk. "No offense intended, of course."

God, could she be any more condescending? So far, Zack hated every part of this plan. It revolved around him essentially seducing a girl he didn't know, gaining her trust, and then destroying her entire life. The idea made his skin crawl. But his uncle needed this. Zack owed him the world. Also, sleeping on the streets sounded like it would suck. "So, how do you suggest I get the newest performer from Vegas' top show to notice I exist?"

"You will use your favorite weapon."

Victoria reached into the left pocket of Zack's vest. Before he could ask, "What the hell are you doing?" she pulled out her hand, along with his red-backed deck of cards. She must have noticed the bulge. Zack always kept a fresh deck on him so he could perform whenever the opportunity arose. When alone, he'd practice his double lifts and false shuffles.

Zack watched in confusion as Victoria cupped the deck between her hands, covering the card box completely. After several long moments, she held the deck between her fingers for Zack to take. He snatched it from her.

"I don't think this is going to work, but I'll try." Zack returned the deck to his vest pocket. "Where would I find her?"

"I will take you to her," Victoria answered through her brown-toothed smile. "Then, your task shall begin."

Chapter Five

For Isis, the best part of putting on the most popular show in Vegas was the VIP treatment from their host resort. This included the hotel picking up their meals at all the restaurants. Famous for its wide variety and delicious food, The Sapphire Resort's five-star restaurant, named The Majestic, held top accolades throughout the city. It was the most expensive and most popular of the four restaurants and buffet on the Sapphire property. Hotel guests had their meals comped along with free show tickets and priority seating in the theater to see The Witches of Vegas. It was a fair deal considering the thousand dollars per night, four-night minimum room rate, and that was for just standard rooms. Suites went for far more. The high rollers in the casino, of course, received everything for free.

Dinner with Sebastian and Selena appealed to Isis as much as their lessons on witchcraft. She loved the restaurant's ballroom environment, with a quartet in the back playing classical music. Everyone dressed in fancy clothing, at least at dinnertime. The acoustics were such that it never felt noisy even when the place was full. Hundreds of people all eating and talking, yet it still felt peaceful.

Isis eyed her dining companions and smiled. She felt closer to them than either of her foster families prior. They made her feel like their daughter and never like a temporary guest. They were, in every sense, her family and it felt right. Although it wasn't due to a foster agency placement, adoption, or through any other official means. Technically, they kidnapped her.

Sebastian definitely seemed calmer than before. Of course, a blood red juicy steak always put him in a better mood. Isis preferred the restaurant's Greek salad and grilled chicken, as did Selena. The topic of Isis' near-fatal fiasco never came up, but there was far more awkward silence, at least toward Isis, than any meal they'd shared prior. Might as well get it out there, Isis decided—break the tension. Hopefully, Sacha's advice was solid.

"Guys, I want to say again how sorry I am about what happened. I thought the flips would look nice up there. I got excited and...I don't know what happened. From now on, I'll run my ideas by you. I'll practice and I'll be more careful."

Sebastian reached across the table and cupped his palm over the back of her hand. "Isis, I'm a witch with great powers and years of training, surrounded by even more powerful witches with even more years of training. Not too much in this world scares me. But watching you almost plummet to your death, now that scared the hell out of me." He threw a quick glance toward Selena. "I know it scared the hell out of my dear wife as well. I beg of you, Isis, don't do that again. You mean too much to the both of us."

Well, damn, add guilt to Sebastian's list of amazing powers. It was one in which he excelled. Between the speech and the look of distress, Isis felt like she could melt away on the spot. Luckily, she had her own ace-in-the-hole so to speak. "Sorry, Dad, sorry, Mom, I won't do that to you again. I promise."

She looked up at Sebastian, and then to Selena, widening her eyes as far as they'd allow. The disappointment melted from their faces. It was the first time she'd ever called them that, and she meant it. Hell, they deserved the titles far more than the others she'd called by those same names. The fact that saying it may have just gotten her out of trouble was an added bonus.

"All right, we can let this go," Sebastian said. "We'll work on your levitations some more tomorrow, first thing in the morning."

"I'll be ready," Isis said. "And I won't do anything on stage that we don't practice first."

"Thank you."

"We understand your excitement, oh, boy, do we." Selena whipped back her red hair. "Always remember, sweetie, our powers are tied to our emotions. The more emotional we get, the less control we have. Sometimes, it could overwhelm us, and other times, we could lose the connection completely. That's why we preach and practice focus."

Isis had heard this about a billion times. She still didn't like it. "It's not fair that our power works that way."

"Life's rarely fair, Isis." Selena shrugged. "Look at me and Sacha. As siblings, the same energy flows through both of us. That means we are connected. If one of us has a bad day, both our powers become erratic."

Isis took a sip of her half-finished soda. A curious thought had lingered in her mind for a long while. It was one she never felt the time was right to ask. Now seemed as good a time as any to throw it out there. "I get why we do the show, but why does Luther? He's always talking about our 'higher purpose.' Performing on stage can't be what we're meant to do, right? Yeah, it's fun and all, but isn't this keeping us from finding that purpose?"

Sebastian and Selena exchanged a glance. Selena spoke first. "You once said when she asked the questions, we'd know she was old enough for the answers."

"I suppose I did," Sebastian replied. "She is fifteen, not a child anymore." He turned to Isis. "No, the show is not our grand purpose. The show is simply a method to keep our connection to the power strong and well-practiced."

"When the hotel was auditioning for a magic show," Selena said, "it was Sebastian's idea to say we were magicians and present our own style of magic." Pride filled Selena's voice as she playfully punched Sebastian's shoulder. "I never thought it'd work, but it has. I agree that it is a lot of fun."

Sebastian continued, "Now, the reason we need to keep those skills at a high level, and I need you to brace yourself for this—"

"—it's because...there's a threat we have to be ready for... The one we need to be ready to stop." Isis caught the confused glances from both. "Luther told me back on my thirteenth birthday. He also told me not to let you know that he told me."

"Did he?" Sebastian growled.

"Yeah, but he didn't tell me what the threat is. He just said that when it comes, the whole world could be in danger."

Selena responded, "He's never told any of us, either. For that matter, neither did my mom. I'm not so sure she really knew."

"But," Sebastian jumped in, "whatever this alleged threat is, we have to be ready. That's one reason we keep doing the show."

His tone didn't escape Isis' notice. "You don't believe it, do you?"

Sebastian shrugged. "I'm not so sure. But Luther believes it, as did Madeline." He nodded toward Selena. "She preached it to them all their lives, and then to me. I heard about this threat every day since they rescued and took me in. That was when I was almost your age." His head dropped. "Her last words were 'stay ready.' It was a warning to us, just before the cancer took her life."

The famous and beloved "Madeline." Isis had heard the name many times. It was always said with passion. She was the sisters' mother, Sebastian's mentor, and Luther's…whatever they were to each other. Isis wanted to know more about the amazing mom that commanded such respect, but even bringing up Madeline in conversation killed the mood. Isis had many questions, like why did they let her die? Well, since they brought up her name…

"Why couldn't witchcraft save her?" Isis asked. "You couldn't just magic the cancer away?"

Selena leaned in. "We are not invincible, Isis. There are things even witchcraft cannot heal. One of those things is a terminal brain tumor discovered far too late."

The glassy gaze from Selena made Isis sorry she furthered the subject. Too late now. "What about

Luther? He couldn't turn her?" That had to be better than dying, right?

"No, he couldn't," Sebastian answered through a bitter tone. "Or, he wouldn't. I never understood why he didn't try—not that he offered an explanation."

"The point is," Selena continued, "our shows serve a purpose besides entertainment. We get to be witches out in the open while hiding in plain sight." She smiled at Sebastian. "It's pure brilliance and I know my mother would have been proud."

"But, why do we have to hide?" Isis asked. "Especially if this is all about helping the world. Why not tell them what we are?"

"You've experienced what happens when we reveal ourselves. I'm sure you haven't forgotten that," Sebastian answered. "People are naturally frightened of what is not part of their normal lives. Their instinct is to lash out. Magic shows, they do understand, at least in concept. Seeing what they assume is illusion beyond their knowledge and know-how falls within normal parameters. Witchcraft, on the other hand, is a whole other story. They won't accept it as something they can have in their lives."

"We have the power to defend ourselves." Isis waved a hand at Sebastian. "You can even change people's minds about wanting to hurt us. You can influence them like you do on stage."

"If it came to that, I could. But frankly, I'd rather just go on taking their money, which keeps our bellies well-fed." Sebastian rubbed his stomach in a circular motion. "And if this threat should ever come, we will have enough of a fight on our hands without needing to start one unnecessarily. Does that make sense?"

"Yeah, it does." Well, kinda. It did make sense. Still, imagine how the show's popularity would grow if the truth was known, that they really were witches and not just pretending. Of course, they do sell out all their shows now. They'd need to find a larger theater. Maybe they'd have to go on tour or something. Isis didn't like the idea of leaving the only place she'd ever called home. Ironic that it was a hotel.

The maître d' approached the table, clearing his throat to get the group's attention. "A good evening to my favorite Las Vegas performers." He clapped his hands.

"How are you, Arthur?" Selena said with a smile.

Isis pressed a fist against her mouth, as she always did whenever he came to their table. At five feet tall and in a black and white tuxedo, Arthur reminded her of a penguin, especially with the way he waddled around the dining room.

"I do hope you enjoyed your meal tonight," Arthur said, "but if you are about finished, I have quite the number of guests awaiting tables."

"We understand, Arthur." Sebastian stood from his chair. "Paying customers should come first."

"I came to your show again today before my shift," Arthur said with pride. He pointed one of his hairy fingers toward Isis. "You were amazing, by the way, young lady. The way you flew across the theater and then back to the stage..." Arthur swatted his hand to simulate Isis' body flying. "You really had me believing you were actually falling." He then threw in, "And, you were so beautiful. Like a flower I just want to sniff and hold against my chest."

"Um, thank you," Isis replied. The compliment

54

would have been a lot less disturbing if he wasn't at least thirty years her senior.

Arthur turned his attention back to Sebastian. "I have a theory on the vampire act at the end. I'm thinking he wasn't ever in that coffin. You had some kind of life-like mannequin or a robot in there. There's probably a trap door underneath the coffin and on the stage floor. You line the trap doors up, and he sneaks through before the coffin travels through the audience. When the stage fills with smoke, the vampire comes out of the trap door on the stage and there he is."

When they first practiced this act, Isis questioned why they needed the smoke. Considering it didn't actually do anything, she thought it would look even more amazing if Luther simply appeared on the stage. It was on Luther's persistent demands that they use the smoke machine. He insisted they leave an iota of skepticism for the audience to ponder. The witches agreed, but only because Sebastian thought the smoke added to the performance.

Arthur placed a hand on Sebastian's triceps. "So, am I close?"

Sebastian offered him a slight grin. "You may be onto something, my friend."

"I knew it!" Arthur stuck his chest out and grinned with pride. "But do not worry. I will not say a word to anyone."

"We appreciate that." Selena stood and stepped away from the table. "It's getting late. We should head upstairs and unwind. After all, we do have another sold-out show tomorrow."

Sebastian placed a hand on Isis' shoulder. "And you have an early morning practice."

"Can I go get some frozen yogurt?" Isis rose from her chair. She batted her eyelashes and held out her palm in front of Sebastian. "It's just a few blocks down the road so I won't be too far."

"What do you say, Sebastian?" Selena asked. "She did perform on stage for the first time."

"On the other hand, she also almost killed herself tonight."

"True, but at least she's looking to get off the property for a while." Selena grinned. "That's something we should encourage."

"I suppose." Sebastian slipped his brown leather wallet from his back pocket. He pulled out a ten-dollar bill and placed it on Isis' palm. "Go enjoy."

"Thank you, see you later." Isis beelined for the restaurant's exit.

Sebastian called, "Make sure you bring back my change this time!"

"I will!" Isis waltzed into the hotel lobby. She didn't get out much on her own, but the yogurt shop was one of the few exceptions. She looked forward to visiting there whenever she could, which wasn't often. She enjoyed watching the people around her interact almost as much as she liked the yogurt and toppings.

Chapter Six

Zack stood outside the frozen yogurt shop staring through the front window for what felt like an eternity. Uncle Herb and Bambi were handling the night's show without him. Tonight, he had his own mission—to approach a girl he didn't know, introduce himself and, somehow, gain her interest. A daunting task considering he had never even spoken to a girl his age for more than two sentences unless he was performing for them outside the hotel. He'd rather be doing that.

Isis was inside the yogurt shop, just as Victoria predicted. Apparently, the tabs she had been keeping on this group of magicians were far more extensive than she indicated. Isis sat at a table by herself eating a bowl of chocolate yogurt with fruit and candy toppings. The smile with each bite suggested she was enjoying it. He didn't want to interrupt, but he'd promised his uncle to at least make an attempt at this connection.

Zack took a deep breath and strolled into the shop. He stared at Isis, ignoring the fact that his entire body sweated under his clothes. Man, after performing on stage in front of hundreds of people, how could starting a conversation with one girl be so difficult?

As Isis worked on her yogurt, Zack approached the table. He had no idea how to open a dialogue with her. "Hi, my name is Zack"? "What's a pretty girl like you doing in a yogurt shop like this"? Ugh, all those lines sounded so geeky. As a performer, she probably had boys their age approaching her all the time. Especially with that exotic olive skin tone which meshed so well with her long brown hair.

Isis looked up from her yogurt. He couldn't stand there with his mouth shut all evening. Time to say something…anything. The words, "Hey, want to see a card trick?" popped out of his mouth before his brain could process a witty introduction.

"I'm sorry…what?" Her head tilted.

"A card trick. I'm a magician, just like you."

Isis pointed at Zack and waved her finger. "Oh, hey, you're the boy I saw in the audience at the show today."

Wow, she remembered and even sounded a bit excited.

"I was directly under you when you almost…" He smacked his hand against the table.

"Not my best moment." Her head dropped with embarrassment, which filled Zack with confusion. The way she stopped in mid-air and flew across the theater—it had to be part of the act. Didn't it?

"Hey, um…do you mind if I sit?" Zack asked.

Isis responded with a nod. "I feel like I've seen you before today, but I'm not sure where. Maybe around the Sapphire?"

"Have you ever been to The Amazing Herb Galloway show at the Galloway Theater? It's in the Felicity Hotel."

Isis shook her head. No surprise there. The number of people who had actually seen their show shrank by the day. "Herb Galloway is my uncle. I perform on stage with him. I also do card and close-up magic outside the hotel."

"Maybe that's where I saw you. I'm sorry, I don't remember."

"My name is Zack. Zack Galloway."

"I'm Isis."

Zack parked himself in the seat across from her. His cheeks felt warm, probably because they were red with awkward embarrassment. He watched her churn her spoon in the bowl. Definite bad sign. He needed to say something to break the silence, and quick. "You don't come off like someone from around here." Ugh, was that the best he could do?

"No, I'm from New York City."

"New York?" An east coaster. Was her entire magic team from there? How ironic that these performers came from the east coast since their arrival here forced all the magicians to relocate there. Did she realize the irony in that? Zack bit his inner cheek. This wasn't the time to have that debate. "What's New York City like?" he asked, trying to keep himself on target.

"Some parts are a lot like here." Isis scooped a strawberry slice with the spoon and placed it in her mouth. "But not so many casinos all around."

"So, how did you end up all the way here with a team of character actor magicians?"

"You mean the witches? They're my family," Isis answered, still staring at her yogurt. "They've been teaching me for a long time." She finally looked up at Zack. "Today was the first time I got to go in front of the audience." An adorable smile formed across her face. It spread from ear to ear. "It was so awesome."

"So, you're a family of performers." Zack nodded

with understanding. "I'm guessing they're not your birth family."

The adorable smile faded. Ugh. Uncle Herb had warned him over and over about his bluntness. So did his teachers in school over the years. "Think before you speak…" If only he had a dollar for every time he'd heard that. Then, they wouldn't have such financial troubles.

"No, they're not," Isis answered. "It's kind of a long story."

"I'd like to hear it, if you're okay with that." Fortunately, Zack hadn't inadvertently ended the conversation.

"Sure. My real mom died when I was five. After that, I was with my grandma for about three years, but she got real sick and couldn't take care of me. It was foster care after that. I never knew my dad, or any other family."

Wow. "So, then you were adopted by The Witches of Vegas?"

"They weren't The Witches of Vegas then." Isis chuckled. "They rescued me when I was nine from a really bad foster situation. They took me in because I was just like them. They've been raising me ever since."

"Oh, really?" Time to dig. God, he hated having to do this. "What are they like?"

Isis grinned. "Selena and Sebastian are like my mom and dad. They really look after me and have since the moment we met. Sacha's like the coolest aunt on Earth. I can talk to her about anything and she always understands."

"And how about that spooky vampire dude at the

end of the show? What's he like offstage?"

Isis shrugged. "A spooky vampire dude."

"I hear that." Not like Zack hadn't met plenty of blood-sucking jerks in his life. One statement she made stood out. "What did you mean by you were just like them?"

"We're witches." Isis licked the back of her yogurt-covered spoon. Her head suddenly popped up. "You know, for the show."

"Oh, of course." Man, Isis was either completely immersed in their onstage characters or, the more likely scenario, she was messing with him.

"You said you perform with your uncle." Isis scooped out the last of her yogurt with the plastic spoon and gulped it down. "Are your parents around?"

"Unfortunately, no. They died in a car crash when I was six. Uncle Herb was babysitting me at the time, showing me magic and teaching me how to perform tricks just like him. I guess he's still doing that."

"Ooh, I'm so sorry." Isis reached across the table and put her hand over his. "We should talk about something else. You said you wanted to show me a card trick, right?"

"Yes, I did!" Zack whipped out his cards, removed them from their box, and fanned them on the table face-up. "As you can see, all the cards are different." He lifted the end card and flipped it, making sure each card caught the next so they all flipped facedown in one smooth motion. "Now, what is your favorite card?"

"My favorite?" Isis licked her lips. "Um, I guess the queen?"

He expected her to offer a suit as well, unless she was intentionally trying to screw him up. He'd dealt with enough volunteers who tried to catch him. Zack knew how to handle it. "You strike me as a Queen of Spades type, am I right?"

Isis gave an uncertain nod.

Zack lifted the fourth facedown card between his right thumb and forefinger, revealing it to be the Queen of Spades. He had also snatched the card next to it and slid it behind the Queen, hoping Isis hadn't caught him. Zack had never performed for another magician other than his uncle. He'd have to be extra careful.

"Now, check this out." Zack waved his hand in an up and down motion. Mid-way, he flipped the two cards so when his hand stopped, the King of Hearts faced Isis.

"Wow," Isis shouted. "That was cool!"

Zack sensed his confidence taking control. He felt as comfortable as when he performed card tricks to strangers at his table outside the hotel. With Isis' attention on the King of Hearts in his right hand, Zack snatched another card from the pile with his left. It was also a Queen of Spades—he had a number of duplicates mixed within this deck.

"The question you should ask yourself is," Zack returned to his patter, "what happened to the queen?"

Zack raised his left hand, which held the second Queen of Spades. He took advantage of his sweaty palm by using the moisture to make the card stick. Isis gasped. It seemed like a legitimate response. Zack handed Isis the queen. Then he slid the fanned-out cards together with his left hand as quickly as he could. He didn't want Isis' trained magician eyes noticing the markings on the back, which revealed each card's value.

"Wow, you're really good," Isis said.

"I'm sure you've seen far better."

"No, really, that looked so awesome!"

"Thank you." Zack had received compliments like this for as long as he could remember. Coming from Isis, it meant so much more, even though they just met. He could entertain her all night—he knew at least twenty more card tricks that were just as impressive, and then several variations of those tricks.

Entertainment, however, was not his goal tonight. He had to keep reminding himself of his mission. "It's just a case of simple misdirection. I'll bet you witches do a lot of misdirection on stage, am I right?"

Isis bit her lower lip, perhaps pondering her answer. "We...don't do a lot of card tricks. We do big stuff."

"Right." Strange, with their level of talent, she must have known all about misdirection, which covered all aspects of magic. What magician wouldn't?

"You're really amazing at that." Isis threw him another smile. Apparently, it was contagious.

"Thanks. My uncle says my hands are like mini-mirror boxes, only with cards instead of rabbits."

Isis tipped her head forward. "What?"

Zack felt his mouth pop open. Was he mumbling and didn't realize it? He did have that habit when he was nervous. "Mirror box," Zack repeated, but Isis still seemed confused. He guessed the trick where the "witch," Selena, disappeared then reappeared utilized an elaborate type of mirror box. Of course, the cluelessness toward basic insider magic terms could have still been her cover. If so, she played it well.

Isis eyed her watch and gasped. "Oh my God, it's

getting late. I have to get back."

Zack snatched his cards, all except the queen of spades—which was still in Isis' hand—and dropped them in the box. "Can I walk you back?" he asked.

"Yeah, I would like that. Thanks." Isis stood from her seat.

Zack did the same. She was only a few inches shorter than him. Her forehead came up to his nose. It was a refreshing change from school where most of the girls his age had a distinct height advantage.

As Isis tossed her empty bowl in the trash, Zack held the door for her. He had a great feeling about this girl and how they connected after just one conversation. Too bad he'd have to spoil it all by betraying her entire family.

Chapter Seven

Zack held out his phone while he and Isis squeezed on either side of the Elvis impersonator. All three gave huge smiles. Zack snapped the picture. He handed the phone to Isis, who gazed at the picture on the screen with a huge grin. Zack reached into his vest pocket and pulled out a five-dollar bill, which he handed to the impersonator.

"A thank ya, thank ya very much," the impersonator said while he straightened his dark sunglasses and dropped the bill in the inner pocket of his all-white suit. He walked away and approached another passing couple.

Isis handed the phone back. "Is it bad that I'm not too sure who he's supposed to be?"

"Probably," Zack said once the two continued on their journey. "He's from a million years ago, but living in Vegas, you should know Elvis. Do you want me to text you the photo?"

"I don't have a phone," Isis answered.

"Really?" To Zack, this was completely insane. Even his old-fashioned uncle had a cellphone. It was an ancient flip phone, but at least he had one. "Why don't you have one?" With the top show in Vegas, it couldn't have been a monetary issue.

"It really hasn't come up." Isis shrugged. "So,

before Elvis, you were telling me how you became a magician."

"That's right." Zack's eyes peeked down when he felt Isis taking his hand. "I started at six years old right after my parents' death. I was devastated to the point I stopped speaking. All I did was cry."

"I can understand that."

"Yeah. Uncle Herb didn't know what to do to get me out of that funk, so he went to what he knows best. He started teaching me card tricks, then other magic. I picked them up real fast." Zack's lips stretched into a prideful grin. "My uncle kept saying he had a future great magician on his hands. Soon, he started using me for his shows, first behind the scenes, then on stage. The rest is history, I guess."

"That is so sweet." Isis' hand squeezed a bit tighter. "Your uncle sounds like a great guy."

"Now that you know my story, I'd like to know yours," Zack said. "You mentioned being in a bad foster situation. What was that all about?"

Isis bit her bottom lip. Zack just hoped he didn't cross a line. After a few moments of silence, she spoke. "It was real bad. First, I was with a family that seemed pretty nice, but the house was crowded with foster kids. They pulled me from there after about two weeks. No one ever told me why. Then, I spent almost eight months with a foster family that didn't want me around."

"Then, why did they become a foster family?"

"I don't know. Usually they just ignored me. My foster mom gave me advice only one time. She told me not to trust anyone outside their community because they were all evil monsters that just wanted to destroy our lives. That was right before she tried to set me on fire."

Zack stopped in his tracks. Isis yanked back as Zack still had a grip of her hand. "Wait, what? You don't mean that literally, do you?"

"She thought I was the devil. They all did." Isis waved her left hand in a dismissive fashion. "Like I said, it was a bad situation."

"Sure sounds it." Zack blinked his eyes rapidly. She must have meant it as a metaphor, right? It could have also been her sense of humor. Talk about an unbelievable story, especially when she told it with such nonchalance. "And after all that, you were adopted by a family outside that community and they're making you a star. I'm guessing you trust them?"

"I do. They've given me every reason since the day they took me in."

Zack's eyebrows rose. "That's quite an ironic story."

Isis raised her arms out as if she were taking in the cheers on stage. "And that's the title of my life—*Quite an Ironic Story*. You like it?"

"It definitely works."

Zack laughed harder than he had ever remembered laughing before. He was having such a great time with Isis that he almost forgot why he approached her in the first place. Oh, right, it was to become someone else in her life that she shouldn't have ever trusted. Man, if only she were a stuck-up bitch like so many other performers he'd met. That would have made his job so much easier. But she didn't fit that description at all.

He found Isis to be sweet, kindhearted, and funny. She had been nothing but friendly and open from the moment they met. She definitely didn't deserve betrayal. He didn't want any part in destroying her entire life.

"Forget it, I'm out," Zack mumbled.

"What?" Isis asked.

"Nothing, I'm just talking to myself."

"You do that a lot?"

"Not really." Zack looked at the time on his phone's screen. "Hey, we're not far from the fountain light show. It starts in ten minutes. You want to check it out?"

"If it's nearby and starting soon, sure. But after that, I really have to go."

"No problem. The show starts every fifteen minutes. It's only about five minutes long."

"I can swing that." Isis smiled.

The fountain was only two hotels away along Vegas Boulevard and easy to find as it took up an entire street. Lucky Zack could find his way there without looking because at the moment, he couldn't take his eyes off of Isis. Every so often, she'd look at him with reddish cheeks and a nervous smile. He found that more intoxicating than he could put into words.

Zack had never felt this way about any other girl in his life, or at least none who he was sure had the same interest in him. He definitely liked her. There was the tightness all throughout his body, from his head, down to parts he never felt react like that before. He'd ask her to marry him right now if it wouldn't make him seem like a freak and scare her off. It was crazy to feel this way for someone he just met, but he totally did.

Zack and Isis crossed the street and made their way to the fountain. It was really more of a pond, but once the faucets rose to the surface and the music started playing, to Zack it was one of the most astounding sights in all of Vegas. He especially liked to come at night when various colored lights tinted the water as it shot out from the faucets. They shined against the multiplex hotel shaped like a tower right behind them. Isis ran ahead of Zack and leaned against the edge.

"Wow," she screamed. "It's so huge! I like it. Thank you for taking me here."

Zack caught up to Isis. Her bulging eyes matched the tourists who were at the fountain for the first time. A weird reaction for someone who had been in Vegas for years. The fountain show was well known, and it wasn't far from the Sapphire Resort. How could this be the first time she'd seen it?

"You really haven't seen the fountain show before?" Zack asked after some reluctance.

"I don't get out much." Isis looked at him. "We get real busy with practicing and all. When there is time, I pretty much just go to the places I know, like the yogurt shop."

"Really?" Zack waved his hand around them. "The strip is a whole world. There is so much to see and explore."

Isis shrugged. "I'm not much of an explorer. I'd rather just hang around the Sapphire. There's a lot to see and do in there, too. We even have a three-floor shopping mall to wander around."

"Most of the resort hotels on the strip have shopping malls." Zack shook his head. "Well, mine doesn't, but others have them. Some of these places even have themed mini-golf courses based on TV shows and rock bands. You'd probably enjoy wandering the other resorts just as much as the Sapphire."

"You're probably right, but I like to stay close to home. I guess I'm kind of lame that way." Isis looked back at the long metal sprinklers rising from the water. "But, I will say, this looks really awesome."

"Wait until you see it in action."

Zack had a few follow-up questions in his mind, but he forgot all about them when both her hands wrapped around his wrist. Her fingers were so soft and smooth. Her right hand rolled down to his hand where their fingers locked. He hoped the calluses he had from years of "flash paper use gone wrong" didn't gross her out.

The metal sprinklers that ran across the pond had stopped rising. This meant the fountain show was close to beginning. A crowd gathered around to see it. Zack only saw about fifteen people—there were usually many more on the weekends—which was why he liked coming during the week. One couple, a few feet away, made him gasp. It was Glen Dobbs with an arm around his girlfriend, high school's curvy blonde bombshell, Angela Russo.

Zack knew Glen from school, and not fondly. In fact, Glen was the bane of Zack's existence in the cafeteria and hallways. Glen was a huge, bulky guy who loved to push people around, both on the football field as the team's defensive tackle, and throughout the school day. Zack was one of his favorite targets. Glen was like the Bluto to Zack's Popeye in a world without spinach. Now, he was out on a date with Angela, the school's "it" girl.

Zack hated their relationship, especially the way

Glen flaunted it in school. It's not that Zack was jealous; he just never understood what Angela saw in Glen. Maybe because she was the head cheerleader, meaning she had to date a football player? If that was the case, why did she choose this football player? Her high-end white blouse clashed against his green with black lettering "I like farts" T-shirt.

"Hey." Zack looked at his wrist even though he wasn't wearing a watch. "It is getting late. I should probably get you back. Maybe we could see the show another time?"

"Sure, whatever you want to do, Zack," Isis responded.

Zack started to turn away from the fountain. He cringed at the sound of Glen's deep voice shouting, "Hey, check it out, Nerdini's here!"

Damn, too late.

When Zack first entered high school, Glen was still trying out for the football team and working on a decent social status among the students. One September evening, Glen came to Zack's table along with his parents and younger brother. They stayed at the table for hours, amazed by Zack's magic, but not enough to go inside and buy tickets. The next day, Glen pointed out Zack to everyone and called him "Nerdini." He said the name over and over again until it stuck.

Zack was no longer invisible—he was now the constant subject of Glen's humor. He hated the nickname for a lot of reasons. One reason was that it was based on Harry Houdini, who was not a magician, but an escape artist.

"Yo, Ang, let's go hang with Nerdini." Glen led Angela over by the arm.

"Is this a friend of yours?" Isis asked.

"Not exactly," Zack muttered. "Actually, no."

"Leave him alone, Glen," Angela said. "Can't you see he's on a date?"

Glen stepped forward, his chest inches from Zack's face. "Holy cow, you really are on a date, aren't you? I didn't know you even liked girls, Nerdini." He threw a backward glance at Isis. "Did you conjure her with your magic or something?"

"Let's not do this now," Zack growled, surprised that Glen even knew the word conjure.

"Why don't we get out of here?" Isis pulled Zack's hand.

Zack nodded. Glen had a habit of making him look like a punk in school. That was fine since Zack didn't care much about what anyone thought of him in that building. But this wasn't school, and he sure as hell didn't want to look like a punk in front of Isis. Best to just leave and not let this confrontation continue.

As they turned and walked away, Glen called to Zack, "The next time you conjure a girl, you should add more meat! And a bigger set of honkers, too!"

"Glen!" Angela shrieked. "That was rude."

"Oh, come on, Babe. Nerdini knows I'm just messing with him."

Isis let go of Zack's hand. She walked to Glen and looked up into his eyes even though he towered over her. Her hands gripped her hips. "You're not a nice person."

"Oh, gee, really? I'm not a nice person?" Glen's mocking tone made Zack's blood boil.

"You are so big and powerful," Isis said in a low, calm tone. "Wouldn't you rather help people instead of just acting like a big jerk?"

Glen burst out into laughter. He put his massive hand on her shoulder. "You want me to help you, sweetheart? Let me help you hook up with a real man. I got lots of friends, and some even have your skin color."

Man, he was such an asshole. Isis' head dipped downward. She mumbled something to herself. Zack stormed over with purpose. "Glen, leave us alone, you hear me?"

It was the first time he had ever stood up to Glen, but it was necessary, and too late to walk away. Zack straightened his back and stood his ground. He didn't want to get into a fight with a guy who had a hundred-pound advantage and could rip him in half. But he also wasn't sure how to get out of it, not with the hostile glare Glen flung his way.

The answer came from Angela, who grabbed Glen's arm and tugged. "Babe, the fountain show is starting." She pointed a finger in his face. "You know I don't want to miss it."

Zack wasn't sure if she was trying to talk Glen down or she really wanted to see the fountain show. From what he knew of her, Zack assumed the latter.

With Glen's attention on Angela, Zack grabbed Isis' hand and gave it a tug. Thank God she took the hint and backed away. "Don't let him upset you," Zack said.

"I'm not upset," she responded. They walked away side by side.

"See ya, Nerdini!" Glen shouted. "Wait until I see you in school tomor—*oh jeeze*!"

A loud thud was followed by a scream from

Angela. Zack spun around to see Glen with his face against the cement. Glen rolled to his side moaning and cupping his hands over his nose. Blood seeped through his fingers. "Oh my God, Glen," Angela shrieked. "What the hell happened to you?"

Zack wondered the same thing. Then, he saw it. Glen's shoelaces were tied together. They definitely weren't before when Glen walked up to them. So, how could it have happened? His head spun to Isis. "Did you…"

"I don't know what happened," Isis replied through a shy grin. "We should go."

"Yeah, sure." It had to be her doing. But how? She'd never kneeled or squatted. She couldn't have used her toes, not with the way her white sneakers were tightly laced up. No wonder her magic show was kicking their asses.

Zack took another look back. Glen was still on the ground. A crowd had formed around him. For Glen, the embarrassment of a sympathetic crowd had to be worse than the actual fall. Whatever Isis did, however she did it, Zack found her even more attractive.

He stepped in front of Isis, interrupting her pace. "Hey, um, I really want to kiss you right now." The words just blurted out.

"I won't stop you," Isis whispered.

Zack pressed his lips against hers. It was his first kiss, and well worth the wait.

Chapter Eight

Luther hated Las Vegas. That determination was made after living in many locations throughout the world for the last five hundred years. Las Vegas was, by far, his least favorite. It wasn't because of the bright lights, the annoying video advertisements on every single building, or the atmosphere of guilty pleasures. It was because of the crowds. Luther had spent most of his life, and afterlife, avoiding large crowds. The Vegas strip, however, was like being stuck in the middle of Woodstock each time he left the hotel.

This was one reason Luther initially opposed Sebastian's idea of relocating to Las Vegas. While the concept of training under the guise of magicians was innovative, Luther expressed several objections. An accidental slip-up causing exposure in front of an audience of thousands was his biggest concern. The crowds, however, were Luther's one selfish reason for hoping they would reconsider. It was not to be as both Selena and Sacha fell in love with the idea.

As much as Luther hated to ever admit when he was wrong, The Witches of Vegas idea proved to be brilliant. It built the witches' confidence in their connection to the power as well as their strength and stamina. Of course, it wasn't the first time Luther had been wrong. At least this time his misjudgment didn't lead to disaster and regret. Still, unlike the witches, Luther never found comfort or joy in the stage's spotlight.

He did find refuge in his nightly ventures through the Vegas desert. It was quiet and desolate which made for a great contrast to the jam-packed theater. His moonlight hunts for the blood of coyotes and mountain lions exhilarated him in ways other than mere survival. While the blood was necessary, the time alone proved just as valuable for his sanity.

Once his thirst was satisfied, Luther had plenty of time before sunrise. At first, it was hard making the time fly—as a vampire he had no need for sleep. He spent his nights wandering the desert, an activity that, while preferable, quickly became monotonous. Two months into their new residency, Luther discovered Boulder City.

Most of Boulder City's concrete townhouses and architecture were built in the early 1930s. Although the houses were constantly renovated, their look and feel never changed. The small town reminded Luther of a quieter and less commercialized era. He spent the nights after his desert hunts sitting on rooftops where he'd focus on his thoughts, undisturbed.

The lack of casinos and tourist attractions assured there were never droves of people walking through the streets, especially at night. This meant Luther could remain unnoticed except by the occasional hobo. Luckily, they were usually too intoxicated to realize a man sitting on a rooftop in the middle of the night wasn't a normal thing. Luther would have recommended long ago they live here if not for the expense, which was considerable, at least compared to the complimentary rooms they had in the Sapphire—

A high-pitched scream came from nearby. Luther stood up, observing two men running down the street. From the layered and filthy clothes, it was a good guess these were part of the Las Vegas homeless. The street dwellers rarely ran toward a scream, yet these two did so with terror written all over their faces.

Luther leapt from rooftop to rooftop keeping the two men in his sights until they stopped in their tracks at the end of the block. A woman in a dirty jacket with uncombed grayish hair pointed at a fellow sprawled in the middle of the street. It was another homeless man with a pool of blood around his head and upper body. The man was clearly dead.

"Oh, no, it got another one of us!" the woman screamed.

Another one? Luther leaned forward and squinted. The man had a hole on the left side of his neck. Luther recognized the aftermath of a vampire's feast. This was most certainly not one of Luther's victims, nor were any of the others the lady referenced. Even when feasting on an animal, Luther would never be so sloppy and leave the deceased where it could be easily discovered. This could only mean one thing—there was another vampire somewhere in the vicinity. This was a reason for concern. His kind was rare, and usually deadly, with few exceptions.

Luther hadn't run across another vampire in over twenty years. Even then, he had only encountered one, and it was by accident. This was shortly after he met Madeline in New York City and agreed to help train her two teen daughters in their recently discovered Wiccan abilities. One night, he came across a friendly young lad wandering the streets of Manhattan. Luther sensed immediately that he was another vampire. At that point, the man didn't yet grasp what he had become.

Damn, what was his name?

Simon. Simon…something. There had been so many names over the centuries, Luther couldn't keep track of them all. But the first name was definitely Simon.

Simon had been turned just prior to their confrontation. According to his story, the turn happened during a backpacking trip in Turkey. When separated from his group, Simon ran into a vampire who survived by trapping tourists and drinking them dry. For some unknown reason, the vampire chose to turn Simon instead of making a meal of him. He then abandoned the new vampire, leaving him in a state of desperate confusion. Luther took the young man under his wing.

Luther taught Simon what to expect over the next several centuries. These teachings included how his skin would turn pale and corrode as it aged. How time would fly by and entire years would feel like days. How a simple piece of wood puncturing a vampire was deadly because it poisoned the blood and inflamed the skin. As Luther learned firsthand in his past, inflamed skin that's deceased doesn't heal.

The most important lesson was how drinking an animal's blood was just as satisfying as a human's. Simon wanted nothing more than to hold onto his humanity.

That was the lesson Simon appreciated most. He was involved in a relationship that, in Luther's day, would have been frowned upon. But he was genuinely happy with his lover. The two lived in a small apartment in Middle Village. They even adopted and raised a young girl.

Luther tried to offer his own experience to dissuade this young vampire from the relationship. "You will watch your lover grow old, wither away, and die," Luther explained to him. "Then, you will go through the same anguish watching your child, her children, and all their children die. Meanwhile, you will simply continue to exist."

This was another of those times Luther was proven wrong.

Despite the warnings, Simon chose his own path. Ironically, it was one that inspired Luther to reconsider his position and stop ignoring Madeline's obvious advances. In the end, Luther watched her die, and far sooner than expected. He was fond of the brief time they had together. So much, in fact, he was still watching over her children. And humiliating himself almost nightly on stage in front of thousands of people. It was all to assist in their façade and make sure they kept up with their training. Perhaps it wasn't the worst way to spend his days.

Although they eventually lost touch, Simon was one of the few people in his later years Luther called a friend. He owed that young vampire a debt of gratitude.

Simon was never a threat. He just wanted to blend in and survive. This made him different from the bloodthirsty monsters Luther knew in the early 1500s when he was first turned. What about this vampire who recently slaughtered a homeless man and left the body in the middle of a public street? Was this one a threat, or was he, or perhaps even a she, also looking to survive? If it were only about survival, the vampire would benefit from learning to hunt in the desert. It would keep him off the radar. Exposure was one thing no vampire anywhere in the world needed.

But what if this was a vampire who killed brutally and without remorse or concern for exposure? If that were the case, then this was a monster that would have to be stopped, and possibly extinguished. This could be a good test for the witches. It would help prepare them should the real threat arrive in their lifetime.

Recently, they'd become lax and complacent, particularly in their training of Isis. They treated her more like a child and less like a witch with the potential to be the strongest the world had ever seen. Someday, the world may need Isis, and the witches were assuring she wouldn't be ready. Perhaps this was the wake-up call they needed.

Either way, Luther would need to locate this vampire and find out the intentions as soon as possible.

Chapter Nine

Isis made it back to the hotel suite far later than she expected. Because of this, she had a hard time waking up in the morning. Her mind and body begged for a couple more hours tucked under the covers. She had, however, promised to practice first thing. Sebastian woke her at sunrise to see that she kept that promise.

After a quick shower and room service for breakfast, Isis found herself in the middle of the living room suite sitting cross-legged a few inches above the couch. She was suddenly the focus of attention—everyone's except for Sacha who hadn't yet returned from her date. Isis' hair hung down her back in a ponytail as she didn't even have time to brush it before practice began.

"Feel the energy, Isis. Feel your connection as it flows through you," Sebastian said. "There are two soda cans and a bottle of water on the coffee table between us. They are full of liquid, but that doesn't matter, you control them. Close your eyes. Visualize them and make them lighter than air."

Isis lowered her eyelids, but it was not the items on the coffee table that filled her mind. It was Zack's face. More specifically, those light-green eyes, which reminded her of the cat from her first foster home. The feline used to follow Isis around the apartment staring at her with that very same gaze. Zack's irises were the same shade of green as the cat's eyes.

"You're losing it," Sebastian said. "Stay focused, feel the energy, lift the cans and the bottle."

Isis couldn't tell if the objects were moving. All she could think about was last night's walk home with Zack. How her hand melted into his. How enthralled she was in his stories about growing up on the Vegas strip. The confused face he made when she gave that big bully exactly what he deserved. Zack's soft lips against her own right after...

A shock went down Isis' body. It came from hitting the couch pillows, back first. She sat up to find Sebastian looking down on her with his hands on his hips. "What's going on with you this morning?"

"I need to start drinking coffee?" Isis asked with wide eyes, raised eyebrows, and a grin. She glanced behind Sebastian where Selena offered her a half smile.

Luther, however, was anything but amused. "I'll tell you what is going on," he cut Isis off. "The girl is constantly undisciplined in her training and easily distracted. That was clear yesterday afternoon when she lost control of the power."

"With all due respect, Luther," Sebastian replied, "you have trained us well, but she is our kid. Let us handle this."

Luther scoffed. "How? By coddling her and treating her like a helpless child at each step of her training? She will never learn to be a witch, especially when the time for that need arises."

"You don't have to browbeat her, Luther," Selena snapped like a lioness protecting her den. "She is young, and it was her first time out on stage. Both of you need to understand that mistakes will happen. She will get where she needs to be."

"We shall see if that is true. I hope you are right, for all our sakes." Luther turned his head in disgust. He stormed out of the living room and into the hotel hallway, allowing the door to slam on his way out.

"What the hell is eating him?" Sebastian asked.

"I *am* going to be a witch," Isis whispered with her head down and bottom lip trembling. "I'll be a good one, too."

Selena sat next to Isis, throwing her arms around her. "Luther was just as harsh with us growing up. Maybe even more so. That's how he shows he loves us, right, Sebastian?"

"We like to think so," Sebastian answered. "He's right about one thing, Isis—you do seem distracted. Does this have anything to do with why you spent so much time at the yogurt shop? And, why it took you so long to get back last night?"

Isis nodded. She figured they had a tracking spell on her—she always suspected they kept an eye on her each time she went out alone. Not that she minded—as long as they were near, Isis felt safe. At least they never directly spied on her as far as she knew. They just kept tabs on her location.

"Did something happen over there?" Selena asked.

"Kind of." Isis picked her head up. "At the yogurt shop, I...I met a boy."

Sebastian raised an eyebrow. "What boy?"

"His name is Zack. He does magic, but not our kind, like real magic."

"Real magic?"

"Well, I mean he's a magician, but a real one, not a

witch like us. He performs at the other show."

"What other show?" Sebastian exchanged a confused glance with Selena.

"The one in the Felicity Hotel. It's not that far from us. It's his uncle's act, The Amazing Herb Galloway Show, but Zack performs with him. He's really good, too."

"Oh my, look at those cheeks blush!" Selena tightened her squeeze. "This Zack must have made quite the impression."

"He did," Isis said through a joker-sized grin. "He made a card disappear in one hand and reappear in his other hand. I have no idea how he did it."

"We've made large animals disappear and reappear on the stage," Sebastian pointed out. "One time, we even did so with a truck."

"Yeah, but we use spells and illusions. He doesn't have any of that. He's doing it without tapping into any of the power."

"Are you sure?" Selena asked.

"Yeah," Isis answered. "I'm pretty sure he's not like us."

"Have you made plans to see him again?" Sebastian's skeptical tone definitely had "concerned parent" written all over it.

"He invited me to see their show tonight. I'd like to go if that's okay."

The front door swung open. Sacha entered the room. There was an obvious spring in her step. She was wearing the same T-shirt and jeans from last night, although a bit wrinkled. She threw an inquisitive glance while pointing a thumb over her shoulder. "What's Luther brooding about in the lobby? I haven't heard the dramatic exhaling sound through his nose in years."

"Isis was a bit distracted while practicing," Selena answered. "Luther berated her and we…stepped in."

"Yeah, that'll do it." Sacha laughed. "What distracted you, kiddo?"

Selena answered, "It's because she met a boy last night at the yogurt shop."

"Oh, really?" Sacha suddenly stopped in her tracks. "Now, that's a story I want to hear."

She looked at Isis with raised eyebrows as she strolled through the living room. "You're going to have to tell me about him, every single detail. I want to hear it all, but if I'm going to perform tonight, I desperately need a shower."

"And a change of clothes." Selena motioned to the stains in Sacha's wrinkled shirt.

"I get it, Sis, I get it." Sacha threw her sister a dismissive blink. She whirled toward Sebastian and leaned forward with a huge smirk across her face. "Wow, so Daddy's little girl met a *boy*. What do you think about that, Sebastian?"

"You're a riot, Sacha," Sebastian replied with an eye roll. "You should start telling jokes on stage."

"Sach, go," Selena snapped. "Now."

"All right, I'm going." Sacha cackled the whole way to her bedroom.

Sebastian returned his attention onto Isis. "Speaking of performing tonight… Are you asking not to do the show so you can attend this boy's show?"

"No. Our show is at eight and theirs isn't until ten thirty." Isis threw her best wide-eyed pleading expression at Sebastian. It was a look she'd mastered to get him to give in. It always worked, well almost always, at least on the small stuff. "Can I go? Please?"

Selena chuckled. "So, what do you say, 'Dad'?" she asked.

"Hmm," he grunted. "I suppose having a friend your own age would be good for you."

Isis liked how that sounded. She'd never had an actual friend her age, least of all, a guy friend.

"Do you agree, Selena?" Sebastian asked.

"Oh, I do for sure," she answered. "Especially if it gets her out of the hotel a bit more often."

After a momentary pause, Sebastian said to Isis, "I'll tell you what, if you can get through your levitation tonight without a hiccup, you can go see the boy's show."

"Really?"

"Yes."

Isis leaped from the couch and wrapped her arms around Sebastian's neck. "I won't fall, and thank you."

"If you do go, be careful." He rubbed the back of her head. "You know what you can't tell him, right?"

"About us, yeah, I know."

"You don't know this boy, Isis, not yet. You need to keep up your guard when dealing with strangers."

"I get it." But to Isis, Zack wasn't a stranger. Sure, she'd only spent a few hours with him, but it felt so meaningful, like nothing she'd ever experienced before. Something inside insisted that she could trust him.

"I'm ready to try again," she said with a smile. Now, she had additional motivation. She couldn't wait to see Zack tonight, and maybe re-experience that kiss.

Chapter Ten

Isis found herself, once again, hovering high above four thousand amazed onlookers while reciting the words "lighter than air." It was a second chance, although in front of a brand new crowd. More important, it was a second chance to show her coven— no, her family—that she could pull this off without any problems. She especially wanted Luther to see that she could do it, just so she could rub it in his smug face.

Come on, focus on the spell, Isis thought, but once again, her thoughts were consumed with Zack. Mostly, about that kiss at the end of the night. It was her first kiss and it was wonderful. With her concentration divided, she expected to fall again. That meant she couldn't go see his show, and she really wanted to be there. As it turned out, Isis was far less nervous than the previous afternoon, and keeping Zack on her mind actually helped her concentrate. Or, at the very least, it kept those distracting random thoughts out of her head.

Isis followed the routine from the day before. She swam through the air over the crowd, and then traveled through the hoop. As she did so, the hoop vibrated on the string. Isis forced her body through. The hoop floated upward; soon it would hit the ceiling. Somehow, she was causing this. Isis shut her eyes and focused. Only her body should float, and nothing else. Isis opened her eyes. The hoop was now perfectly still. Whew.

It was time to bring the act to a close. This time, however, Isis refrained from the back flips and somersaults. She wasn't taking any chances, not with her evening plans on the line. Instead, she floated to the stage and let her body sink until her feet touched the ground. The crowd applauded, although not as loud as the last time.

"Ladies and gentlemen, let's hear it for the witch who defies gravity, *Isis*!" Sebastian waved a hand toward Isis, allowing her to soak in the cheers. She remained in place with her hands folded against her chest. She glanced at Sebastian. "Get your cheers in now, folks," he said into the microphone while returning her glance, "she has plans tonight and needs to go get ready!"

Isis mouthed the words, "Thank you" to Sebastian through a wide-eyed grin. She took a final bow toward the crowd and then made her way backstage. Isis appreciated that Sebastian changed the show's order so she'd go on earlier.

Sebastian jumped into the next act, clipping the microphone onto its stand, then reaching into his jacket and pulling out three huge katana swords. He tossed the three swords high in the air. Six swords fell, all of which Sebastian caught, one at a time. The crowd loved it, mainly due to the perceived danger. They'd never guess that the swords didn't exist. They were all Sebastian-created illusions, but damn, they looked real.

Soon, Sacha would come out and lean her back against a wooden stand. Sebastian would "throw" the swords at her, each one being a near miss. The crowd would gasp with each throw. The final sword, however, would shoot directly through her chest. A panicked scream always filled the audience. Then, the sword would disappear. Sacha always received loud cheers when she'd reveal herself without injury. Isis loved to listen to the reaction, but not tonight. It was time to head to Zack's show.

Once backstage, a cold, undead glare stopped Isis in her tracks. She hated that expression as it was usually followed with sarcastic criticism. Maybe she needed to stop being so sensitive toward his comments, at least that's what Sebastian and Selena kept telling her.

"That was better," Luther said.

"Really? It was?" Whoa, a rare compliment from Luther. If it weren't attached, her lower jaw would have fallen from her face and hit the floor. "Thank you."

Luther looked up to the ceiling and grunted. "I know I am hard on you, young one, but I feel it is necessary. You have the potential to be a powerful witch, but with that must come responsibility."

"You called me immature and too unfocused to be a witch."

"Those were not my words, although they happen to be accurate. Isis, you must come to realize the more power you take from the energy around us, the more it could corrupt you if you are not careful…"

Luther went on for a while. Isis stood in place and pretended to listen, even offering the occasional nod. She wanted to be respectful, but her mind once again wandered to her anticipation for the evening. Isis was about to go on her first date. Well, technically, she was only invited to see his show, but it could be seen as a date. God, the mere thought made her more nervous than flying in front of the sold out theater.

An elbow leaned on Isis' shoulder. "Forgive him," Sacha sneered. "Luther likes to think of us as soldiers in an upcoming war, and little else."

"My goal is to help you stay alive," the vampire snapped. "In my time, I've seen too many witches extinguished because they suffered either from being horribly unprepared or they became corrupt in their powers."

Isis had heard this numerous times before. Luther reminisced a lot, and usually about his association with various covens. That was all hundreds of years ago. Today, Isis hadn't met any witches other than her own coven. Not like she got out a lot, but she also never heard them talk about other witches either. "There were more witches back in your day, weren't there?" she asked.

"There were many throughout history."

"What happened to them all?" Isis asked. "Why are there, like, none today, except for us?" She didn't even want to get into the fact that Luther was the only vampire she'd ever met, or even heard about.

"Oh no, don't get him started," Sacha said through pinched lips. "To sum it up, Luther believes it's because of technology. He thinks because everyone in the world focuses on TV screens and phones, they don't focus on themselves, so even those with the gift never realize their connection. Isn't that right, Luther?"

"I'm amazed you were paying attention. Now don't you have somewhere to be, like on the stage?" Luther growled at Sacha's teasing.

"I'm on my way, but first, I was sent to deliver a message." Sacha looked down at Isis. "I am to tell you not to dawdle too long. They want you back home shortly after the show ends."

Isis knew who sent Sacha with that message—Sebastian loved the word "dawdle." He constantly looked for a way to use it in a sentence. "Tell them I promise to do my best," she said.

Sacha threw her hands onto Isis' shoulders. She gave her a friendly shake. "Have fun on your very first date, kiddo. You deserve it." She flashed her usual smirk. "Try not to do anything rash or impulsive, okay?"

"Hmph," Luther grunted as he turned away shaking his head in disbelief.

Isis eyed Sacha with raised eyebrows.

Sacha sighed. "Yes, I admit I went through a bit of a phase when my mom died and we were suddenly being raised solely by Mister Warmth." She waved a hand toward Luther.

"They are summoning you," Luther barked. "Go make yourself useful and impress the audience."

"I should be going," Isis said.

"Of course." Sacha gave her a wink. "Don't want to keep the cute boy waiting."

Isis' lips stretched into a huge grin. Her cheeks burned.

"Remember, they will be waiting up for you. Trust me on that." Sacha backpedaled toward the curtain. "The last thing you want is a couple of frantic witches tearing apart all of Las Vegas looking for you."

Isis responded with a nod. She was sure that wasn't an empty threat. But she hoped to have a good reason to stick around just a little bit after the show.

Chapter Eleven

"Keep an eye on the coin, ladies and gentlemen!" Zack held up a quarter between his thumb and forefinger for everyone to see. With his free hand, he pulled a playing card from his vest pocket.

He had seven people in front of his rectangular table, which was covered by a slick black tablecloth. He counted around sixty people in total throughout the night. Sixty was hardly a record, but it was still a decent showing. He hoped it translated to a good crowd for tonight's show. He had the youngest of his current audience, a girl of around six in a pink dress, holding out her hand, palm up. Zack had found that an audience always showed more excitement when he used their young children as volunteers. He placed the quarter on the little girl's open palm.

Zack waved the playing card just above her hand. It was an ace of spades. "Keep a close eye…" He yanked the playing card away, revealing a now-empty palm.

The crowd shouted a collective, "wow." One man, presumably the dad, checked the girl's hand to see if the quarter had gone through her skin.

In the excitement, Zack palmed the coin off the back of the card and slipped it up his sleeve. He had pulled off this trick at least a hundred times. In fact, it was possibly the easiest of his entire repertoire. No one ever suspected the playing card had a glue stick line underneath the design on the back.

Zack caught the sight of another onlooker a few steps behind the group. It was Isis. Part of him had doubted she would actually show. He almost hoped she wouldn't. Zack hadn't told his uncle yet that he wanted them to pull out of the charade. He felt as much guilt over disappointing his uncle as he would if he went through with the plan. Then again, maybe he wouldn't have to either. Neither of them had seen or heard from Victoria Hunter the entire day. Hmm, maybe it didn't need to be a charade, but a genuine relationship.

"Okay, folks, I am done for now, but if you enjoyed what you've seen here, and would like to experience even bigger and better magic, The Amazing Herb Galloway Show begins in less than one hour! Tickets are still available at the hotel's front desk!"

The crowd applauded. "Are you Herb Galloway?" one gray haired lady asked.

"I'm his nephew, Zack, but I'll be on stage as well." He gathered his playing cards along with the tip cup filled with single dollar bills. "Believe me, though, The Amazing Herb Galloway is far better than I could ever hope to be."

"Well, I think you're pretty amazing," she said.

Zack appreciated the compliment, but he'd appreciate it even more if it led to the group going into the hotel and buying tickets. He hustled around the crowd toward Isis. Now that he'd seen her, he was thrilled she had come, especially in those tight blue jeans and green T-shirt. "Hey, you came," he said with excitement.

"Yeah!" Isis grabbed Zack's hands and gazed into his eyes. "I'm really excited to see you perform."

"Thanks. We don't have the real cool props like your show. We do a lot of traditional stuff. It's still a fun show."

"I'm sure it'll be awesome." Isis wrapped her arms around Zack's triceps. "Would you believe this will be the first time I've ever seen a real live magic show?"

Zack's mouth gaped. "You mean…besides your own, right?"

Isis let out a nervous giggle. "Well, yeah. Duh."

A high-pitched voice squeaked Zack's name. Bambi waved Zack over as she stepped through the hotel's double glass doors. From the corner of his eyes, he caught Isis eyeing Bambi's tight white skirt, which barely covered an inch of her legs.

"Hey, Bambi, what's up?" Zack walked in her direction. Isis followed.

"Herbie's asking for you to come inside. He told me to get you."

"I have my phone." He tapped his right back pocket. "Why didn't he just call me?"

"I don't know, I didn't ask." Bambi glared at Isis. "Who's *this* girl?" She pointed a pinky finger at Isis. "I'm not getting replaced, am I?"

"No, Bambi, this is my friend, Isis. She's here to see the show, not be a part of it."

"Oh." She offered Isis the fakest smile in human history. "Nice to meet you." Back to Zack, she said, "I'll be in there soon. I just need a quick smoke."

"I really want to turn her into a frog," Isis whispered as they left the vicinity of Bambi's smoke break and entered the hotel.

"Can witches really turn people into frogs?" Zack went along with her character play.

"No, not really."

They laughed. Zack brought his arm behind Isis to place it around her shoulders. He quickly pulled it back. What if she wasn't ready for that sort of intimacy? Then again, they had shared a passionate kiss last night.

"When I hit the stage, the first thing I do is stick Bambi in the Zig-Zag box," Zack said. "It's an old effect, but still one of my favorites if you pretend it's real."

"I can't wait to see it."

Isis took Zack's hand as they walked in. Apparently, she was ready for the intimacy. He looked into her brown eyes. He could stare into them all night if he didn't have a show to perform. "Wish me luck," he said.

"Good luck, Zack." Isis gave Zack a quick peck on the cheek. A warm sensation traveled through his body. For a moment, he considered asking Isis about ditching the show and going out on another date. No, he couldn't do that to his uncle, or himself. Being alone with Isis excited him, but not at the expense of tonight's performance. He didn't know why he even considered it in the first place.

****

Loud instrumental music and a smattering of applause filled the theater. The Amazing Herb Galloway stepped onto the stage. For Isis, getting to watch the show from the audience instead of peeking through the back curtain was a rare treat. The theater looked more like a large nightclub than an auditorium. The stage was one half the size of the one Isis called home. Still, the place had an intimate feel to it. In fact, a number of audience members greeted one another as if they came to the show on a regular basis.

There was only one level of seats while her theater had two. Most of the front sections were filled while only few scattered seats in the back had people. Isis stood in the aisle toward the back so she could take in the full ambiance. Maybe she'd pick up some ideas she could bring back to Sebastian.

Zack's uncle opened the show by taking off his magic hat and pulling out a long red handkerchief. He placed the hat back on his head and then proceeded to stuff the handkerchief into his right fist through the thumb and forefinger. He then yanked it out from under his pinky fingers. Now, the hankie was a bright blue. Herb slowly opened his fingers to reveal his empty hand—the red handkerchief had either changed or disappeared completely. The crowd applauded and so did Isis.

After years of watching Sebastian work the crowd through the mic, Isis found it strange that Herb Galloway performed without a microphone. Each trick was put to music without a word uttered. What impressed her most was the fact that The Amazing Herb Galloway was not a witch, at least as far as she knew. Maybe they were witches and Zack kept it to himself, but that was doubtful. Despite being a mortal human, Herb was able to make objects such as foam balls and red roses move, disappear, and reappear. He did it all without spells.

Next, Herb presented a small table with a black tablecloth. He brought a girl a few years younger than Isis from the front row to the stage and had her hold the other end of the tablecloth. The table floated up, off the floor. It looked like it wanted to float to the ceiling if not for Herb and the girl holding the tablecloth ends. The young volunteer peeked at the bottom, but the widened eyes she threw toward the audience suggested she didn't see anything that would explain this miracle.

Once the girl stepped away, the table seemed to have a mind of its own, trying to get away from the magician. Herb kept pulling it back. One time, the table even tried to fly well over his head until he yanked it back by the tablecloth. It reminded Isis of her "lighter than air" spell. If Herb accidentally let go of the tablecloth, would the table fly off like a helium balloon? Nah, she had a hunch he had full control of the table, although she had no idea how he was doing it.

Finally, the moment she waited for—Zack came out. He rolled a large, thin rectangular box on wheels. The silhouette of a woman's body was painted on the red surface door with four holes for the head, both hands, and one foot. Zack placed the box in the middle of the stage. He ran offstage, then returned leading Bambi by the hand to the box.

Herb unlocked a latch and opened the box's door. Isis squinted, but she couldn't see a lot of room inside for Bambi, who stepped in anyway. Herb shut the door and locked it. Bambi stuck her head, hands, and one foot through the holes. The music boomed from the speakers while Zack stepped offstage again. Bambi, meanwhile, wiggled each of her hands and foot as Herb pointed to them one at a time.

Zack returned, holding the black handles of two huge blades above his head. Each measured the length of the box. Zack smacked the blades together. The loud clang echoed throughout the theater. He handed one to Herb who held it up for all to see.

Herb slid it directly through the box around Bambi's chest area. Zack followed by sliding the second blade into the box near her waist. Only the handles protruded. Both magician and magician's nephew spun the box around so the audience could see the end of the blades coming out of the back. Once they turned the box back, Bambi wiggled her hands and foot once again. Isis couldn't even fathom a guess as to how their assistant could have avoided those blades, at least not without witchcraft.

Zack peered out to the audience in dramatic fashion. Isis took it to mean something amazing was about to happen. She moved down the aisle to get a better view. Zack did not disappoint. He placed his hands on the side of the box and pushed the center out, almost separating it from the top and bottom sections. The crowd gasped in much the way Isis often heard during her own shows. Zack waved his hands between the top and bottom sections. Bambi winked to the audience. She waved her hand, which still stuck out of the center section even though it barely touched the other two sections.

"Where is her body?" Isis whispered to herself.

"They are quite talented," an adult female voice with an accent whispered in her ear.

"Yeah, they are," Isis answered, never taking her eyes off the stage.

"Especially, the boy," the woman said.

Isis smiled. "Yeah, he's real goo—"

A cloth suddenly covered her nose and mouth. The pressure against Isis' nose caused her eyes to water. She tried to pull away but couldn't. A powerful hand held the cloth in place. She grabbed the person's feminine wrist, but it was too strong to budge. She tried to scream, but it was a pointless attempt and only came out as "Mmph." Even if she could scream through the cloth, no one would have heard her over the loud music and applause.

"Sleep, little witch," the woman's voice whispered into her ear.

Isis threw back her elbow. It connected to some part of the woman, but even that didn't make her budge. Isis tried again, but this time her arm moved much slower. Her eyes sagged.

"Sleep," the woman said again. Her voice was almost rhythmic.

Isis wasn't sure what to do. The thought, *block the poison*, ran through her head. She had the power to do just about anything. Maybe if she could cause her body to block the effects of this smelly stuff, she could escape. Her attempt at a spell refused to work. That hadn't happened since she started her training at nine years old.

Isis felt her legs giving out. She wanted to throw another elbow, but her arms wouldn't listen. Her eyelids fought the attempt to keep them open. The last thing she remembered seeing through blurred eyes was Zack raising his arms on stage.

Chapter Twelve

Zack took one last bow to the audience as the lights came up. Uncle Herb and Bambi both did the same. Bambi took off for her dressing room, which was actually an out of order hotel room on the second floor; Herb and Zack had an actual dressing room behind the stage. It wasn't a large room, by any means, but it was big enough for clothes and some of their props.

The crowd dispersed to the back doors. Zack felt good about tonight's performance. Not that they had more of an audience than usual, but there was one particular audience member he wanted to impress—Isis. Knowing she was out there inspired him. He felt that inspiration in all his moves and mannerisms throughout the performance.

Zack scanned the theater, searching for Isis. A few people still lingered, but she was not among them. He expected to see her either waiting in the back or making her way to the stage. She wasn't in either location.

"Are you sure she came?" Herb asked, reading Zack's confused expression.

"Yes, she was here. We walked in together." Zack took another look at the stands. "Could she have left early?" Was Isis losing interest in him already? Every instinct in his body told him that she felt the same way he did. Then again, what did he know about girls? From what he'd seen, they preferred guys like Glen over him.

Herb put a hand on Zack's shoulder. "Maybe it's just as well. None of this sat right with my conscience. If Victoria comes around, I'll tell her we're pulling out. Best it ends before it begins."

"What about our show, Uncle Herb? What happens if they kick us out?"

"We'll come up with something." Herb stroked the back of Zack's neck.

Zack was pleased with his uncle's change of heart. He was really hoping to see Isis again, only this time not under false pretenses.

Herb removed his black magic hat and stepped into the back, heading toward their dressing room. Zack, meanwhile, took one last look at the theater where the last of the crowd cleared out. Damn, he really thought she'd have stayed after the show to see him. Maybe his uncle was right. Maybe it was time to forget about her, if only he could—

"*What the hell?*" Herb screeched.

Zack sprinted for the dressing room. A million paranoid thoughts ran through his head as to what could have made his uncle scream like he'd never heard before.

He stopped short. "Oh my God!" he exclaimed. This certainly wasn't anywhere on his radar.

Isis was slumped in a wooden chair, her eyes shut tight as if she'd been knocked out. Her hands were tied together behind the chair. Victoria stood in front of the chair. She looked over her shoulder at Zack and Herb with an annoyed scowl on her face.

"You abducted her?" Herb cried out. "Are you out of your mind?"

"What is your contention?" Victoria crossed her arms. "You want to find out their secrets, as do I. This is how it happens."

Her nonchalance made Zack's blood boil. She nodded his way. "You've done well, young man. Congratulations."

"How are you learning her secrets? You knocked her unconscious!" Zack clenched his fists. His heart rate sped up by several beats. "Uncle Herb, we can't let this happen." He wanted to do something, anything. But what?

"You do not want her awake." Victoria's tone became short and fierce. "It would be far too dangerous for you."

"Because you think she's a witch?" Zack shouted.

"Your lack of belief does not make it less truthful." Victoria brushed her hair to the side and sneered, forcing Zack to take a step backward. "Your part in this is over." She pointed to the door behind them. "Now, leave us alone. Your payment will be the end of their show, as we agreed."

"Uncle Herb, this woman is clearly insane," Zack said, realizing that they had just made a deal with the proverbial devil.

Herb motioned for Zack to clam up.

"Think this through, Victoria," he cried out. "You've just abducted this girl. Whatever you believe she is, it's still wrong, not to mention, a felony!"

"Is it your goal to continue wallowing in mediocrity, Herbert Galloway?" Victoria scoffed. "The very bane of your existence will be eliminated by night's end. All you have to do is nothing. Just leave."

Zack opened his mouth to protest, but his attention

was caught by a groan that came from behind Victoria. Isis' eyes slowly opened. She gazed around the room in a dazed state.

"Where...where am I?" she said with a yawn.

"You are awake. Excellent." Victoria smiled toward Isis. "I've been looking forward to meeting you."

"What's going on?" Isis tried to stand. She realized that she couldn't. Her head tilted with eyes wide as saucers. "Why am I..." Isis locked eyes with Zack. "Oh my God, Zack, did you do this to me?"

Zack's head drooped with guilt. He wanted to apologize, but at this point, it was far too late for that.

"I will ask you one last time..." Victoria growled like an angry dog protecting its supper. "Leave us."

Herb took a deep breath and stepped forward. "This is not continuing. Zack, untie her. Now."

Zack's head picked up with vigor. Finally, he and his uncle were on the same page regarding this Victoria woman. "With pleasure."

Herb pointed a finger at Victoria. "As for you, lady, don't make me have to physically throw you out of my theater—"

Victoria stepped in Zack's path. "I...said... LEAVE!"

Victoria's eyes turned black like charcoal. Her lips parted revealing two teeth longer than the rest. Each protruded from opposite sides of her upper jaw. A heavy wind formed and plowed through the dressing room. Clothes flew from their hangers. Furniture, including chairs and the Zig-Zag Box, tipped over. The wind took hold of Zack and Herb. It lifted them off the ground and tossed them out of the dressing room.

The door slammed shut. They fell to the stage floor. "What the hell just happened?" Herb screamed.

Zack jumped to his feet and, with a running start, slammed himself against the dressing room door. Nothing happened except he jammed his shoulder.

"She has Isis!" he yelled at his uncle. "We have to do something...we should call the police!"

"We can't call the police." Herb struggled to his feet.

"Why not?" Zack punched the door. The wood refused to budge.

"We are accomplices to this, Zack," Herb shouted back at him. "We would be charged with conspiracy to kidnap a minor."

"But we didn't know."

The moment he said it, Zack knew that defense would not get them far. They had to do something, get help from somewhere, because Uncle Herb was right. They were responsible for whatever harm this woman would inflict on Isis. The thought tore at his insides like a wolverine swimming through his bloodstream.

It was up to them to save Isis. But, how? Even if he could get the door open, how could they stop this woman who could somehow create wind?

Then, it hit him. Victoria may have been lying to them the entire time, but maybe not about everything.

"I know what to do." Zack leaped off the stage and ran up the aisle. "I'll be back with help!"

"What help? Where are you going?"

Zack didn't respond. He hated to leave his uncle in such a confused state, but time was of the essence, and he had to move fast.

Chapter Thirteen

The trip between the Felicity Hotel and the Sapphire Resort usually took twenty minutes by foot. This time, Zack made it in less than ten. He nearly got hit by cars while running through streetlights on two separate occasions, but at least he made it faster than ever before. Now, he had to find Isis' family. Victoria had said that they were witches, a statement Zack found ludicrous since he didn't believe witches existed at all.

Hell, he still wasn't sure he believed in anything supernatural, but he couldn't rule out the possibility, not after everything that just happened. He and his uncle were thrown from their own dressing room by a violent wind that churned from nowhere. Apparently, the only truth Victoria left out was that she, too, was a witch.

Breathing heavily and sweating profusely, Zack ran through the lobby and into the theater.

"Sir, can I help you?" the clerk behind the front desk shouted.

Zack grabbed the door and pulled. Thankfully, it was unlocked. Hopefully, they'd be in there.

He ran halfway down the aisle before realizing the entire auditorium was empty. Isis had told him they practiced on stage all the time, even at night, but with the curtain closed. The curtain, however, was wide open. It was as deserted as the theater itself. How would he find them? He didn't know which room was theirs. He only knew they stayed somewhere in the hotel. Even if he did know where to find them, what would he say? "Hey, folks, I hope you're really witches because I just helped abduct your adopted kid through trickery and deceit." Yeah, that would go over about as well as a winter cruise to Antarctica.

Zack's vision blurred. He didn't feel sick or lightheaded. It felt more like the theater itself fell out of focus. A pressure filled his stomach as if he were sitting on an airplane during takeoff. He shut his eyes tight, hoping that would clear whatever was happening to him. When he reopened them, he found himself against the wall in a large living room. His mouth opened. He wanted to either start asking questions or just scream. Nothing but dry heaves left his throat.

Zack was surrounded on three sides by two adult women and a man. One creepy-looking man with really white skin stood behind them. He remembered each of them from the show—these were The Witches of Vegas. He couldn't let them see him lose it, but every muscle in his body suddenly felt like Jell-O.

He finally found it in him to speak. "How…how did you do this, b-bring me here?" His jaw trembled with each word. "Is this…your hotel room?"

"Isis was right," the one Zack remembered as Sacha said. "He *is* cute."

Zack stepped forward. "Oh, thank God, I've been looking for you—"

Sebastian snatched two handfuls of Zack's shirt and slammed him against the wall. "Where is she?" Spittle hit Zack in the face.

"Dude, chill," Zack shouted. "That's what I'm here

about—"

"She went to see *you*, and now we can't sense her anywhere!" Sebastian leaned in.

Zack smelled the meat and potatoes Sebastian had for dinner. "Where the hell is my kid?" His eyes narrowed with rage.

"She's in trouble. That's why I'm here." Zack could see the air shooting out of Sebastian's nose.

"Sebastian, wait…" Selena placed a hand on his shoulder. "I'm getting a vibe from his left vest pocket."

Sebastian's eyebrows pulled together. "Whatever you have, take it out, and do it slow."

"It's nothing, I swear. It's just my cards." Zack reached into his pocket with his thumb and middle finger the way he saw people do it on television when a cop wanted to see what was in their pocket. He removed the cards as if he were playing the crane game and held it up for all to see. "See? No threat here."

Selena took the cards and examined them. Her angry eyes then shot at Zack like darts. "These have been enchanted with a love spell."

"Is that why Isis went so gaga over this boy?" Sacha barked.

"You put a love spell on her?" Sebastian's grip on Zack's shirt tightened. The collar tightened against his windpipe. He gulped hard. "Who the hell are you?" Sebastian growled.

"I don't know what you're talking about!" He couldn't remember a time he'd felt more nervous or confused. His entire body shook. "What the hell is a love spell?"

"Sebastian, wait. This spell goes both ways." Selena stared down at the deck of cards against her palm. "He's under it as well."

Sebastian's grip relaxed, but he still kept a tight hold of Zack's shirt. "Am I…am I really under a spell?" Zack took a hard gulp. His heart slammed against his chest. They had to be kidding. Just thinking about Isis made his heart flutter, but those feelings were real. Weren't they? They had surfaced fast, faster than he ever expected. He couldn't get her out of his head even when he tried. But maybe that was how love worked. It wasn't like he had a point of reference or experience in this area.

Selena handed the deck to Sacha, who dropped them in a metal bowl. She widened her eyes and concentrated her gaze. A flame shot up from the bowl. There was no match involved. That was a magic trick Zack had done many times, but with flash paper. He didn't catch any concealed in Sacha's hands. Unless some gimmick slipped by his notice? If not, then this woman made fire with her mind.

"Okay." Sebastian let go of Zack's shirt. "I need you to look at me." He grabbed Zack by the chin. "Look into my eyes." Sebastian's blue eyes brightened.

Zack couldn't turn away from them. It was like looking into a river that flowed upstream. Soon, everything around him had a blue tint.

Sebastian's voice echoed. "Tell me, everything. Tell me the truth."

A wave of euphoria filled Zack's head. He suddenly felt as if he was in a dream. He was there but not in control. His mouth was moving and, even though he heard his own voice, it sounded like someone else was speaking. "Victoria said she wanted to expose you, to run you out of Las Vegas. She said she was a reporter who debunked magicians and that you are all witches. She said if I befriended Isis, she'd let the secrets to your illusions slip. We thought she was just some loon until her eyes went black and she created wind, actual wind. It carried us out of our dressing room and then made the door slam shut. Victoria lied to us. Now she has Isis."

Through the trance, he heard Sebastian's voice. "Why do you want to run us out of town?"

"You hurt our show," Zack heard himself say. "We can't draw good crowds anymore. We're getting desperate. This was the only way."

Another voice spoke, this one was deep and spooky. "Sebastian, release the spell. Now."

Zack's head cleared. The room came back into focus along with all the faces staring his way. That included one pale, pinched expression. It was the vampire who ended the show. Isis had mentioned his name. Luther.

"Describe this woman," the man said.

"Um, weird accent, black eyes, and two sharp teeth when she gets pissed. Seriously pale skin." Zack took a close look at Luther. He realized this man was not wearing any sort of stage make-up. "Her complexion was just like yours."

"Oh, no," Luther gasped. "Not now, not yet."

From the terrified look on his face, Zack realized the name would have made Luther white as a ghost, if he didn't already have that skin tone. What could Victoria have done to bring pause to a man who looked like he came out of an old black and white monster movie himself?

"Luther, what is it?" Selena asked with concern.

"The homeless man," Luther mumbled, more to himself that anyone else in the room. "It had to be her."

Selena took a grip of his arm. "Luther, who are you talking about?"

"It is Valeria. She has returned," the vampire replied.

Sebastian turned away from Zack. His interrogation suddenly shifted to Luther. "Who is Valeria?"

"Pale skin, black eyes, and I'm guessing...fangs? She sounds like a vampire." Sacha raised her shoulders along with her eyebrows. "But then there's the love spell and he said she created wind. Since when does a vampire have the powers of a witch?"

The room grew awkwardly silent with all eyes on Luther. Zack was sure if he had a knife, he could cut the tension in the air.

Finally, Luther exhaled. "Valeria was a witch, and a powerful one. Before she was turned."

"Turned? Like into a vampire?" Zack exclaimed. "So, you really are witches and vampires? None of this makes any sense."

"Quiet." Sebastian shot Zack an evil eye. Zack took the hint and stopped talking. Sebastian returned his attention to Luther. "Who would ever turn a witch? An immortal with that sort of power—" Sebastian paused in mid-sentence. When Luther didn't respond, he asked, "Did *you* turn her?"

"I did," Luther responded, confirming what even Zack had figured out.

"For God's sakes, Luther, why?" Sebastian threw a hand over his forehead. "Don't tell me she's yet another soldier to fight the supposed impending threat you've been preaching at us for as long as I can remember—"

"Listen to me!" Luther roared. It seemed Sebastian's air quotes enraged him. His eyes blinked pure black. "Valeria *is* the threat!" He stepped eye to eye with Sebastian. "She is an immortal witch with the power and the motivation to destroy this world as we know it. She is the one I have feared could return, and you are not nearly ready to face her."

Selena placed a hand on Sebastian's arm and pulled him a step back. "Why would you turn her?" she asked Luther. "You wouldn't even turn Mom when it would have saved her."

"I made a terrible error in judgment." Luther's eyes blinked. He looked ready to tear up, except his faucets had apparently died out, probably a really long time ago. "We were…together, and in love."

"I'm assuming this was before you were hooked up with our mom?" Sacha said.

"This was centuries before your mother. We lived in Salem, Massachusetts in the late 1500s. It was a different time and there were far more witches out there fighting for their lives than even exist today."

"Okay, so you've always had a thing for witches," Sebastian interrupted. "But that doesn't answer the question. Why did you turn her?"

"I went through many relationships that ended due to sickness, old age, then death. Experience it enough and loneliness sets in. I wanted a partner by my side where we could share eternity. I believed Valeria was that partner."

"It went bad, didn't it?" Selena asked, revealing a hint of sympathy.

Luther nodded. "We formed a coven, all of which

we had saved from the trials. We couldn't save all, but we saved some and kept them safe. That wasn't enough for Valeria. She didn't just want to save witches or punish those who led the mobs. No, she wanted witches to rise and enslave or extinguish all of mankind. Very few of our coven stood with her while many disagreed with this course of action. She murdered one young witch in front of us as a warning. She killed her own kind without hesitation or mercy."

"What did you do?" Sacha asked the question on everyone's mind. "How did you stop her?"

"I collaborated with those who survived her wrath to surround, overwhelm, and incapacitate her." Luther's eyes closed. "I could not bring myself to kill her. None of us could. She did save so many of the coven. We understood her goals were not evil, but they had become corrupt. One witch, in experimenting with teleportation, felt the presence of another dimension. She called it the Other World. The witches combined their control of the energy to open a portal into the Other World and exiled her. On this plane, there was no evolved life, just animals she could hunt for blood and survive. With Valeria cut off from the energy of this planet, we hoped she would never find a way to return."

"But we were the back-up plan just in case she did," Sebastian said.

"You are but the latest. There were others over the centuries."

"Okay, let me see if I'm following this," Zack chimed in. "You're actually a bunch of witches and a vampire who go on stage and pretend to be witches and a vampire? You know that's so messed up, right?"

"So, this chick is, like, a super powerful witch and

an immortal vampire," Sacha said, which let Zack know he wasn't part of this conversation. "And, she's got a mad-on for you." She pointed at Luther.

"And, she has Isis," Selena added. "We have to find her."

"She has Isis at the theater!" Zack shouted. Finally, the group turned his way, acknowledging he was still in the room. "I mean, my theater, not yours."

"Take us there," Sebastian stated. "Now."

"That's why I came here, so you can save her." Zack stepped away from the wall. "We need to get there fast. Do you have a car or a broomstick or something?"

"We can get there much faster." Selena placed her hands on Zack's head above his ears. His immediate instinct was to back away. "Relax," she said and firmed up her grip. "I need you to think of the location. Visualize your theater where Valeria has Isis. I can use your thoughts as a beacon to take us there."

"And witches don't fly on broomsticks," Sacha barked. "FYI, we don't wear black pointy hats, either."

Zack rubbed a hand along the goosebumps that formed across his arm. He'd already teleported once— no reason to get nervous now. He focused on the theater that he knew so well. It was where he last saw Victoria or Valeria…whatever her name was.

Soon, the room blurred just as it had before.

Chapter Fourteen

Isis closed her eyes tight. "Untie," she whispered over and over again. The chant didn't help. No matter how much she concentrated, focused, and everything else she'd been accused of not doing during practices, the ropes around her wrists wouldn't budge. A loud snort made her head jump.

"You are confused," the pale-skinned lady said from the doorway. She had a slanted-eyed look as if Isis had food stuck to her face. "Did your coven not teach you about enchanted crystals?"

She tapped her foot twice on the floor. A shiny diamond-like crystal about the size of a toe rested between Valeria's feet. Although Isis hadn't used them, she had learned about crystals from Sacha, who had more knowledge on their use than even Selena or Sebastian. In fact, Sacha had a purse full of them hidden in her closet. Five crystals, enchanted with a spell, needed to be placed at equal lengths in a pentagon shape. Within that shape, a witch's influence over the energy increased. They could do many things, including the ability to cut another witch's connection to the energy.

"I'm powerless," Isis mumbled.

"You are."

"You're a witch, too." Isis had never met one

114

outside of her own circle.

The woman laughed. "That, and so much more."

Isis straightened her back. She scrunched her face in an attempt to look tough. "Let me go."

The woman reached out and slapped her hand across Isis' face. Isis winced. The palm felt rough like tree bark. "It is about time we met. My name is Valeria. I am your new mistress. The first rule you must learn is that you are never to make demands of me. I am the teacher, you are the student, and I will teach you all you need to know."

She grabbed Isis by the hair and yanked her head. Two teeth, which looked like fangs, protruded from her top lip. "My training will be harsh, if necessary, but there is much for you to learn. Do you understand?"

Isis' guts raced up into her throat. She wanted to defy this woman in the worst way, but without powers and tied to a chair, defiance wouldn't do much good. She'd probably just get slapped again. Best to play along, at least for now. "I...I understand," she said through gritted teeth.

"Then we are off to a good start." Valeria smiled. Her teeth were various shades of black and brown. She loosened her grip of Isis' hair. "Tell me, Isis, do you know why Luther and his coven sought you out? Of all the witches in hiding across the globe, why did they choose you?"

"They said..." Isis pushed against her inner cheek with her tongue, trying to alleviate the stinging sensation. "They sensed me. They never sensed any others."

"I'm sure that is not true." Valeria leaned in, bringing them nose to nose. Her breath smelled like worn socks. "They sought you because your connection with our world's energy is strong. I can sense it and I'm sure they could as well. You have the potential to become very powerful. Power enough, in fact, to change the course of history."

Isis had been told many times about her great potential. She had taken it as simple hyperbole meant to motivate her during training sessions. "They say I have a purpose." Isis' voice barely carried beyond a whisper.

Valeria slapped her hands together. "On that, I agree. On said purpose, I am sure Luther and I wholeheartedly disagree. You were not gifted with such power to be a court jester."

"How do you know Luther?" The question, and nasty tone, blurted out before Isis could even consider it. She flinched, expecting to get slapped again. Instead, Valeria smiled.

"You are insolent. I will need to break you of that." She threw Isis a curious expression. "I am surprised Luther would tolerate such behavior. Have hundreds of years softened him so?"

She stared down at Isis for several moments, apparently waiting for an answer.

Isis decided to give her one. "They're going to come for me, and for you," she said through an angry glare. It earned her another hard slap. This one almost knocked her, and the chair, over.

"I know they will." Valeria gave Isis a glare of her own. "I have been planning for that meeting for a very long time."

Isis shifted her gaze to some green smoke that poured into the room from under the doorway. The smoke caused Isis' eyes to burn, forcing her to blink rapidly. Apparently, it had the same effect on Valeria, who used a forearm to shield her face. Could this be her family riding to the rescue?

The door kicked open. Zack's uncle Herb stormed in with a revolver in his hand. He pointed it at Valeria, who waved her hands at the smoke.

"I don't care what kind of crazy you are," he roared, "this ends now!"

"Please excuse me," Valeria quipped toward Isis, "this will only take a moment."

Herb moved forward and brought the barrel of the gun inches in front of Valeria's face. The gun suddenly turned into a small green snake with the tail in Herb's hand.

"What the hell?"

The snake showed its fangs and lunged for his wrist.

Herb stumbled back. He flung the snake against the wall. Once it hit the floor, the snake turned back into the gun.

This had to be an illusion, Isis realized. Those were Sebastian's specialty, but she'd never seen him create one so fast, and without a verbal spell.

A flame formed in Valeria's right palm. It grew into a ball of fire. With Herb off balance, Valeria pulled her hand back like a pitcher about to deliver a fastball. As her arm went forward, Isis kicked Valeria in the back of the knee. The fireball exploded against the ceiling. Herb charged in, firing a right clenched fist to Valeria's jaw.

"Yes!" Isis cheered.

The celebration didn't last. Valeria shot to her feet and growled. Faster than the eyes could see, she reached out with her right hand and grabbed Herb by the throat. Despite his clear weight advantage, Valeria slammed him through the doorway. She then floated high above the stage, taking Herb with her.

"Wh-what are you?" Herb managed to eke out through a closed windpipe.

With a high-pitched shriek, Victoria released her grip. Herb fell to the stage floor. His body crashed through a table. Herb rolled onto his back, clutching his left arm. His arm lay crooked, possibly broken. Isis gasped.

"It's been hours, time to eat." Valeria floated downward, landing on top of her intended meal.

A shriek from across the theater grabbed Valeria's attention. "Uncle Herbert!" It was Zack's voice. He was here and he hadn't come alone.

The cavalry had arrived.

Chapter Fifteen

"Well, well, it's The Witches of Vegas! Cue applause."

Valeria stood at the end of the stage as if she were the star of her own show. Behind the numerous rows of seats, Luther glared at her like an animal ready to pounce. Sebastian had made his way to Luther's left while Sacha and Selena went right. It looked like a western standoff at the OK Corral.

Zack sprinted down the aisle. He leaped onto the stage in one hurdle and kneeled by his uncle. He helped Herb pull his left arm against his chest. The movement made Herb cringe. "Zack, what the hell's going on here?" he asked.

"We're stuck in the middle of something big," Zack replied.

"Valeria, I know you have seethed vengeance for over four hundred years," Luther said in a surprisingly calm tone. "However, I will make a plea to your better judgment. This is a different time. The world has changed. Witches are no longer burned alive as public spectacles. There is no longer a reason for what you are looking to do."

"Guys, it's a trap!" Isis screamed from the dressing room. She struggled, seated in a chair, her hand bound behind her. "She was waiting for you! She's planning something—"

Valeria waved her hand. The door slammed shut.

"From what I've seen in the years I have been free, nothing has changed," Valeria shouted across the theater. "Witches are close to extinct and those who are out there remain in hiding. That makes my resolve even stronger." She looked across from Sebastian to the sisters. "If this misguided coven is your way of hindering me, then they will be unfortunate casualties in the creation of a new and improved world."

"I will not allow you to harm them!" Luther's voice was filled with intensity.

"Is that care and concern I hear in your voice, Luther?" Valeria laughed. "There was a time you cared about *me*, before you and our witches betrayed and banished me to an empty, desolate realm."

"Oh my God, what are we waiting for?" Sacha shouted. "Let's take this bitch down!"

"Do not force this, Valeria," Luther warned.

"Consider these events forced, Luther!" Valeria placed her hands behind her back. "Just as you forced me to fight for my life for hundreds of years!"

"Hundreds of years?" Zack asked more to himself than anyone else.

Valeria removed a wooden stick from her belt. It was a foot long and had a sharp point at the end. She tucked it between her left arm and lower back. It was a subtle move that went unnoticed by Luther, or anyone else other than Zack.

"That planet was devoid of intelligent life," Luther said.

"Yes, intelligent life." Valeria's jaw clenched, as did her fists. "The planet where you exiled me was full

120

of animalistic creatures."

"So you could feast and stay alive."

"They were hunters and predators. Many attacked in packs. I would corner one for its blood, but hordes of them tried to rip me apart."

"No, we peered into the Other World. The animals were docile. They were easy prey for you to satisfy your hunger."

"That was hundreds of years ago!" Valeria shouted. "Over time, they evolved, as all species do. You clearly did not consider that when you stranded me there for all of eternity."

"No, we did n-not," Luther stammered, revealing a twinge of guilt. "We thought we had placed you in a safe environment."

"Do not fret, Luther. Those creatures couldn't kill me—I'm already dead," Valeria said. "But they did bring me harm. They tore my skin to shreds. The only thing that helped me survive and conquer that world was one lingering thought—the moment I return to accomplish my goals. And the moment I would destroy all you love right in front of your face."

A ball of fire formed in Valeria's right hand. She raised her arm and brought it over her head. Her body shifted to the right. She had the fireball aimed in Sacha and Selena's direction.

"Leave them!" Luther's eyes went dark. His fangs showed. He leaped, clearing every row of seats, and landed on the stage. He lunged at Valeria with both hands reaching for her throat.

"Look out!" Zack shouted, but it was too late.

In one quick motion, Valeria swung her left hand and jabbed the wooden stake into Luther's abdomen. It stopped the vampire dead in his tracks. His body went lifeless. He fell to the floor.

"Luther!" Selena cried. It was followed by gasps from Sebastian and Sacha.

"It's funny…" Valeria stepped over Luther. "Since my return, I've read all these books written by mortals on vampires. Most of the details they get wrong, such as we turn to bats and water blessed by a holy man can kill us. One thing they did guess correctly is our weakness for wood." She let out a loud cackle. "Can you imagine beings of such strength, yet we can be overcome by something as simple as a splinter?"

Sebastian yelled to the sisters, "Let's take her out fast!"

"*Ignis!*" Valeria pointed an open hand toward the sisters.

Another fireball formed, then shot out. It sped through the theater and hit the last row of seats. The backrests in its path spattered in several directions. Selena grabbed Sacha's arm and pulled her away, just beyond the fire's reach. Like a cat, Valeria ran across the top of the seats, row by row, making her way to the sisters.

"Quick," Herb said to Zack, "free the girl."

Zack raced across the stage for the dressing room door. He snatched the doorknob. It wouldn't turn. A kick also had no effect. He rammed it with his shoulder, but the door fought his every attempt to make it budge. He knew the door well in that they had to refurbish it three times over the last five years. It had never been so sturdy.

Zack's eyes shifted to the battle. A thought of getting the hell out of there crossed his mind. He immediately dismissed it. No way was he going to abandon Isis or Uncle Herb. Valeria leapt over the flames, which had filled the back row. She stood face to face with Selena and Sacha. The sisters needed a moment to regain their composure. Sebastian waved his arms. A chair rose out from the row and flew at Valeria. With a flick of her hand, she changed the chair's trajectory so it slammed against the wall. She did the same with the second chair that hurtled her way. The third, she sent back at Sebastian, who dove to the floor, barely escaping its attack.

"You go high, I'll go low," Selena said to her sister.

As if hearing her, Valeria turned her gaze their way.

Suddenly, the earth shook under Valeria's feet, throwing her off balance. Sacha pushed against the air with her right hand. Valeria fell to her knees as if she were suddenly under someone else's control—probably Sacha's. The vampire pointed her palm at Sacha. To Zack, who observed everything from the stage, it looked like a battle of wills, one Valeria was winning if her hand pushing forward and Sacha's pushing back was an indication.

"Together!" Selena hooked her arm around Sacha's.

It was now Valeria against the combined might of both sisters. The struggle lasted for several long seconds, neither willing to budge.

Finally, Valeria's hand turned so her palm was inches from her face. "No!" she shouted. "I will not allow this!"

Despite Valeria's bluster, the witches had her on

the ropes.

"Sebastian, go!" Selena screamed.

Sebastian leaned to the right of Valeria. He spoke into her ear, "Look at the lines of your hand. Notice how the thick and thin lines merge into one another. Notice the levels of light, see the shadows around those lines." Valeria's hand inched closer to her face. "Nothing around you matters except the lines on your hand."

Valeria's body crumpled, her shoulders slumped. The fire along the back row faded.

Zack took another shot at the door to free Isis. He grabbed the handle. It turned, but only slightly. Damn, he had one task. So far, he was failing miserably. The witches, however, were being far more successful in their part.

"The lines remind you that it's been a long time since you slept," Sebastian said. "It reminds you that you are tired...drowsy..."

Suddenly, Valeria's head lifted from her palm to Sacha, making direct eye contact. "*Timor*," she said.

Sacha's eyes widened to the size of grapefruits. She stumbled backward, away from her sister. "Sacha, don't break the connection," Selena exclaimed.

But she did. Their hands disconnected.

"Oh, boy," Sebastian said.

Valeria stood up. Zack suddenly charged off the stage. If he could ram his shoulder into Valeria's back, take her down or just distract her so The Witches of Vegas could recoup...

Valeria raised her arms in the air. "*Gutta caeli*," she shouted.

A tornado shot from the ground. Zack flew

upward, his body twisting in the air. It was like being in a zero-gravity chamber, or at least what he figured that would feel like. It wasn't just Zack, either; his uncle and the witches were in the air as well, looking just as petrified. Besides Valeria, only Luther remained on the floor, unmoving. The end of the wooden stake protruded from his stomach.

Zack flailed his arms and legs. It didn't help. He worried most about his uncle, who was up there as well, but with what Zack presumed was a broken wing.

Valeria dropped her arms. Zack found himself plummeting to the floor. He hit hard, head first. Bright stars filled his eyes. Zack rubbed them, trying to clear his vision. All around, the others were sprawled across the floor.

"I like your sleep spell idea." Valeria stood over Sebastian. She spread her arms. "I think I will use it, myself."

Zack tried to push his upper body away from the floor, but his arms gave out. His eyelids became heavy. Valeria strolled his way. She flashed a huge grin. Soon, Zack could only see the insides of his eyelids.

Chapter Sixteen

Luther hiked through the deep Pennsylvania forest, his feet dragging through muddy turf. He had to push himself with each step due to the huge carcass of a wild boar hoisted over his shoulder. The meat of the animal did not interest Luther, but the blood inside its body would be quite satisfying. Of course, it would have to be consumed quickly before it went sour. The window of time was usually around six hours after the body stopped breathing.

It was the first day of January in the year 1600. This was not the first time Luther experienced the turn of a century. It certainly wouldn't be his last. As an immortal—or vampire, as folklore had come to call his kind—he would experience many more milestone dates. He had a feeling those milestones would eventually lose their prestige and end up becoming just another day.

At least now he wouldn't have to live through it all alone, because last week he made a decision. He chose to turn his current lover—already a powerful witch in her own right—into someone just like him. It meant he had to kill her first, but only momentarily. This was not a decision he made lightly, or without much thought and conversation with her. Now, Luther would have a partner he could love and depend on for all eternity. He was glad she was a willing participant. This was a decision that would change his continued existence for the better. Now, he'd know love that wouldn't end in a flash.

Luther arrived at his destination, a log cabin deep in the woods. It was the only one of its kind, at least in Pennsylvania. Word had it that these types of homes had become popular in Delaware and Massachusetts. Luther didn't care about making a statement, or getting ahead of a trend, he simply wanted to live undisturbed. The woods were best for solitude.

Luther tossed the boar next to the door, then entered the cabin. Valeria was seated in a hardwood chair staring at a similar chair across the room. Her gaze was wide-eyed and tear-filled. Was she second-guessing the turn? At this point, there was no going back. Now, it was this or a permanent death, and death would not come easily.

"How are you feeling?" Luther asked.

"A mouse ran across the floor," Valeria said, never looking away from the empty chair. "I levitated it into the air and, with a snap of my fingers, broke its little neck."

"What did you do then?"

Valeria turned to face Luther. Blood stained her lips and chin.

"I could not help myself," she said. "The thirst, it overwhelmed me. It gnawed at my stomach like a bear trying to claw its way out."

"You will learn to deal with the hunger over time."

"That is but one concern I have, Luther."

"You know you can ask me anything, Valeria."

"That pale skin of yours." Valeria stood from her

seat and wiped a sleeve across her mouth. "Along with your two fangs. Is that the fate which awaits me?"

"Eventually, yes." Luther took Valeria's hand and placed it against his chest. "It happens over time, but you have many years before you need worry about your complexion."

Valeria took a deep breath and gripped Luther's hand. Her gaze dropped to the floor. "Forgive me, my love. I am still coming to terms with what I am now."

"Are you having regrets, my dear?" Luther asked.

Perhaps they should have discussed it further before Luther turned her. He should have given her time to think about it. Instead, he jumped at her immediate agreement. Part of him worried that if he gave her the time to contemplate, she would eventually refuse.

"No, it's not that," Valeria answered. "I do prefer the knowledge that I, although technically deceased, exist forever. But I am conflicted on how I am defined. I can still feel the planet's energy, perhaps even more than ever before. Does that make me still a witch?"

Luther nodded. "You are that, and much more."

A stinging pain shot through Luther's stomach. It felt sharp and deadly. He spun his head. There was nothing around them except for four walls, two chairs, and the dirt floor. He couldn't recall any reason for such a painful sensation. Surely, he'd remember if something had punctured his skin.

"You are being coy with me, Luther," Valeria snapped. "But, think about what we could do were we to stop hiding from the world in this log house." Her eyes widened. "We could determine the future, assure witches like me are no longer hunted. As immortals, we can make sure that course is never altered."

Her words worried Luther. He could never embrace the idea of abusing their immortality. He was once surrounded by a clan of vampires who looked to do just that. This was back when he was first turned, and then recruited for their army. They saw themselves as gods. Their corrupt selfishness led to war, in-fighting, and the near-extinction of his kind. Now, Valeria wanted to make the same mistakes. These misguided ideas would need further discussion.

"Oh, Luther," Valeria moaned. "I can see in your eyes you disagree."

"Our immortality is not meant for controlling the flow of history."

Her eyebrows rose. "Then, what is our immortality for, Luther?"

"What matters," Luther answered, "is that we will face the world together, forever."

Her eyes suddenly changed. They grew narrow and angry. "Do you mean that, Luther?"

Luther meant every word, yet somehow, he knew this love wouldn't last. Although he had the best intentions, they would never be able to overcome their conflicting beliefs. Valeria's immortality, coupled with her Wiccan connection to the planet, would corrupt her soul to the point they would end in conflict. This was clear to him, but how?

Because this had already played out. At first, Luther thought he was seeing into the future. Then, his mind suddenly reminded him that this was the past. In fact, it was centuries ago.

Luther opened his eyes. As a vampire, he couldn't sleep, but apparently, he could dream—or was he hallucinating? His mind had wandered to the memory of the worst mistake he had ever made. Now, centuries later, the consequence of that mistake hovered over him while a demented smile flashed across Valeria's face.

Luther tried to sit up, but his body wouldn't cooperate. He peered down at his gut where a wooden stake protruded. It had traveled through his abdomen with the sharp end touching the skin on his back. His skin around the wound flared, causing necrosis to set in. Without the fresh blood he had consumed flowing through his body, he would die, just like a mortal.

His last memory was of a battle in an auditorium, a battle they lost. Once again, his judgment was off when it came to Valeria. He thought he could catch her unprepared and end the fight quickly. He should have realized she had been preparing for that fight for hundreds of years. Luther, on the other hand, had become domesticated.

Between the hot sun overhead and the sand under his body, Luther realized he was no longer in that auditorium. Valeria had moved him outside, to the desert perhaps? The sound of water suggested otherwise. Where had she taken him and why? What the hell was she up to?

For Luther to survive, the stake would need to be removed, and soon. Then, he'd need a new dose of fresh blood to heal. He couldn't accomplish either of these tasks on his own, not in his current condition. He needed help, and fast.

It was a struggle to turn his head, but what he observed offered no relief. The witches he had raised and trained for this battle were all facedown and, he presumed, unconscious. At least he hoped they were unconscious and not dead.

Finally, one of the people stirred. It was the mortal boy. His head picked up from the sand. Although they'd only met once, Luther could tell the boy was resourceful, at least for a mortal without any sort of extraordinary abilities. Unfortunately, he wouldn't be much help against Valeria. To stop her, they needed...

Luther's eyelids rolled closed. With that went all feeling in his body. Soon, his ears were filled with nothing but the sound of the ocean and the heavy groans of those around him...

Chapter Seventeen

Zack woke facedown with a mouth full of sand. He spit it out. As he opened his eyes, he realized that the sand was everywhere. It covered his arms, legs, and clothes. He had no idea how long he had been asleep here—or back at the theater—but based on the grogginess, it must have been a while.

The sound of waves hitting the surf filled the background. "Beach?" he murmured.

A large tree in front of him, however, made him second-guess those suspicions. Its bark had a slight green tint and long branches that stretched out several feet. It was also the largest tree he'd ever seen. Round pink fruits with green stems hung from the branches. Zack scanned the area with a hand over his forehead to shield the bright sun. Three more of those trees scattered throughout the area. Not far off, the witches all lay facedown in the sand.

Selena was the first to wake. She lifted her head and peered around, getting her bearings. She placed a hand on Sebastian's knee and gave it a shake. He stirred and lifted his upper body, squinting in the bright light. Then he gasped.

Sacha was the next one up. She crawled over and kneeled next to Luther. The vampire was on his back, his eyes barely open. The end of the wooden handle projected from his midsection. Luther was always pale white, but now he had tints of red in his face as well. From the way Sacha was squeezing his hand, Zack could tell those red blotches were a bad sign.

A loud groan came from Uncle Herb, who used his one good hand to pull himself into a sitting position. Zack pushed through the sand and made his way to his uncle's side. He hooked him under the armpits and helped him lean against the tree.

"Are we on a beach?" Herb asked.

Zack looked back and forth. The area was oval-shaped with water hitting the sand from every direction. "I think we're on an island," Zack answered.

Yes, it definitely was an island, albeit a small one. It couldn't have been bigger than the hotel lobby. How they came here, he could only guess, although it didn't involve any traditional means of transportation.

An elongated shadow formed in the sand. Zack peered up at Valeria, who hovered three feet in the air. She faced the witches with her back to Zack and Herb.

"Ahh, I see you are all awake," she said. "Excellent."

Valeria now had the attention of everyone on this small island.

Only Selena was on her feet. "Where are we?" she asked with what sounded like forced bravado.

"I was exiled for the duration of many lifetimes," Valeria hissed like an angry snake. "And now, the same fate has fallen upon you. This is your new home."

"This is the Other World?" Sebastian picked up a handful of sand and let it run through his fingers.

Valeria held her arms out in a welcoming fashion. "It is similar to our own world with various regions and seasonal changes, but no people. Animals control the Other World, hunting in packs. There are, however, uninhabited areas. This is an uninhabited area." Valeria hovered down to the ground until her feet hit the sand.

"Why are we here?" Sebastian asked.

"Call it a merciful end. It is because you are fellow witches that I am choosing to leave you here as opposed to outright killing you. But I do need you out of my way."

"While you destroy our world?" Selena snapped.

Valeria raised her hands and looked to the sky. "While I restructure the food chain so the most powerful take their rightful place as the dominant species. It is as I would have done hundreds of years ago, had I not been banished by my own coven."

"Let me guess, this restructuring will be under *your* rule?" Sacha shouted, shaking the sand out of her red hair.

"For a time, yes," Valeria answered. "It seems necessary to lead our fellow witches on the correct path. Do not fret. I may someday come back for you, so you may benefit from the new world you sought to prevent."

"No, I don't think so." With determination written across her face, Selena threw out her arm and pointed a finger at Valeria. Nothing happened. "Huh?" She gasped and gaped at the end of her finger.

Valeria grinned. "The energy is different in the Other World. It took me almost four centuries to connect to it."

She waved her hand at Selena, who toppled backward as if she were hit by a moving vehicle. Sebastian grabbed her arm, preventing her from rolling farther across the sand. "So, instead of outright killing us, you're going to leave us here to die slowly?" he shouted at Valeria.

A fruit ripped from its branch. It floated from the tree into Valeria's outstretched hand. "These native fruits are filled with enough liquid and nutrients beneath the shell to keep you alive. I do suggest using them sparingly—the supply is not unlimited. Should you run out, I cannot be sure which of the insects around us are edible."

"What about Luther?" Sacha screamed. "He's hurt and dying. I'm betting those fruits won't help him survive."

Valeria let out a loud laugh. Zack suddenly found himself dragged through the sand by an invisible force. Like a puppet getting yanked by its strings, he rose to his feet. Valeria grabbed a handful of his hair. "I have supplied him with mortal blood, as you can see. This, too, will need to be consumed sparingly." She threw Zack to the ground. He landed on all fours.

Valeria turned as if she were about to walk away, but stopped. "Oh, one more thing," she said, holding the shelled fruit in her palm. "In case you have ideas of leaving this island for the sake of exploration..."

Valeria tossed the fruit in the air like a football. It traveled several feet from the island. The moment it hit the ocean, fire shot from the water like a volcano exploding. Next to it, another fireball erupted, then another next to that one. A fourth went up as well. Each explosion made Zack's ears ring. His throat closed up. He struggled to squeeze air through his windpipe. Did everyone else feel the same way?

"As I said," Valeria said with a grin, "things work

differently. I recommend you stay put for your own safety."

A blurred circle formed behind her. It had to be a portal of her creation. She stepped through. It faded away. The portal, and Valeria, were gone.

"Sebastian, help me!" Sacha used both hands to yank the stake that went straight through Luther's body.

Sebastian jumped to his feet. He ran over and wrapped his hands around the wood stake. Together, they pulled on the sharp stick until it slid out of Luther's body. The end was covered in black soot that Zack guessed was long-expired blood.

"He won't heal," Sebastian said. "Not without fresh blood to rejuvenate him."

"Do...not...do not fret over me." Luther's words were garbled; his eyes refused to stay open. "Isis is alone against Valeria. She is not close to ready."

"We'll find a way to get to her." Sebastian looked up to Selena. "We have to find a way."

"Did she actually take us through space to another planet?" Zack tapped a foot against the sand to see if it were real.

"Not exactly," Selena answered. "It's another plane of existence. There are worlds that occupy the same space, but on different frequencies." Selena looked up at the bright hot sun. "Luther and my mom used to tell us about these worlds. We always thought they were just stories. I guess we were wrong."

"And now, we're there," Zack said. "Trapped."

Selena put a hand on Sebastian's shoulder. "What do we do?"

"I don't know." The way his head drooped, Zack had a feeling this was the first time he'd ever uttered that phrase.

Chapter Eighteen

The ropes looped off of Isis' hands and fell to the floor. She was finally free. She jumped from the chair and ran for the door, eager for a chance to escape. An ear against the thin wood confirmed the noise on the other side had stopped. That had to mean the fighting was over. Her side must have lost. Otherwise, they'd have come for her. Certainly Valeria would return as well, unless she was busy burying the bodies. Or worse. It was time to get the hell out of there and run as far away as possible before Valeria made her way back.

Isis gripped the doorknob. She pulled open the door and ran out of the dressing room, and stopped in her tracks. Somehow, Isis was no longer in the theater. She was in a brown wallpapered hallway that ran from a kitchen into a living room.

Isis recognized the hallway—it was Nikki and George's house.

Standing here brought back horrible memories she didn't want to experience again. It wasn't the friendliest of environments, but Isis had tried to make the best of it while hiding magical powers she couldn't understand at the time.

A young girl's muffled struggles radiated from behind what Isis remembered as the bathroom door. She reached for the rusty handle, but her fingers passed through the panel. She yanked her hand back and rolled it in front of her eyes. Her flesh was solid, at least as far as she could tell. That meant everything around her was not.

"This isn't real," Isis mumbled to herself.

She stepped through the door where five adults— three men and two women—were gathered around the bathtub.

Nikki—Isis' former foster mother—kneeled over the filled bathtub. She had her weight pushed against a young, skinny child's backside. With both hands, Nikki held the child's head under the water. Isis remembered this moment well. That child was her...from over six and a half years ago, although it felt like a whole other life.

Isis' heartbeat raced, just as she remembered it did back then. She had put the entire experience behind her but had never forgotten a single moment. She remembered trying so hard to pick up her head after swallowing what felt like a gallon of the lukewarm bath water.

At least half a minute passed before Nikki pulled the girl's head out from the water. Young Isis coughed as the one man in a clergy uniform, the priest from the neighborhood church, and Nikki's long-time friend, held a large cross against her chest. The girl was wide-eyed; her entire body shook. Isis remembered thinking the bathroom was icy cold that day, like being trapped inside a meat locker. Now, she realized the bathroom was tepid. It was the fear of death that had chilled her body.

"In the name of our lord, I command thee, Devil, be gone of this child," the priest chanted.

"Please, just leave me…alone!" the girl cried.

Her face mirrored her rage. The cross flew out of the priest's hand and hit the mirror. It shattered the reflective glass. The frightened priest leaned back with wide eyes.

Nikki grabbed a wooden brush from the tub and slammed it across the side of the girl's face. All this time, Isis had thought it was a fist or a slap that hit her. She never realized it was the head of a wooden back scrubber.

Nikki wrapped a towel around young Isis' face. She struggled, but the priest held her hands. One of the other men snatched her feet. The third man took her by the waist. They easily hoisted her up, despite her struggles, leaving no room to budge.

"Come on, I know where we could put her." Nikki ran out of the bathroom.

The three men and one woman followed, running through Isis as if she were a ghost, dragging her younger self with them. Isis knew exactly where they were going. She had relived this day too many times in the middle of the night.

Nikki waved them to the open door down the hall from the bathroom. It led to the basement. Like a slab of meat, the men tossed the girl through the doorway. Each part of her body hit a step as she tumbled down the staircase. Isis recalled the striking pain in her left knee, both elbows, and lower back when this moment actually happened.

The towel flew off the young girl's face. Isis stepped through the doorway onto the top step. She peered down at her younger self. The door slammed behind her.

"Please help me," the younger Isis screamed, looking up at her older self while blood dripped down the side of her face. But Isis knew the girl wasn't calling out to her—it was to the people who had done this to her, who believed she was a threat. They were as afraid of Isis as she was of them. Watching her younger self lay her head on the ground and cry forced Isis' eyes to tear up.

"I know you remember this moment well." Valeria appeared at Isis' left side.

Isis jumped and swiped the tears from her face.

"I do," Isis sobbed.

"This is but one example of human nature. It was the same even in my time," Valeria explained. "I see from your experiences, mortals haven't changed at all. Even at your young age, you knew they wanted to kill you because of what you could do."

"Not everyone is like this," Isis said, repeating the lessons of the last six and a half years. "Most people are decent, good. It's just the few—"

"And yet, your coven forces you to hide your true self, masquerading as an entertainer." Valeria motioned Isis to look down the steps at the younger version of herself. "This is the fate all witches avoid by hiding. I say, with the power given to us by Mother Nature, our path is clear. Why should we live in fear when it is they who have every reason to fear us?"

"No, we need to fear *you*," Isis growled like a dog protecting a bone.

"Is that what they have told you?" Valeria laughed. "I look only to improve the lives of young witches like the one locked in this basement."

Isis' eyes locked onto the younger Isis. She wanted

to turn away, but couldn't. It was as if the moment was frozen in time. Suddenly, the entire basement faded like a huge fog had rolled in and overtook the area. Once it cleared, the basement was replaced by a wood door and a coat rack with several outfits meant for male magicians. It was the theater dressing room. Isis was back sitting on that uncomfortable chair. The rope squeezed her wrists behind her back, reminding her that she was still a prisoner.

"We were seeing the past," Isis said to Valeria, who stood over her. "How?" She never thought time travel was possible, even for a witch.

"Are you not adept at illusion?" Valeria asked.

"Not yet." Isis hadn't worked her way to those lessons yet, although Sebastian promised they would soon. God, how she wished he and the others were here. They would know how to beat this woman. Isis, on the other hand, had no idea what to do.

"You will need to master that, along with many other abilities." Valeria kneeled in front of Isis, bringing them to eye level. "I need to make you strong so we can succeed in our mission."

"What mission?"

"To fix the natural order of nature, my dear. To make right a universal wrong." Valeria folded her arms and shook her head. "They took you in, thinking your power could help them stand in my path. It is irony that we will now walk that path together."

Valeria's dark purple irises undulated as she spoke. She kept licking her lips while she waited for Isis to respond.

"Where…where's my family?" Isis' jaw trembled once she asked the question.

"You need no longer be concerned about them. They are no longer relevant to you."

"Did you kill them?"

"No. Well, not yet. But anyone who stands against us will meet death. Be it mortal, witch, or vampire."

Isis swallowed hard. It was time to take a stand. If her family were truly prisoners somewhere, she certainly wasn't going to help the person who caused it. Maybe she could bargain for their lives. She looked Valeria straight in her psychotic eyes. "Free my family or I won't help you."

Valeria stroked her fingers through Isis' hair. "You are very brave, my new young apprentice. And quite insolent."

Isis raised her eyebrows. "Apprentice?"

"Yes." Valeria held her palm under Isis' chin. Heat radiated like a candle near Isis' skin. Her nostrils stung. Isis pulled her head as far back as possible. "Wh-what are you doing?" she asked.

Her jeans tore from thigh to knee. The two sides of the opening spread wide, exposing Isis' light brown skin.

"Insolence...however," Valeria said, "can be trained out of you."

Valeria turned her hand over and pressed her palm on Isis' exposed upper leg. For Isis, it felt like a branding iron drilling through her thigh, down to the bone. Her skin sizzled. Her eyes dripped like a leaky faucet. In her entire life, Isis had never felt such pain. The only sound in the room louder than her scream was Valeria's cackle.

Valeria's hand lifted from Isis' leg. It offered little relief from the intense sting. Isis' head was yanked back by the hair.

"You will learn, little witch," Valeria said with a confident grin. "You will."

Chapter Nineteen

Selena kneeled next to Herb, who kept his head and back leaned against the largest tree. She pressed a finger along his arm. The slight pressure made him flinch. The arm was held across his chest with Zack's vest buttoned around it. One of the armholes wrapped around Herb's neck, which made it work like a makeshift sling. It probably wouldn't last, but without a hospital on whatever plane of existence they were stuck in, this was all they had.

Zack was impressed with Selena's ingenuity. She was able to come up with solutions even without her witchcraft. So far, she seemed to be the only one of the group that had knowledge and skills beyond their hocus pocus.

"My medical knowledge is limited, but I'm pretty sure this is a fracture," Selena explained to both Herb and Zack. "Under normal circumstances, it would have to be treated."

"So, you're not going to feed us to the vampire?" Zack asked.

"No, sweetie," Selena answered. "Of course, we are not sacrificing you."

"Although we probably should," Sebastian blurted while he and Sacha were by Luther's side. "You are responsible for us being here."

"We couldn't have known what she was," Herb replied, "or what she was looking to do. How could we have known? I still have trouble believing any of this."

"Your intentions with her were certainly not honorable." Sebastian rose to his feet and faced Herb like a prosecutor confronting a witness. "It was with the intent to hurt us."

"You hurt us first," Zack shot back.

"*We* hurt *you*?" Sebastian stepped forward, leaving a footprint in the sand. "How do you figure that? All we did was put on a show, just as you have done."

Herb straightened his neck and looked up at Sebastian. "You came into our industry, which we have poured our hearts and souls into, and turned it on its ear. So many magicians along the Vegas strip lost the only livelihoods they've ever known because your show was better, and a lot cheaper, than anything we could ever hope to match. We couldn't compete without draining our resources, so we died out."

"Not you," Sebastian snapped. "Obviously, your show survived."

"Barely. Since The Witches of Vegas came into town, we have been suffering. You perform illusions that rival ours and charge your audience next to nothing to see it. We've had to lower our ticket prices three times, yet we still can't match yours and keep the show running. Because of this, we barely bring in enough of an audience to pay the bills, let alone improve," Herb scoffed. "I never understood how you did it, but now I do. As it turns out, you were cheating all along."

"Cheating?" Sebastian's eyebrows rose.

"We don't have the benefit of witchcraft to create our effects. We only have human ingenuity and hard work. Not to mention expense. Everything we create has to be built from scratch. That cost isn't an issue for people who can create miracles out of thin air."

"So, for revenge, you colluded with a deranged four-hundred-year-old witch with a grudge against mankind." He waved a hand at Luther. "This man helped raise us and now he is dying. We have been exiled to this place, surrounded by water that bursts into flames." He turned away for a moment, then spun back. "And then, there's Isis, who I had made a Wiccan vow to protect. Now, she is in the clutches of this powerful maniac, and so is our entire world. All this, because we stole your audience?"

"We were desperate," Zack said. "We didn't know any of you then." He dipped his head. "I didn't know Isis."

"She approached us as a reporter looking to debunk magic," Herb followed. "We suspected she wasn't being completely forthcoming, but never that she was a witch. We never considered you were anything but amazing magicians. Hell, as a magician, I never believed in the supernatural existing at all…at least, not until today."

Selena stood from Herb's side. Her eyes glanced upward, connecting with her husband's eyes. "Sebastian…"

"I know that look," Sebastian said to her. "You're about to disagree with me, aren't you?"

"I am, because I have to. They're right. On everything." She walked up to Sebastian and took his hands. "We can't blame this on them. They were manipulated just like us. You must see that as well."

"Perhaps," Sebastian replied. "It's not like they

created Valeria, then exiled her when she went out of control."

"You're blaming Luther."

"You saw her eyes, Selena—she is clearly deranged. Maybe she always was, but I'm guessing four hundred years of isolation made her condition far worse." Sebastian turned his head and leered at their injured mentor. "Damnit, why didn't he kill her when he had the chance?"

"Because he loved her." Selena put a hand on Sebastian's cheek. "Could you kill me?"

"With the world at stake, I...don't know. Probably not, but an eternity of isolation is probably a far worse punishment than death." Sebastian stepped away from Selena. "Sacha, how is he?" he called, making it obvious he wanted to change the subject.

"It's hard to say." Sacha touched Luther's forehead with the back of her hand. "His skin is ice cold, but it's always ice cold. As time passes, he's getting weaker. He doesn't have enough blood in his system to heal."

"Hey," Zack said to the group, "you are going to get us home, aren't you?"

Sebastian answered, "We need access to this planet's energy or we can't even begin to open a portal."

"Even then," Selena said, "finding a destination could be impossible. We'd need a point of reference from here to there, and we've never crossed dimensions before."

"Then, how the hell did Victoria...Valeria... whatever the hell her name is, do it?"

"It took her four centuries to figure it out," Sebastian answered Zack. "We obviously don't have that sort of time."

"Then we'll have to be quicker about it," Sacha said with a nervous grin. "We have to."

Sebastian and Selena joined Sacha in sitting positions around Luther. The depressed and defeated expressions on the witches' faces didn't fill Zack with confidence.

"We could just wait," he said. "She did say she'd come back for us."

"I wouldn't count on that," Herb called out.

Needing a moment with his thoughts, Zack walked to the shoreline. The horizon looked exactly as it did back home, although he hadn't been on a beach since his parents took him to California when he was five. On this beach, however, he had to keep enough distance so the water wouldn't touch his feet. He remembered what happened to that fruit and certainly didn't want to personally experience the same spontaneous combustion. This was not the way Zack saw himself living the rest of his life. Hell, he didn't even like going camping.

Zack reached into his back pocket and took out his phone. It wouldn't do much good here, but at least he could look at photos while he still had battery life. Zack pulled up the selfie he had taken with Isis and the Elvis impersonator while walking her home from the yogurt shop. It cost five bucks to get the lookalike in the pic, but it made Isis smile, so it was worth it. Man, what was she going through without anyone to help her right now? Zack's heart raced at the thought. He was worried about her. It wasn't an in-love worried—he was pretty sure the spell had passed—it was more of a caring kind of worried.

He stared at the photo on his screen for several seconds. Then, he noticed it… "Oh, man," he exclaimed. "Uncle Herb!"

Zack ran in his uncle's direction with renewed vigor. Their situation wasn't as hopeless as they thought.

Chapter Twenty

Isis had never seen burnt skin before, not even on TV. Now, she was staring at it, and smelling it on her own thigh. The skin had turned three different shades of red. What she thought were bubbles spread randomly along the area. She realized those were blisters. It stung like hell. It was about a million times worse than the sting she got on her hand from a bumblebee as a kid. The very sight of it made her stomach turn.

As if she hadn't been through enough, Valeria wasn't done with her yet.

"It is such a shame." Valeria stood over Isis with her hands on her hips. "Your connection to the Earth's energy is so strong. Someday, you could even be more powerful than I." Her lips curled as her head shook. "They've done you such a disservice in your upbringing."

Valeria's comment about Isis' family was nasty, but it also mimicked objections she had heard from Luther over the years. He, too, thought Isis should have been raised as a warrior. She loved and appreciated the life they had given her even if she never came out and told them that. Right now, however, she kind of wished Luther had his way. Maybe she would know how to fight back. Then she wouldn't be so frightened.

"I think you've been tied up long enough." Valeria

clapped her hands. The ropes slipped off of Isis' wrists.

Isis rubbed her hands across her face. She leaned forward and tried to stand from the chair, but the throbbing in her thigh took over. She fell forward, hitting her elbows on the floor. "Ow!"

Her screech incited a laugh from Valeria. "Stand up," the immortal witch stated.

Isis placed her palms on the floor and pushed her upper body up, stretching her arms. "I…I can't stand up," Isis groaned. "My leg, it hurts…"

An object rattled on the floor in the corner. It was Herb's gun. It levitated in the air, then floated across the room, stopping inches in front of Isis. The barrel pointed between her eyes. "If you cannot triumph over adversity," Valeria said, "then you are no good to me. Now, stand up. Immediately."

The gun's hammer pulled back. Isis' throat went dry. She brought her knees to her stomach and pushed. Her thigh throbbed to the point she stifled a gag. Somehow, she lifted herself and straightened her legs.

"Good, good." Valeria applauded. "We will be testing your fortitude quite a bit. You have been raised weak, and I need you to be strong."

"I…I'm not going to hurt people for you," Isis said with as much strength as her hoarse voice would allow. "The world is different now, it's not like when you—"

"Is it? Luther always preached about how the world would change if we simply did nothing. Our kind was being murdered by far lesser beings on a regular basis while we hid."

Valeria grabbed Isis by the shoulders and shook her. "Tell me, young fool, can you imagine the shame of finding a world so far removed from the one you knew, just to realize it hadn't progressed at all?"

"We…we don't have to hide. Not anymore—"

"LIE!" Valeria's scream made every muscle in Isis' body tense. Her grip tightened. "You have experienced the lack of compassion from mortals when they tried to murder you. Even now, you and your coven, powerful as you are, hide by demeaning yourselves entertaining children."

Valeria let Isis go, and then paced across the dressing room, taking long, hard steps. Isis moved a step back. This woman was scary and full of hate, but she did have a point. As much as Isis loved performing on the stage for thousands of cheering fans, they were hiding out of fear of exposure and persecution. It was exactly why she had been warned never to reveal herself as an actual witch, just a fake one on stage.

"It is time for the balance of power to change! Witches need to reveal themselves and rule this entire planet with an iron fist!"

Valeria lunged at Isis. She grabbed for her chin, stopping Isis from jumping back. "This is an objective we can share." She suddenly eyed Isis with a vicious grin. "Earlier, I took a tour of your memories. Would you like to experience mine?"

"No."

"*Procidat deceptionem.*"

The dressing room faded again, forcing Isis into another illusion. She suddenly found herself standing on wet grass and surrounded by trees in the middle of a forest. It was nighttime, but the full moon high above illuminated the area. A woman screamed. Instinctively, Isis ran toward the screams, dodging the trees. What she witnessed made Isis come to a screeching halt and almost fall over.

The screaming woman was completely naked and hanging by the wrists from a high branch. Thick brown rope was tied so tight her hands had turned blue. The tree was surrounded by at least twenty men, with a few women scattered in the crowd. The men wore tall broad hats and brown jackets that, from the back, looked like capes. The women wore long dresses that Isis had only seen in history books. Half the crowd held Bibles in the air with both hands.

One man raised a long torch made of straw high over his head. In response, the ruckus stopped. "I hereby declare this woman guilty of performing witchcraft!" His accent, which was not quite British, sounded similar to Valeria's. "A crime punishable by death!"

The crowd cheered.

Valeria took shape beside Isis. "Take a good look at your roots, young witch." Her sudden arrival made Isis' skin nearly jump off her body. "This was the late 1500s in Salem, Massachusetts. Do you know what took place during this time period, Isis?"

"Yes," she whispered. "The Salem witch trials."

"They've taught you your history. At least they did something correct." Valeria pointed to the woman hanging from the tree. "Did you know many witches and accused humans were released as their witchcraft could not be proven in court? No, it was not the trials that led to the deaths of the accused. It was mobs of mortals who did not agree with the courts' decisions. They took it upon themselves to execute the accused. Now, pay attention."

In an act of defiance, Isis tried to close her eyes.

The lids wouldn't budge. Valeria's doing, no doubt.

"Tonight," the man in charge shouted, "for our sakes and the sakes of our family, we watch another witch BURN!"

The man held the end of the torch against the woman's stomach. Her skin caught fire. Her screams became louder and even more pain-filled. Isis spun 180 degrees, only to find she was still looking at the woman on fire.

"This is part of your education," Valeria roared. "You do not get to look away!"

The flames spread across the woman's body, to her legs and chest. Soon, it engulfed her completely. Her screaming stopped. The people cheered. In an act of defiance, Isis spun her body away again. This time, she found herself in front of a solid brick wall. She was back in that damn dressing room.

"You claim the world has changed," Valeria whispered into Isis' ear. "I have no doubt they tell you this as they keep you isolated. And yet, I can sense that, deep down, you know otherwise. Mortals will execute anyone across the globe suspected of being more powerful than they. This is why we must take the initiative and lead witches everywhere in a worldwide revolution."

"You want to go to war with everyone on the planet?" Isis asked.

"Mother Earth has given us access to its energy for a reason," Valeria screamed at Isis as if she were scolding her. "It is a sign that it has declared us the dominant species. Now, we must exercise that dominance. The mortals will accept their place in the natural food chain. If not, then we shall eradicate all those who dare oppose us."

"Eradicate?" Isis gasped.

"We can create fire, yet we fear being burned alive. We have sixth sense, yet we fear being hunted." Valeria's gaze pointed to the ceiling. "It is long past time the inferior fear their superiors as opposed to the other way around."

Isis wanted to dispute Valeria's stance, explain to her why she was wrong about humanity and their prejudices. Then again, her former foster family did try to kill her once they discovered her power. That was exactly Valeria's point. Maybe she was right on some level, but Isis couldn't see herself purposely setting people on fire in order to teach them respect. Plus, her family now, the only family that ever made Isis feel wanted, would never approve. They'd stand against her.

"I will have your support, Isis, but I would prefer it be willingly," Valeria said with a veiled threat in her tone. "That is your choice to make."

"I don't...I don't think witches will go for this," Isis answered. "Many will fight to stop you."

Valeria pointed a closed fist at Isis. A force shoved Isis against the wall. Her arms and legs wouldn't move. A peek down revealed that she was inches off the ground. The pressure across her chest increased as Valeria closed the gap. It felt like those knuckles were about to go through her.

"Let me tell you something about witches that I'm sure your former masters did not teach," Valeria said.

"They're not my..." Isis could barely get the words out with her chest sandwiched between the wall and Valeria's invisible force.

"Listen carefully. If you shoot a witch, they die. If

you stab a witch, poison a witch, or even drown a witch, they die." Valeria touched her ice-cold nose against Isis' cheek. "However, if you burn a witch, then engulf their entire body in flame, that's when a magical reaction takes place. Their pores open and the energy flees their body as their life force extinguishes. It is through intense heat that a nearby witch can absorb the connection."

Isis looked into Valeria's eyes. The pupils were wide and dilated, as if they had been near such intense heat and smoke many times over. Isis had to wonder how many dead witches she had absorbed. How else could she be so damn powerful? A thought from the past struck her. She remembered early on when Sebastian and Selena taught her about the Salem witch trials. They talked about how people acted out of fear, burning anyone suspected of witchcraft, whether true or not. The executions started as hangings but quickly became setting witches on fire. So many innocent people were burned to death in those years.

At the end of the lesson, Isis had asked them a question, "How did it start? Who thought to set witches on fire?" She couldn't imagine what would give someone the idea to engulf a living being in fire as a form of execution. Neither Sebastian nor Selena knew the answer. The look on Luther's face, however, made her suspicious even at her young age. Luther was there. Isis had a feeling he knew but didn't want to say.

Isis could barely keep her jaw steady. Even at the risk of a further beating, she had to ask. "Did...did you cause the—"

"Oh my God, what are you two doing back here?" The high-pitched voice made them both look up.

157

Isis recognized the distinct squeak. It belonged to Bambi.

Valeria's head slowly turned to the dressing room's doorway. Bambi stood in her skimpy denim shorts, a white T-shirt that cut off at the waist and high heels with her arms folded. "This area is for the talent *only*!"

Valeria snorted. Her eyes turned pitch black.

"Bambi, you have to leave! Now!" Isis shrieked. "Run!"

"I have to leave? What are you talking about?" Bambi gasped. "Oh my God, he *is* replacing me, isn't he?"

Valeria stepped face to face with Bambi, who looked the vampire-witch up and down. "You should have heeded the girl's advice," Valeria said through a wide grin. "It's too late, now."

"Where is Herb?" Bambi stamped her foot. "If he's replacing me with some sort of horror-themed freak show, he needs to tell me to my face."

"Bambi, she's a vampire!" Isis screeched.

"Vampire?" Bambi's eyes slanted. She shook her head at Valeria. "Sweetheart, I have done the vampire thing, and yours needs a lot of work. Now, where is Herb?"

"Valeria, please!" Isis pleaded. Tears rolled down her eyes. "She's innocent. Let her go—"

Valeria raised a finger at Isis, silencing her. "Have you not been paying attention, young witch? No one is innocent!"

Valeria wrapped both hands around Bambi's throat and ran her backward out of the dressing room. Bambi fell to the floor with Valeria on top of her. The pressure that kept Isis flattened against the wall disappeared. She dropped to her knees and elbows. Isis widened her eyes as Valeria lunged for Bambi's throat with her mouth. Isis cringed when those two sharp fangs dug into soft flesh.

Isis shut her eyes and turned her head, unable to watch the massacre. Blood splattered around the stage and across her face. Bambi's scream sounded like a siren, until it halted, and was replaced with an obscene slurping sound. Valeria was feasting—a thought that turned Isis' stomach. After her meal, Valeria made a loud noise that may have been a belch.

Isis was finally able to open her eyes, but she couldn't lift her head to see what was left of the woman she barely knew. A few steps in front of her, a tiny crystal lay on the floor. She couldn't see the other four crystals in the room, but she didn't need to. She only needed to move one to get her powers back and escape.

It was time to act.

Isis swatted the crystal across the room, breaking the pentagon. She wanted to teleport the hell out of here. It was a witch's power she had learned, but never really practiced. Once, she did teleport, but only a few feet within the same room. Now seemed like the right time to try and take herself to a different location. But where? She decided on her own room at the Sapphire, the one place she felt most safe. Make it there, get her bearings, and then figure out the next move.

"Teleport," Isis said under her breath.

Everything went fuzzy. Valeria spun in her direction. She looked pissed. "*Hic manere*," Valeria said as she faded away, along with everything around her.

Isis rose to her knees, keeping a hand pressed

against her burned thigh. Everything gradually came back in focus. She was still in the dressing room—she hadn't gone anywhere. "How?"

Two hands gripped her shirt and pulled her to her feet.

Valeria's eyes were still dark. Her fangs, like her mouth and cheeks, were covered in fresh blood. She breathed heavily, like a rabid dog.

Isis braced herself for the beating she expected to receive.

That's when Valeria grinned. "I understand," she said between heavy breaths, "I feel cooped up in here as well."

Valeria grabbed a handful of Isis' long brown hair. She then lifted Isis, letting her body dangle. Isis reached with her toes, but she couldn't feel the floor. "Let's take a road trip, you and I," Valeria said. "*Lacus.*"

Once again, everything faded away. This time, however, it wasn't Isis' doing.

Chapter Twenty-One

"We should let them in on this, right?" Zack whispered.

"Can you fathom a single reason not to tell them, Zack?" Herb replied. "Help me up. I'm done leaning against this tree."

Zack took hold of Herb's good arm and yanked him up. He remembered his uncle being much heavier at one time. Then again, it may have been that Zack was younger and still growing. He held Herb's right arm, waiting for his uncle to gain his balance while keeping the fractured left arm in place. The vest-turned-sling barely held together as the buttons started to rip past the holes.

They approached the witches, who were now standing in a semi-circle around Luther's upper body. Luther's eyes kept shutting until he forced them open, as if he were willing himself to stay alive and aware.

"—between the three of us," Sebastian was saying, "we should be able to figure a way to connect with the energy of this planet. We just need to find a way to break through."

"Maybe with meditation, we could connect," Selena responded, "but it's going to take time. A lot of time."

"Time Luther doesn't have. Or Isis, for that

matter."

"Hey, guys, you really need to hear this," Zack announced.

"I seriously doubt that," Sebastian snapped. Annoyance covered his face like a bad sunburn.

"Sebastian!" Selena scolded.

"I'm sorry, but there isn't time for pleasantries," Sebastian said to her. "We need to figure this out fast, and we are at a loss."

Herb's sudden roar snapped the three witches to attention. "In that case, how about you drop the arrogant, demeaning attitude for one moment and let the lowly mortals contribute to the conversation?"

"I meant no disrespect," Sebastian said, although Zack was pretty sure he did. "But I'm upset right now. Without a plan, we could be stuck here forever."

"I understand the situation very well!" Herb shouted. "But, your witchy magic is on the fritz. So, perhaps you need to rely on our magic to find a way out of this mess."

A slight grin formed on Zack's lips. He couldn't remember the last time he saw his uncle handle himself with such confidence. It used to happen all the time when The Amazing Herb Galloway show was the talk of Las Vegas. Years of the show falling apart had taken its toll on his health and his ego. But this man, right now, was the confident magician who brought Zack up.

"Do you have a magic trick for opening a dimensional portal?" Sacha asked with a smirk.

Herb pointed a thumb from Zack to himself. "Our magic tells us that Victoria Hunter, besides being a crazy psycho vampire-witch, is also a magician. Part of magic is setting a scene so the audience buys into what we are telling them. Accepting falsities as fact goes a long way into fooling them into seeing things the way you've presented it. Right now, we are her audience."

"And all this means what?" Sebastian asked.

"It means Valeria fooled us. Despite what she said, we are actually not on another dimensional plane." Herb waved his hands out as if he were presenting the finale of his show. "We are most definitely still on *our* planet, good ol' Earth."

Sebastian raised an eyebrow. "It's an interesting theory, but—"

"It's not a theory!" Zack retorted. "It's a fact."

Selena placed a hand on Sebastian's arm, stopping him before he could respond. "How can you be so certain?"

Herb waved his nephew on. "Tell them."

Zack held his phone up with a huge smile. "I'm getting a signal."

"What? Are you sure?" Sacha gasped as both Sebastian and Selena stood, stunned, with their mouths hanging open.

"Only one bar, but it's a signal." Zack pointed to the display on his phone's screen.

"Unlike my nephew, I don't know much about how phones work," Herb explained, "but I presume it only works on planet Earth, am I correct?"

"I would say that's...probably accurate," Sebastian replied.

Sacha walked over and elbowed Sebastian in the ribs. "Admit it, you're impressed."

"Enough, Sacha, let's see if they're right." Sebastian leaned down and snatched one of the strange fruits that had fallen off the trees. Like an Olympic javelin thrower, he ran to the shore and tossed the fruit high in the air. The fruit arched, then dropped into the ocean. The impact caused a splash, but no explosion, no fire.

After the ripples faded, Sebastian looked over his shoulder with red in his eyes. "It was a damn illusion. I should have realized this. Illusions are my forte."

"As I said," Herb replied, "she painted a scene and we accepted it as truth. That's Magic Presentation 101."

"Do the two of you have a magic trick for finding out exactly where we are?" Selena asked with her hands cupped together.

"For powerful witches, you don't know much about modern tech, do you?" Zack poked his thumbs against the screen. "Hocus pocus, map app."

The grin suddenly disappeared as Zack's screen reacted. His eyes widened. "Oh, man. According to this, we're in the Caribbean, on an island eighty miles south of Saint Croix." He looked up. "The island isn't even named."

"So, we are still on Earth, but literally in the middle of nowhere." Sebastian rubbed his thumb and forefinger against his temples.

"I still don't understand," Selena said. "Why the ruse? She obviously has the power to open a portal. Why not actually put us there?"

"Maybe she doesn't," Sacha answered. "Luther said it took a number of witches to open the portal to send her in. Somehow, she was able to open it from the other side herself. Maybe she can't do it again?"

"Or, is there something in that world she's afraid of?" Selena suggested.

"A question for another time," Sebastian said.

"Right now, we have bigger priorities. Like, if we're still on Earth, why are we not connected? How did she cut us off from the power?"

"Some sort of magic spell?" Herb asked.

"No, it's not that." Sacha's head dropped in thought. After moments of silence, she gasped. "It's crystals!" Her head turned back and forth. "We're inside a pentagon."

"That makes sense," Selena said to Sebastian. "I can't believe we didn't think of this."

"Um, what are we talking about?" Zack asked.

"Enchanted crystals," Sacha answered. "When five are placed at equal distances in a pentagon shape, they focus and strengthen our control of the energy within them. Right now, Valeria's focus is strengthened here and she's using it to break our connection."

"So, if we find them, you get your powers back?" Zack asked. Selena nodded. "Then, we have to find them. What do they look like?"

"Look for something small, shiny and diamond-shaped," Sebastian replied. "They can be any size, but they're usually tiny and colorful. Check the shorelines."

"If she buried them, they could be anywhere," Herb said.

"No, they won't connect if they're buried." Sacha took a handful of sand. "But as Sebastian said, they can be any size—even the size of a grain of this sand."

"Remember, we only need to find one," Selena said. "Break the pentagon, the spell within breaks as well."

"No, Sis, we have to find all five," Sacha shot back. "We can use them to freeze time around Luther, keep him alive until we figure out how to save him."

"You can actually freeze time?" Zack asked.

"Yes! Well, maybe, but only in a small space and within the crystals." Sacha stared down at Luther. His body convulsed as if he was either freezing or having a seizure. "I believe Selena and I can freeze the space around Luther, although we've never actually done that to a person before."

"All right, let's start searching," Sebastian responded. "If you find one, let the rest of us know, but don't move it. We can follow a straight path to find another crystal, then use both locations to figure out where the others are."

Sebastian came up behind Zack and Herb. He put a hand on each of their shoulders. "Good job, you two." Zack threw Herb a slight grin. He was sure he heard an apology in Sebastian's tone.

Sebastian and Selena spread out in opposite directions. Sacha leaned down near Luther. Zack made his way to another part of the shore. Where he stood, the water rolled past his shoes. At least he could take assurance in that it wouldn't cause him to explode. He wanted to feel confident, but the situation was far more dismal than Sebastian let on. In order to escape, they'd have to find the proverbial needle in a haystack. Actually, a needle in a haystack would be far easier to find than small crystals somewhere on an entire island of sand. To make things worse, the sun was going down.

Chapter Twenty-Two

Isis found herself surrounded by high-rise apartments that hadn't been cleaned, renovated, or fixed up since long before she was born. She looked up at the building, particularly at a dark window three floors above the stoop. She knew this apartment well, along with the wooden bench in front of the building that she had sat on many times. She trembled, finding herself once again on her knees in the middle of this neighborhood. She promised herself long ago that she'd never come back here, ever.

At first, Isis questioned why Valeria would take her back into the same memory. She suddenly realized that this time, it was different. This time, she smelled the garbage scattered along the street and from the metal bins next to the apartment buildings. This time, she felt the roughness of the asphalt streets against her knees. This wasn't an illusion. Valeria had actually teleported them across the entire country. But why?

"I presume you know where we are," Valeria said, standing behind Isis.

"Yes."

"You say there are innocent mortals who deserve our mercy, but it was here you discovered otherwise, even if you do not wish to admit this to yourself."

From the corner of her eye, Isis caught Valeria's

long, red fingernails wrapping around her forearm. The fingers squeezed, digging into Isis' skin.

"It is here that you learned how our kind is treated by an arrogant yet inferior species," Valeria said.

"It wasn't everyone," Isis replied. "It was just them and their friends—" Isis found herself yanked off the ground and dropped onto her feet.

"Look around you!" Valeria screamed. "All these buildings, all these windows. How many mortals live here?"

"I...don't know."

"TAKE A GUESS!"

"H-hundreds?"

"More like thousands!" Valeria's saliva hit Isis in the left eye. "Now, how many of these onlookers tried to stop it? How many called the authorities? How many took pity on the scrawny child who was locked in a basement for days with nothing to eat except the occasional cockroach that crawled past her? Or, when they surrounded her on the street and tried to burn her alive?"

Isis looked up at all the windows surrounding her on every side, illuminated only by the lampposts throughout the neighborhood. She couldn't imagine how Valeria knew the details of what happened to her all those years ago. "They...they thought I was the devil," Isis said in a tone barely above a whisper.

"Yes, these mortals have always looked to their precious religions to justify torture and murder." Valeria pointed up at Isis' former home's window. "Did you know they reported you a runaway? The police and the social workers spent three days trying to find you, then they all moved onto other cases."

"I...I didn't know that." Isis had never given them, or how the foster agency handled her disappearance, a single thought until today.

"Meanwhile, your foster parents never answered for their heinous acts." Valeria shoved Isis forward. The force almost sent Isis to the ground. "I think it is time they faced their actions."

"No!" Isis moaned. "I don't want to see them—"

"*Eos deducere.*"

Valeria snapped her fingers. A bright light flashed in front of the stoop. Nikki and George appeared, lying on the ground next to each other as if they were in bed. In fact, based on Nikki's pink pajamas and George's black boxers, that's exactly from where Valeria plucked them. Isis stood over them, her head pounding. It was hard to complete a single thought between the pain in her thigh and the anger she thought was long behind her.

Nikki's eyes opened. First, her face scrunched in confusion. Then, she sat up and shrieked. Her dark brown skin went pale. George rose to a sitting position in reaction to Nikki's screech. His head darted back and forth. "What the hell? How did we get outside?"

"George." Nikki tapped him, her brown eyes locked on Isis.

Isis stared down at her former foster parents. Memories of the most horrible experience of her life— or at least the most horrible experience until she met Valeria—ran through her head.

"Isis?" George's eyes opened as wide as his mouth. "Is that you?"

Over the years, Isis had thought about what she would do if this confrontation were to happen. She didn't need it or want it, but if it happened, Isis expected she'd let them see how happy she was and walk away with her head held high. Her life, after all, turned out great. In fact, it was far better than theirs—but this was in spite of them. Now that she was face to face with these people—these monsters—her vision went red. She wasn't looking to walk away.

"Isis, wh-what the hell is this?" Nikki stuttered. "What do you want? How are we outside?"

"Who is that behind you?" George sounded just as stunned as his wife.

"You tried to kill me," Isis snarled. Her glare never wavered.

"Is that why you're here?" George asked. "For revenge?"

"SOMEBODY HELP US!" Nikki screamed.

But they were alone on the street. Most of the windows within shouting distance remained dark, just like when Isis needed someone to save her.

"You called me the devil." Isis took a step forward. "I was nine years old!"

Nikki sat up and folded her hands. Her eyes shut. "O my Lord, forgive us our sins, deliver us from this evil—"

"It is time!" Valeria said. "Your new path begins here. These inferior mortals harmed you. It is time to pay them back in kind. Let them be the first to fall to your superiority."

"NO!" George climbed to his feet. "If you're here to kill us, I ain't going down like a punk!"

He clenched his fists and lunged. Isis stuck out her right palm. A wave of force knocked George back down as if he had run headfirst into a solid wall. This was one of the first uses of the power Sebastian had taught Isis. He would toss a ball at her and she would have to send the ball back to him without touching it. Eventually, it went from balls thrown to Sebastian lunging at her. Despite all the lumps it caused him, Sebastian made her practice this over and over until she could do it by instinct. This was the first time she had ever needed to protect herself from an actual attack.

"Oh my God, George!" Nikki put a hand on his chest. She looked up at Isis. "Please, Isis, let us go. We thought we were doing the right thing to save our community and your soul."

"My soul," Isis repeated, her stare never wavering.

"It is past time for your vengeance," Valeria said, her arms folded across her chest. "Let the ground swallow them up. Bury them far down so they can reflect on their transgressions until the moment they take their final breaths!"

Isis' entire body grew warm from the inside—it was the power building. A tingle went through her fingers, to her hands and then her arms. Valeria was right, Isis was angry—no, she was enraged—and she did thirst for vengeance...

But not at Nikki and George. Their rejection led to Isis finding a family that loved and cared for her. Valeria was the one who took Isis away from them. If anyone deserved to be buried...

Isis turned from Nikki and George and faced Valeria. "Into the ground," Isis roared.

Valeria sank through the earth as if it were quicksand under her feet. It took her by surprise, which may have been the only reason Isis' attack worked. The ground swallowed Valeria until she was waist deep.

She didn't spend time on self-congratulations.

"Run!" Isis shouted at Nikki and George. The two pulled themselves to their feet and took off down the street.

Nikki's scream for help was loud enough that it should have woken the entire neighborhood, if anyone cared.

Valeria's eyes turned black. Her fangs showed. For Isis, her advantage would only be momentary. She had to think fast. Her head spun back and forth until she laid eyes on the wooden bench near the stoop. Isis focused her thoughts on the bench until it hovered and fluttered as if possessed. The bench flew in the air like a javelin thrown at Valeria. The ancient witch struggled to escape. The bench slammed against the ground inches in front of its target. The bench fell over, covering Valeria.

"Crap!" Isis exclaimed. She hoped to impale the wood into Valeria's exposed upper body, not just bury her underneath. Either way, it was time to get the hell out of there.

Isis ran for her life, just as she did the last time she had been in this neighborhood. She couldn't build up much speed, not with the severe burn on her exposed thigh.

Once around the building, Isis stopped and leaned against the wall. She held her hand over the burn. "Heal," she said between heavy breaths. Her skin moved, but far slower than ever, most likely due to her emotions going crazy with fear and exhaustion.

"Come on," she mumbled. The movement across her skin stopped. Her healing stopped working. It was due to panic. She had to relax and ignore the fear. She needed the power to respond fast so she could get as far away before—

The sound of what she thought was an explosion from below made Isis scream. Valeria shot through the ground, sending pieces of soot and gravel in all directions. She landed in front of Isis. With the speed of a leopard, her right hand shot out and wrapped around Isis' throat. Her grip felt like a vise cutting off Isis' air. Isis tried to teleport. It didn't work, not with her heart beating faster than it had ever beaten before. One of Valeria's fingernails dug into her neck.

"I foresaw you making a great apprentice to my cause. But now I see you are too naïve and defiant. You are no good to me alive. It is time for plan B." Valeria raised her left hand. It ignited, suddenly surrounded in fire.

"B-burn...me...here." The words barely squeezed out of Isis' throat. "No...one...to...see."

The whites in Valeria's eyes returned. She gazed up in thought. "You may have a point. I can absorb your connection, and your death could be a message for all to see if I make this a public execution. Yes, I like this idea very, very much."

Valeria released her grip. Isis fell to the ground coughing and clutching her throat.

"You wish to die in Las Vegas instead of in this decrepit neighborhood?" Valeria asked. "Very well, then, let us grant your final wish."

Chapter Twenty-Three

"Zack, what are you doing?" Herb asked. "We're supposed to be finding these...crystal things."

Zack looked up from his phone as the ocean water rolled over his feet. "I tried calling Bambi. She could tell us if there's anything happening in the theater."

"I doubt she could," Herb replied. It was a valid point.

"Either way, she didn't pick up. Probably lost her phone again." Zack put a hand under Herb's elbow and lifted his arm to chest level. He re-hooked a button on the back of the vest so the arm would no longer sag. "I thought about calling the police, but what the hell would I say to them?"

Herb replied, "I guess telling them a vampire abducted a witch and teleported us to the Caribbean wouldn't work. Even if they didn't take it as a prank, how long would it take anyone to get here? We certainly couldn't count on local authorities to save the girl."

"After dismissing the idea of calling anyone, I realized why I was fooled so easily by her story. It was because I came across her videos debunking magicians shortly before we met her." Zack waved the phone in the air. "But now I can't find them anywhere online. It's like they've completely disappeared."

"You should save your battery," Herb said. "Soon, it will be nighttime, and if we don't find those crystals, we could be here for a long time."

"Luckily, my phone has a flashlight, but even then, the chances of us finding a crystal the size of sand on an island of sand—"

"Zack."

"—they're astronomical, especially since we have to find it by sight—"

"Zack!"

"—and without their witchcraft, they're no better off than us in finding them—"

Herb snatched Zack by the wrist. "ZACK, YOUR PHONE!"

"I know, I know, shut it off."

"No, listen to me," Herb shouted. "You just said you have a flashlight on there."

"Yes, but so wha—" Zack widened his eyes. "The crystals. If they're like glass—"

"—they'll cast a glimmer from the light." Herb looked toward Sebastian and Selena on the other side of the tiny island. They were on their knees, sifting their fingers through the sand. "Get on it, Zack. I'll let the others know what we're up to."

Despite his body barely balancing and leaning to the left, Herb moved quickly. That was the first time since meeting the witches that his Uncle Herb didn't refer to them as "the witches."

Zack dropped to his knees and placed the phone on its side against the sand. With one screen tap, the light shined and formed a straight line. He eased himself forward, sliding the phone along with him. He moved several feet before seeing a tiny shadow. Excitement coursed through Zack's veins as he crawled on his knees and elbows to the shadow. The crystal was barely larger than the sand surrounding it, but it was definitely diamond-shaped and shiny with a turquoise hue.

"You found one," said Sebastian, who now stood over Zack.

"Yes, I did."

Zack rolled his left hand through the sand until it was underneath the crystal. He then lifted his hand and took the crystal with the fingers from his right hand. "I feel it," Sebastian said, staring out toward the ocean. "The pentagon is broken."

"We need them all, right?" Zack asked.

Sebastian took the crystal from Zack and stepped into the exact spot it was found. "Use me as a starting point and walk straight. I expect one will be placed on the complete opposite end of this island."

"I'm on it!" Zack jumped to his feet and ran across the beach. He constantly glanced behind at Sebastian, using his position to pinpoint the next crystal. The others looked on as Zack dropped down and placed his cellphone against the sand. Once again, he used the flashlight.

****

Twenty of the longest minutes in history had passed, but the job was done. Zack had located all five crystals. Selena stood across from Sebastian where the second crystal was located. Herb took the third crystal's spot. Once they found the first three, the last two proved relatively easy to locate. To Zack, it was amazing that these five objects, which all together fit in the palm of his hand, could be so powerful.

Sacha and Selena placed the crystals around

Luther's body. They chanted "time freeze" in unison while holding their hands out over him. Beams of light similar to the one from Zack's phone suddenly shot out from each crystal and formed a five-sided, three-dimensional shape over Luther's body. The vampire stopped moving. It looked to Zack as if he were actually frozen in time, just as the witches described.

As the sisters worked, Sebastian paced. "We have to get back. That madwoman could be doing who knows what to Isis."

"This is a problem," Sacha said while staring down at Luther. "I don't know how Valeria keeps her spells active from thousands of miles away, but we can't, even with the crystals." She turned her gaze toward Selena. "We leave, our control breaks and Luther dies."

"What about teleporting some wild animal here?" Sebastian asked. "Luther could take its blood."

"We barely even know where 'here' is," Sacha answered. "Or, where there's an animal to teleport here. We could end up wasting a lot of time and energy for nothing."

"I agree we've spent enough time here already," Sebastian shouted in a frantic tone. "We need to get back, now!"

"Sebastian, we can't just run in guns blazing," Selena snapped. "We need a plan or she will destroy us."

Zack chimed in, "For all we know, Isis could be dead already." And it was all his fault. He led Isis right into Valeria's trap.

"Even if she's not dead," Sebastian added, "we don't know what Valeria is doing to her, or to the rest of the world."

"You have to go." Selena grabbed a hold of Sebastian's arms. "Buy us some time until we can figure out a way to save Luther and come up with a way to stop Valeria."

"And then what?" Sacha asked. "She's a vampire. It's not like we can kill her."

"You thought this was another planet, one she was trapped on before." Herb stepped between the three witches. "Can you send her back there?"

"We wouldn't know how to open the portal," Sebastian answered.

"No, we wouldn't." Sacha pointed down at Luther. "But he would. He could guide us. He was there when the witches first sent Valeria through."

Selena took Sebastian's hands. "Sebastian—"

"I know. I have to face her." He leaned in and whispered, although loud enough to be heard by all, "I'm not powerful enough to beat her alone. The two of you would have a shot."

"You don't have to beat her. You just have to rescue Isis and keep Valeria distracted until we arrive with Luther and a plan." Selena touched her forehead against his cheek. "You may not be the most powerful among us, Sebastian, but you are the most innovative and the most resourceful. That's why you're the leader of our coven." She pulled her head back and offered him a smile. "If anyone can find a way to succeed, it's you."

"You're buttering me up, aren't you?"

"Is it working?"

"It's not hurting." Sebastian grinned. His eyebrows rose. "I may have an idea or two. But I can't do it alone." He turned to Zack. "I will need your help."

"Anything!" Zack shouted. "I'm game!"

"Whoa, whoa!" Herb raised a hand in a stop motion. "I'm not comfortable putting my nephew in danger."

"The whole world's in danger, Herb," Sebastian said. "But you don't have to worry. I am not looking to use him as bait."

"Then, what is the plan?" Herb asked. "How are you going to draw her out?"

"I'm the bait." Sebastian turned to Zack. "I just need you to be sneaky. Can you do that?"

Zack scoffed. "I'm a magician. Sneaky is part of my job description. I got this—"

"Hold on," Herb interrupted. "Sebastian, if you're the bait, what's the trap?"

"I'm counting on my powerful family to spring it in time." Sebastian offered his hand to Herb. "Before I go, and if I don't survive, I want to say right now, I'm sorry. When we started our show, I saw it as a victimless endeavor."

"There were a lot of victims, Sebastian," Herb replied. "There was a time you couldn't walk six feet along the Vegas strip without bumping into another magician just trying to get their name out. Now, they're all gone, indirect victims of your witchcraft."

Sebastian nodded his understanding. "This is the first time I've ever met one of our...victims."

"Had you known, would you still have done it?"

As Herb asked the question, Zack's head popped up. He wanted to hear the answer as well. Despite their differences, Zack saw a good man in Sebastian, just like his uncle. The answer would confirm or deny that belief.

"I wish I could tell you no," Sebastian said. "But I would do anything and everything to take care of my family."

Herb gazed at Zack, and then down at Luther. "I can respect that." He took Sebastian's hand and shook it.

Selena placed a hand on Sebastian's back. "You should get going."

"Right. Are you ready, Zack?"

Zack nodded, then looked toward Herb, who hadn't moved an inch. "You're not coming with us?"

"No, I'm going to see how I can help here. Let them heal my arm."

"Really?"

"Yes. Trust me on this."

Zack couldn't think of a single way his uncle could help, unless it was with ideas. Maybe something from one of his unique stage plans could translate to this situation? Even so, why wouldn't he look to get off the island as soon as possible? Maybe he saw his broken arm as a liability if the battle started immediately upon their return?

Zack tried to maneuver to Sebastian's side, but he was intercepted by his uncle who wrapped his one good arm around him and offered a hug. It took Zack by surprise as Herb was never much of a hugger. Those sentimental moments were usually reserved for the anniversary of his parents' death. Even those stopped a few years back.

Zack wrapped his arms around Herb's back, returning the embrace. "I'll see you soon."

"I know you'll be fine." Herb released his hold, allowing Zack to position himself next to Sebastian.

"All right, let's send them back, Sis," Selena said to Sacha.

"You should consider how many magicians attend your show just trying to figure out how you pull it all off," Herb said to Sebastian. "It's a matter of time before one thinks outside the box and figures out your secret."

Sebastian nodded. "That may not matter if we can't stop Valeria."

"I have faith that we will."

"We've dawdled long enough." Sebastian straightened his back, bracing himself for the sisters' spell. Zack followed his lead. "Send us along."

Herb took a step back. Selena and Sacha took hands. "We'll send you back to the last place we saw them, your theater," Selena said. "Focus on it, Zack."

"Got it." He knew the drill. He focused on the stage side area between the front row and the stage.

"Transport home," the ladies said in unison.

Everything went hazy, then faded away.

Chapter Twenty-Four

Zack opened his eyes to find himself back home, surrounded by the familiar stage in front and the seats he knew well behind him. With everything he'd gone through, the stage seemed far smaller than before. Magic was always something special to him, but that was before he learned that real magic and supernatural powers actually existed in the world.

Zack clenched his stomach and gagged. It was the fourth time he had been teleported by his new witch companions. This time, however, it left him nauseous. It could have been the distance, or the stress. Or, maybe it was due to the sunburn on the top of his head. It gave him a terrible headache.

Sebastian stepped forward, looking back and forth, all over the empty auditorium. With the curtain wide open, they could see the dressing room's door open. That was where Valeria had Isis tied to a chair. Now, there was no battle waiting to be had. There was only the chair.

"They're not here," Zack said.

"I didn't think they would still be here."

"What?" Sebastian's reply caused Zack's jaw to clench. "If you knew, why the hell did we come here?"

"I didn't know. I suspected," Sebastian answered. "But I need a starting point. If I can pick up their trail, I may be able to communicate with Isis…assuming Valeria hasn't killed her."

"That's my worry." The thought sent a chill down Zack's spine. "But I was thinking about it. Valeria could have killed her before instead of abducting her. She must have kept Isis alive for a reason. She needs her alive for something, right?"

"That's what I'm counting on." Sebastian shut his eyes and pointed his nose up. "Now, let me concentrate."

"Right." In other words, stop rambling. But Zack had that habit, especially when he was nervous.

Zack stopped in his tracks and gasped. Bambi's body lay in the middle of the stage, her blank eyes staring up at the ceiling. Her lips and skin were exceedingly pale and lifeless. Dried blood covered her neck, T-shirt, and the stage floor around her. "She…she feasted," Zack said to himself as Sebastian's attention was focused somewhere other than inside the theater.

Zack jumped onto the stage, but kept his distance, not wanting to get any closer than necessary. This was the first dead body he had ever seen. Bambi looked like something he'd seen in zombie movies, except she wasn't animated. Zack heaved. It was lucky he hadn't eaten anything in hours. Zack grabbed the edge of the curtain and walked from one end of the stage to the other. The curtain followed along its pole high above, blocking the stage—and Bambi's corpse—from view.

There had to be something more he should do, but what? Pray? Take the body and bury it in the desert? They did have a trap door under the stage. Bambi used it many times when they'd perform a disappearing act. Nah, bad idea. Hiding Bambi's corpse in the same hole she utilized during performances seemed way too morbid. Plus, Zack didn't think he could bring himself to drag or roll the body under the stage floor.

He could let her next of kin know, although Bambi never talked about a family. His Uncle Herb would know what to do, if only he had come along as Zack expected he would. Hopefully they'll be off that damn island soon enough.

A pressure built between Zack's eyes. He massaged his temples with his right thumb and forefinger. Be strong, he told himself. There was no time to panic. Through the pain, he heard a knocking sound. Then, it happened again. It was coming from the side door that led to the stage. Damn! Who could it be?

At least it wasn't Valeria returning to kill him and Sebastian. If that were the case, she wouldn't bother knocking. It could have been a cop, or even worse, the hotel manager. Didn't they have a show scheduled for tonight? Zack grabbed a long green sheet from backstage and draped it over Bambi. Whoever was knocking didn't need to see a corpse sprawled out in the middle of the stage.

Zack hesitated, but then turned the doorknob. He pulled the door open. Definitely not Valeria, unless she'd turned male, grown short black hair, a goatee, and fifteen-inch pythons shooting out of his muscle shirt. Zack was happy to see a familiar face in the doorway. Kris had been a trainer in the hotel gym for over a decade. In that time, he and Herb had grown close over afternoon drinks in the bar.

"Kris, is everything okay?" Zack's question was in reference to the trainer's determined pace as he walked through the doorway. He was a man on a mission.

Between the gym muscles and the possibly dyed slick hair, he looked much younger than his actual age of forty-seven.

"I came here looking for Herb…and you," Kris responded in his east coast accent. "There's a new street show setting up and it's happening right outside this theater."

"What kind of show?"

"I think it's a magic act, but with that new wave torture performance stuff. This pale, creepy-looking woman is tying a girl to a tree." He threw a slanted look at Zack. "I don't know how they got a tree in the middle of the street. I know it has to be artificial, but it looks real, like it's actually sprouting from the ground."

"Okay, thanks for letting me know," Zack said. This had to be them.

"There's also a huge torch out there," Kris added. "I'm thinking a fire trick? Right now, it looks like they're still setting up. There's already a crowd forming."

Sebastian, now on the stage, walked between them. He grabbed Zack by the arm and pulled him a few steps away. "I've spoken with Isis. She's in trouble," he whispered in Zack's ear. "But they're close—"

"—right outside the theater, I know."

"Hey, Zack," Kris called. "You want me to go out there and tell them to pick another street corner? Let them know this is Herb Galloway territory?"

"That's okay, Kris, let us handle this," Zack said to him.

"He should stay far away from them," Sebastian whispered. "We don't know how she would react to interference. She may kill him on the spot."

"Right." To Kris, Zack said, "I'd suggest staying away from that area, and try to keep the guests away from it as well."

"I hear you, buddy." Kris pointed at Zack. "We don't want them stealing your audience." Kris gave Zack a wink, then marched through the doorway.

"Holy crap," Zack said to Sebastian once Kris was out of earshot. "She's going to set Isis on fire out there in front of everyone?"

"I projected a thought to Isis," Sebastian said. "I let her know we're close."

"Why in the hell would she do that?" Zack looked down to see his fists clenching and unclenching against his will. "I-I get that she's crazy, but to set someone on fire—"

"She wants Isis' power, and she's looking to put an idea out there."

"An idea? What idea? What kind of game is she playing?"

"She wants to inspire witches to reveal themselves, band together, and fight. She's doing this by setting a witch on fire and putting it on display. It's a reminder to all witches of a dark time in our history. It may take years, even decades, for this idea to evolve, but she has the time to wait."

"But this isn't human prejudice," Zack replied. "This is a witch setting another witch on fire."

"When the story becomes legend, it won't matter who did what, only that it happened. The details rarely follow a narrative."

Zack shook his head. "I don't see how we can beat her. She handled all three of you pretty easily the last time."

"You let me worry about that." Sebastian held his hand up with his fingers separated. The wooden stake they had pulled out of Luther appeared in his hand. "We both have our jobs out there. Yours is to free Isis while Valeria is focused on me. Do you understand?"

"I... Yeah, I do." Zack's throat closed. It felt dry like the last time he was sick.

Of course, this fight was Sebastian's, not his—at least until the others showed up—and he was confident in his own ability to sneak in unseen. Only now, it was about to get real. In fact, it was more real than anything Zack had ever dealt with in his entire life. So many doubts, like the fact that Sebastian was horribly outmatched power-wise against Valeria. His entire plan relied on surviving until the other witches saved Luther and showed up. Neither had any idea how they'd do it. What if they couldn't actually revive him? What if they didn't show up in time, or at all—

Sebastian dropped the wooden stake on the floor. The sound echoed throughout the empty auditorium. Zack nearly jumped out of his skin.

"Listen to me." Sebastian took Zack by the shoulders and looked down into his eyes. "I know you're scared, but you have to put that aside. This isn't just about you, your uncle, or even Isis. This is about saving the entire planet from a dark future where everybody dies."

"She could kill Isis. She could kill us—"

"Not just Isis. Not just us. Everybody!" Sebastian gave Zack a shake. "To stop her, I need you to man up and do your part. Do you understand?"

Zack's tense muscles loosened up. His throat opened, allowing himself deep breaths of air. It wasn't the best plan he'd ever heard, but it was the best they had. Right now, Zack believed in Sebastian's ability to make it work. If his sudden confidence was because Sebastian was using his witchcraft, then Zack appreciated it, because the speech wasn't that great.

"I understand," Zack said.

"I'm heading out there right now. Can I count on you?"

"I'm ready. Just give me a minute to grab a few items. I think they'll help."

"Just don't dawdle. We have to go save our girl."

Chapter Twenty-Five

"You need to learn to control your emotions. Emotions affect your ability to control your powers."

Isis had heard these instructions far too many times since she was nine. At fifteen, she understood them well. Anger made the control erratic while fear could disconnect her completely. This was a huge problem because Isis had never been more scared in her entire life, and that covered a lot of fearful territory.

Isis hung from the branch of a tree that Valeria had created. Somehow, it started underground and broke through the street. Each end of the rope that hung over the branch dug into Isis' wrists. Her arms felt like they wanted to pull out of their sockets. Her toes barely touched the ground.

"Patience, young witch. We will begin shortly," Valeria said in response to Isis' struggling.

What made this even worse were the dozens of men, women, and children who had gathered and formed a semi-circle while keeping a safe distance. No one looked nervous, outraged, or concerned. The faces behind the phones snapping pictures or taking video all depicted curiosity as to what would happen next. The people of Vegas had become accustomed to every occurrence on the strip being part of a show—even a fully grown tree showing up in the middle of the street didn't faze them. Normally, they'd be right, so why would they think otherwise? This was one of those times where they were wrong.

A voice raced through Isis' head. Sebastian's voice said, "We are near." Thank goodness they had escaped whatever trap they were in. Valeria said she didn't kill them, but Isis hadn't been sure if that was the truth or not. She took a deep breath and focused on one thought, "Please hurry."

"Yes, people of Vegas," Valeria shouted to the growing audience in the street and sidewalk around them, "use your precious devices to send my message to the entire world!"

Another voice whispered her name. First, Isis thought it was in her head. But the second time it came, she realized it was behind the tree. "Zack?" she whispered. "What are you doing here?"

"I'm getting you out of this," he said.

"No, you have to go. If she sees you—"

"I speak to all the witches who can hear my words," Valeria announced. "The time for hiding our true selves has long passed! We must stand together against the weak mortals who will take their places beneath us!" Valeria turned to Isis. "And against those who would dare stand in our way!"

Valeria held out a hand as if she were reaching for something that wasn't there. On command, the torch, lit with a heavy flame and rose in the air. It hovered in front of Isis' face.

She turned her head away from the heat and black smoke. She still sensed Zack behind the tree. So far, Valeria hadn't picked up on his presence. She was too intoxicated in the moment to notice him. It was clear he came to help. Brave boy, but what could he do other than put himself in danger?

"Rejoice, young witch," she said. "The sacrifice you make today will benefit our kind for many generations to come."

The torch leaned against Isis' chest, but the flame extinguished before it touched her. Valeria stared at it in confusion, then at Isis. "Did you just—No, it wasn't you." Valeria spun around. "They are here!"

"No, not all of them." Sebastian stepped through the crowd. "It's just me."

"The weakest of the three." Valeria tossed the burnt-out torch at Sebastian's feet. "Where is the rest of your coven?"

"They are still on the island where you stranded us." Sebastian moved closer. "They are mourning Luther and burying his body."

"Mourning?" Valeria's head snapped back. "You spared the mortals and sacrificed your mentor?"

"We look to serve the greater good, just like you." Sebastian made eye contact with Valeria. They were now within inches of one another. "We don't wish to harm this innocent world."

"Innocent world?" Valeria suddenly sounded less angry and more curious.

"Look inside your soul," Sebastian spoke with a rhythmic flow, "and you will find your belief in the greater good. You have the power to help people—it is what you've always wanted to do. Look deep inside and you will see that your anger is not the answer."

Valeria's eyelids fluttered. "It makes...sense. Why is this only dawning on me now?"

"It is never too late to change your mind, Valeria,"

Sebastian said. "You can begin a new path starting now—"

"I can…I can…" Valeria's eyes suddenly went dark with rage. "You are in my head!"

Valeria swung a roundhouse right that connected with Sebastian's jaw. The force and the surprise of the punch staggered him. Before he could recover, a gale-force wind hit him in the chest. It took him off his feet and sent him crashing to the ground at the feet of some onlookers. The people scattered, moving back several feet, but staying close enough to watch the show.

Valeria leaped in the air and landed at Sebastian's feet, her fists clenched and glowing.

"No, please, don't!" Isis screeched.

"Don't worry…" Zack sneaked around the tree now that Valeria had her attention on Sebastian. "He has a plan. My part is getting you out of these ropes."

"How?" Isis asked. "You don't have any powers."

"That's the problem with you witches." Zack pulled a switchblade from his back pants pocket and unlatched the knife blade. "You think your powers are the answer to everything." Zack sawed through the rope.

As he worked on the ropes, Isis peeked at Sebastian. There was suddenly eight of him lying side by side. Valeria looked back and forth at each of the Sebastians. She then let out a loud cackle. "You try to trick me with illusions? This is why you are the weak one."

Valeria clapped her glowing hands. Seven of the Sebastians faded in puffs of smoke, leaving only one, the real Sebastian, who rolled to his knees and then rose to his feet. Valeria raised a hand, which levitated

Sebastian several inches off the ground. A pistol materialized in her free hand—it was Herb's gun. She pointed it at Sebastian's chest.

Zack's knife finally cut through the rope. Isis fell to all fours. The rope landed in front of her. "Come on, we have to get out of here!" Zack kneeled and wrapped his arms around Isis' waist and pulled her to her feet.

"We-we can't just leave," Isis sobbed. "She's going to kill him!"

"I told you, he has a plan." The sharp wooden stake flew past them, making a beeline for Valeria's back.

Zack flinched. "And there's his plan!" he howled.

Isis' eyes widened with excitement. She wanted to see the one object that could harm a vampire shoot through Valeria's hate-filled heart. However, just before the stake could plunge her skin, Valeria spun 180-degrees and waved a hand in the air. The stake shattered into small wood chips.

Sebastian fell to his feet, taking a moment to regain his balance. The gun, however, remained in mid-air, pointed inches from his chest. "Oh, no," he screeched.

Valeria peeked over her shoulder. "Oh, yes," she said. A deafening bang filled the area.

Valeria snatched the smoking gun from mid-air. She stared Sebastian down as blood seeped through his white shirt. Sebastian clutched the right side of his upper chest, just under his shoulder. His legs went wobbly, and then he fell to the ground.

"NO!" Isis screeched.

"Men and their toys. That's never changed." Valeria tossed the gun over her shoulder. Her head turned to Isis and Zack. "Now, where were we?"

"Oh, damn!" Zack yanked on Isis' arm. "We have

to run. Now!"

A sudden force slammed Zack to the ground. It didn't come from Valeria.

Isis marched in the vampire's direction. "No, I'm not going anywhere!" she growled through clenched teeth.

Valeria came her way. Her eyes narrowed. Isis no longer felt fear, only anger. No. Rage over Valeria possibly killing the only father she'd ever had. And Isis had done nothing to stop it. She left him there to fight alone while she cried and cowered. The tingling in her body felt stronger than ever before. It meant the power was flowing through her veins like the water from a broken pipe. It was time for this bitch to die.

"You've found your spine. Good." Valeria mimicked Isis' narrowed eyes. Valeria raised her hands in the air. "You should die on your feet like a true witch—"

"I'm done being afraid of you," Isis roared. "Heavy hands!"

She focused her gaze on Valeria's hands, calling on the power to make the air around them heavy, too heavy for Valeria to fight the effects. It worked. The air dragged Valeria's arms to her sides. The vampire's eyes widened to the point that they looked ready to explode out of their sockets.

"Rope!" Isis shouted. She made the rope by her feet rise in the air as if it were a third arm. She could move it as easily as her fingers and toes.

The rope was thick and strong—Isis still felt the sting from burns around her wrists. She threw her hand forward. The rope soared at Valeria. Before the immortal witch could react, the rope wrapped around her throat. Isis lifted her hand high in the air. In response, the ends of the rope shot up, lifting Valeria.

Valeria, regaining use of her hands, clawed at the rope wrapped around her throat. Her face revealed more surprise than fear. As a vampire, Valeria didn't need air, but Isis was able to will her to experience choking. The crowd cheered as if realizing—even while believing this was all an act—that Valeria was the villain in this battle.

Isis finally had the advantage. It was time to give her a taste of her own medicine. "Fire!" she screamed.

Three heavy flames shot out of the ground, but none were underneath Valeria. One sprang up in front of Isis, the others on each side. Onlookers scurried back. That included Zack, who jumped to his feet and moved to safety. Now, Isis needed to create another flame—this one would be a gift for Valeria. She had to focus without letting her temper rattle her control. Stay calm, she told herself, time to do to her what she wanted to do to me...

"Isis, the fire!" Zack screamed. "It's out of control!"

To her left, one gray-haired lady in an orange dress with a blue flower pattern had fallen on her backside. She couldn't get up. The woman's hands clutched her right ankle as flames spread in her direction. Unlike all the faces in the crowd, Zack didn't hesitate. He ran to the woman, grabbed her by the waist, and attempted to pull her away. Unfortunately, she was too big for Zack to budge. No one from the crowd made a move to help. Either they were afraid for their own safety, or a more likely scenario, they thought it all was part of the show.

Isis had to make a decision. She had Valeria on the

ropes, literally. Focus on her advantage, create another fire, and hopefully this one would hit its target. It would save all the future lives Valeria would destroy. But this one woman would die right now—not to mention possibly Zack and others as well—and it would be Isis' fault. She peeked over at Sebastian who was on his back, his eyes closed. His chest was covered in blood. She didn't know if he was alive or dead, but she could hear his advice in her head. *Always make the choice you can live with at the end of the day.*

"Damnit!" Isis turned her attention to the flames. Her focus away from Valeria caused the witch to hit the ground with a thud. Isis focused on the fire. "Fire, fade."

On her command, the flames on all three sides evaporated into a yellow fog. Through the fog, Isis could barely make out Valeria on the ground holding her throat and shaking her head.

Zack kept shouting to the crowd for help. Finally, two men heeded his call. They ran over and helped Zack pull the woman off the ground. They were able to move her back. Everyone was safe, at least for now. Time to make sure they stayed that way by ending the real threat. Hopefully, she hadn't gotten her bearings yet.

Isis turned back in time to see a red car door flying through the air at her. Before she could react, the loud CLANG thundered through her ears as the door slammed against her face. It forced her eyelids to shut. When she opened them, Isis found herself on her back with Valeria standing over her. A boot pressed on her chest. Apparently, the impact had knocked her unconscious.

A hand against her forehead revealed blood. Valeria peered down and grinned. Isis wanted to defend herself, but she could barely think straight let alone tap back into the power. Smoke emanated from Valeria's hands.

"You truly do have a great connection to the power. Mother Earth thought much of you, indeed." Valeria leaned down and took a handful of Isis' hair. "However, I cannot have one such as you imprudently trying to stop me from saving our kind. So, if there are no other witches here to stand in my way, I must end your existence."

"There's at least one more here to stand in your way," a voice shouted.

Isis rolled her head to see Zack standing several feet back. His hands were cocked at his sides. "Back off or suffer my wicked wrath!"

Valeria straightened and stepped away from Isis' body. She faced Zack. "You are a witch?" She let out a loud laugh. "I do not think so."

"I'm the baddest witch in Vegas, lady," Zack replied. "This town is under my protection, so back down or be destroyed!"

"The baddest witch in Vegas." Valeria looked Zack up and down. "You are clearly not a witch at all."

"Try me." Zack raised his left hand in the air. A red light glowed between his fingers.

Chapter Twenty-Six

"You claim to be a witch." Valeria's voice hesitated. "I can sense the relationship in those who are true witches. I sense not a drop of connection within you."

"I've been using a magic spell to hide my true self." Zack waved his left hand, waving the red glow from his fingers in a circular motion. "I've been waiting for the right time to reveal myself."

"And this is your moment." Valeria cackled. "Foolish child."

"Yes," Zack stated. "Stand down or I will disintegrate you."

Valeria took a step forward. Zack took one back. He needed to make sure his hand never stopped moving while he kept enough of a distance. He didn't want Valeria noticing the hollow, rubber fingertips he had covering his thumb and middle finger. Each had a small red lightbulb inside. They made for a great act on stage as the magician could make the light appear, reappear, and even jump from one hand to the other. Right now, they needed more time, and the light trick made for a good distraction, but if Valeria noticed, the jig would be up.

"If you are truly a witch, then show me your power," Valeria said, an indication that she wasn't buying his act. "And do so quickly, because I am about to kill you."

Valeria hovered inches from the ground and floated in Zack's direction. Zack put his right hand behind his back. A wad of flash paper stuck out of his back pocket. As Valeria came closer, he flicked the lighter hiding between his fingers to ignite the flash paper. The moment fire hit paper, Zack dropped the lighter, yanked out the flash paper, and tossed it at Valeria's eyes. She threw a hand in front of her face as the flame scattered, then disappeared.

It worked as Zack expected. He hoped it would give him enough time for his next trick. His life might depend on it.

From his right sleeve, Zack revealed a metallic finger-sized cane that shot out another three feet. He swung it with all his might. It made contact with the side of Valeria's skull just above her ear. He had bought the metal appearing cane from an online magic shop a year ago. His Uncle Herb thought it was a waste of money. "The plastic ones at half the price look just as good on stage," Herb had said. But Zack wanted a strong metal one for his collection. Today, it practically paid for itself.

Valeria stretched out her arm. The pistol slid across the ground as if answering her call. Zack tossed the cane at Valeria. She swatted it away with ease, but that was okay—he meant it only as a distraction. Zack dove for his uncle's pistol. He snatched it with his right hand, then stood up and pointed the barrel at Valeria while balancing his right hand on top of his left palm. Time for the grand finale.

Zack's only experience with this gun was a few

times on the shooting range. Herb would shoot huge targets from fifty feet away. Once he finished, he'd offer the gun to Zack to try. Zack took him up on the offer only two or three times over the last few years. He never thought he'd actually shoot a live person. Then again, Valeria was anything but a live person, and it was necessary.

Zack squeezed the trigger. The gun fired and the bullet pierced Valeria's gut. Smoke emanated from her stomach where the bullet hit. From such a close distance, that bullet would kill any human being. Zack hoped it would at the very least knock Valeria to the ground. All it did was stagger her like a weak punch to the stomach.

Valeria straightened her back, exposing sharp fangs and eyes black as night. With space between her feet and the ground, she looked almost seven feet tall.

The gun flew from Zack's hand.

His shirt unbuttoned itself and then ripped from his body. It flew far away along with everything he had stashed in his shirt pockets, which included another switchblade, a few smoke bombs, and a few more sheets of flash paper. So much for convincing her that he was a witch.

"Oh shit!" Zack tried to run, but his feet wouldn't move—her doing, no doubt. "Um, how about we just call it a draw?" he asked with wide eyes and raised eyebrows.

"Young fool, I am going to enjoy drinking you dry," Valeria roared. Guess she didn't have much of a sense of humor.

Isis sat up. Her upper body rocked as she pressed a hand against her forehead. "N-no, leave him alone!"

"No worries, Isis," Zack shouted. He could feel control over his body return. "I got this." Although he had no idea what the hell he could do.

Zack held up his fists, a futile display considering he had avoided fights his entire life. Figures his first one would be against an all-powerful witch. He expected to die, but at least he'd go down swinging. The space between Valeria's boots and the ground closed. With great effort, Zack took a step back. Valeria swatted her hand. As if in response, Zack's feet yanked forward. He landed on his backside.

"It is time for your brief life to end," Valeria stated.

Zack braced himself for whatever was coming next. It would probably hurt a lot.

Valeria suddenly blurred as if Zack was looking at her through water. For a moment, he thought he was teleporting again, but everything around him was perfectly clear. A blurred circle had formed between himself and Valeria. It made her tremble.

"What? How?" Valeria gasped. She made a quick 180-degree turn.

Her answer, and Zack's salvation, stood several feet away.

Sacha held her hands out with her fingers touching at the tips, forming a circle. Selena stepped in front of her and stared down Valeria with angry, slanted eyes. Selena screeched a loud high-pitched scream and threw her arms straight out. A blast of air—or force—smacked Valeria in the chest. It pushed her toward the portal.

"No!" Valeria screeched. She dug her heels into the ground and extended her arms, sending a defiant force blast of her own. Waves of energy clashed in the space between the witches, causing random sparks throughout the air. "I have been a witch for four hundred years!" Valeria shouted over the hum of energy. She took a step forward. "You think you have it in you to defeat me?"

Valeria's boots scraped the ground. Now, it was Selena taking a step forward. "You hurt my family," Selena roared. "You're damn right I have it in me!"

"Come on, Selena," Zack said under his breath. Her sweat-filled face revealed that she was struggling far more than her bravado let on. But she wouldn't relent. Unfortunately, neither would Valeria.

"Selena!" Sacha called. "Say the word, I can close the portal, help you, then re-open—"

"NO!" Selena snapped. "Stick with the plan, wait for my signal!"

Zack crawled to Isis, who watched through wide eyes. Her upper body teetered, struggling to stay in a sitting position. Zack put his hands on her shoulders for support. The sound of thunder from the colliding forces was earsplitting even over the sounds of hundreds of people cheering and screaming. Something had to give, and soon. Would anyone in the area survive?

Selena's arms trembled. A line of blood dripped down her forehead. Despite this, she refused to budge. As impressive as Selena was in battle, she couldn't last much longer. Especially against Valeria, who took another step forward.

And another.

With each step, Selena's face scrunched.

"Push her, Sis!" Sacha shouted. "You have to, for all our sakes!"

"I…I will. I must." Selena's eyes turned into slits. Her arms visibly quivered as she pushed forward.

Selena's body shook. Her forehead had drapes of blood and sweat. Zack was sure she wouldn't last.

An idea suddenly sprang into his mind. "Isis!" He shook her until the shock on her face disappeared. "When I first saw you, it was at your show. You made yourself float in the air, remember?"

"L-lighter than air," Isis answered. Her voice trembled as she watched the battle through glazed eyes. "I can make myself float, but how would that help?"

Zack pointed at Valeria. "Can you do it to her?"

Isis' head spun to Zack. She looked back at Valeria with a huge smile and renewed life. Isis threw her hands forward. "Lighter than air," she chanted. "Lighter than air…lighter than air…"

Valeria lifted in the air. Her body floated as if someone had suddenly turned off the gravity around her. The smugness left her face. Without her feet dug into the street's asphalt, the immortal witch's body flew backward past Zack and Isis, rocketing toward the portal.

"Yes!" Sacha screamed with delight. "Get her in position, Selena, you got this!"

Selena let out a long howl as her arms and body straightened. The force blast hitting Valeria increased in both sound and sparks.

Valeria threw her palms back, aiming her force blasts at the portal. It stopped her in mid-air, inches from the blurred circle. "I will not…return!" The glow around Valeria's hands increased in brightness. The struggle between two powerful witches resumed.

"NOW, SACHA!" Selena's entire body shuddered from the pressure. Her head slowly turned toward her sister. "DO IT NOW!"

Sacha unlocked the circle her fingers had formed, stretching out her right arm. "Luther, appear!" she shouted.

On command, Luther materialized in mid-air, flying at Valeria as if he had been fired out of a cannon. He was no longer hurt or injured. The vampire was completely revitalized. "Close the portal!" Luther yelled to the witches.

Luther rammed his shoulder into Valeria's ribcage. Her arms flew up. The glow around Valeria's hands disappeared. Both vampires zipped through the circle of blur. "CLOSE IT, NOW!" Luther called as both he and Valeria disappeared. The noise caused by the force blasts stopped.

"Sacha, we have no choice," Selena said through a deep breath. "Close the portal."

"Right." Sacha's voice cracked. She placed her palms together, which made the circular portal shrink, then disappear. "Goodbye, Luther," she sobbed.

Selena staggered near Sebastian, who was still laid out covered in a crimson puddle. She collapsed to her knees. Zack stood to get a good look as well. Sebastian's eyes were shut, but his chest rose; he was still alive.

"Sacha!" Selena rolled her hand under Sebastian's head. "I can't heal him, I have nothing left," she said between heavy breaths.

"I can heal him!" Sacha ran over and kneeled next to both of them. "My God, he's lost so much blood." She looked back at Selena. "I'm going to have to teleport that bullet out of him, then get his blood cells to multiply while I close up that hole."

"You can do this," Selena responded. "You have

to."

Sacha nodded and placed her hands on Sebastian's chest over the open gash. She shut her eyes and concentrated. "Heal Sebastian," she chanted. "Heal Sebastian."

"Nothing is happening," Selena gasped. "Why is nothing happening?"

Sacha's eyes opened. They turned to her sister. "It's you, Selena. I can feel your panic."

"You're right, I—" Selena looked back at Zack and Isis. "I'm going to check on Isis."

Selena took a deep breath and forced herself to her feet, leaving Sacha to her work. With slow anguished steps, she made her way to Zack and Isis, and kneeled in front of them. "Isis, are you—"

"Mom," Isis cried out, then let her upper body fall against Selena's chest. Even with her eyelids shut, Isis couldn't prevent the tears from rolling down her face like raindrops on a window.

"It's okay, baby," Selena whispered, embracing Isis with hands against her head and back. "It's all over now. We won. Valeria is gone."

"Dad?"

"He's alive," Selena replied. "Sacha is healing him now."

Zack peeked over Selena's shoulder. Sebastian sat up and reached for his chest. He was surrounded by blood, but none of it looked fresh. "She did it. Sebastian looks healed." Zack echoed Selena's sigh of relief. He stood. "I'll head over, make sure he's okay."

"Thank you," Selena responded. Zack expected to see eyes filled with excitement, or even exhaustion. Instead, he saw sorrow. He couldn't imagine why.

Could it have been over having to exile Luther along with Valeria? He was like a father figure to them and now he was gone. Suddenly, her sadness made sense, sort of.

As Zack raced to Sebastian and Sacha, he glanced around, taken aback by all the eyes surrounding them. The crowd of dozens had become hundreds, and then even more on top of that. It was as if every tourist on the Vegas strip had made their way to this particular spot. Many were still pointing their phones and cameras. This meant the day wasn't over for the witches, but maybe they'd never again have to worry about protecting their secret. Of course, that would cause them a ton more problems.

Zack kneeled by Sebastian's side. His shirt was torn and bloodstained, but his skin was sealed. "Thanks," Sebastian said to Sacha.

"Hey, you're practically my big brother," she replied with a sarcastic smile. "I sure as hell wasn't going to let you die."

"Sebastian," Zack groaned. "We have a problem."

"We just finished with a problem," Sacha groaned. "What now?"

Zack waved his hand to the crowd. He could have pointed in any direction as they were surrounded on all sides.

"Oh, no," Sebastian yelped, looking back and forth. He glanced across to Selena, who returned his concerned expression with one of her own. "We need to leave, and fast."

"I'm too pooped to teleport us out," Sacha said. "That means Selena can't, either."

"If not with our powers," Sebastian replied while

peering back and forth, "then we'll have to make a run for it."

Zack threw his arm across his eyes, blocking the blinding flashes from all sides. The ruckus was getting louder. Zack realized what they wanted, the same thing that every audience wants.

"Sebastian!" Zack tapped his arm. "Sell it!"

"Huh? What are you talking about?"

"For the show! Sell it!"

Sebastian's head lifted. He stood up and looked around at the crowd. "Got it." He stepped forward, showing that he understood Zack's meaning. Good. "Ladies and Gentlemen," Sebastian shouted out for all to hear, "this town has just been saved by the magic of The Witches of Vegas!"

The crowd filled with numerous reactions, from laughter, to relief, to applause.

"You can see amazing effects like these, and so much more," Sebastian continued, "four nights and three afternoons a week in the main theater at the Sapphire Resort, just a few blocks down the strip! Go and get your tickets now while they are still available!"

The crowd erupted in a cheer. Sebastian stretched his right arm, taking in the crowd's reaction. They didn't seem to notice that his left hand was pressed against his chest where the bullet had pierced his skin. Apparently, a witch's healing spell didn't remove the pain of an injury, but Sebastian's facial expression hid it well. He turned back to Zack and Sacha, then to Selena and Isis. He let out a deep exhale.

"Good call, kiddo," Sacha said to Zack.

Zack gave Sacha a slight grin. He'd have appreciated the compliment much more if his knees weren't shaking so much.

"Glad to help," Zack replied. "Now, we should get the hell out of here."

Sebastian exchanged high-fives with a few members of the audience.

"Good idea," Sacha said. "Let's go somewhere quiet. We have a lot to talk about."

Zack took another look at where the portal to the other world once stood. He wanted to make sure it was truly gone. It was—as if it never existed in the first place. Now that the danger was over, Zack wasn't interested in rehashing or talking about what happened. He never got why adults always wanted to talk everything out after the fact. Apparently, that was even the case with adult witches. Right now, Zack just wanted to see his Uncle Herb, make sure he was okay, and then go sleep for a week.

Chapter Twenty-Seven

The five-foot drop separated Luther from Valeria. His body rolled across a ground made up of dirt and what felt like dead grass and rocks. He managed to stop his momentum inches from a cliff's edge, a cliff that had he gone over, would have dropped him what looked like a far distance. It wouldn't have killed him, but, despite the urban myths, vampires can feel pain. In fact, it was one of the few sensations that remained long after death.

From his knees, Luther looked up to where the portal had closed. The only traces left were the electrical sparks in the damp air. Soon, those last traces of home would disappear forever, leaving just the grayish sky that tinted the entire area.

He had no idea what to expect when he went through the portal. He supposed there would be a sense of euphoria, but that belief proved to be incorrect. In truth, passing through the portal didn't feel like he had gone anywhere except a few feet forward. It made him think everything, including the plan and his instructions for opening the portal, failed. The proof, however, surrounded him on all sides as he no longer stood in Las Vegas. Instead, he was here, in what he assumed was the Other World.

"The plan worked," Luther said to himself.

In truth, he hadn't known if Sacha and Selena would be able to create the portal, even with his instructions—instructions that came from a memory over four hundred years old. But Madeline's daughters were far more powerful than he, or they, realized. He shouldn't have doubted them.

Luther had trained many witches throughout the centuries, but he hadn't grown as close to any in the past as with this coven. They were a true family, and they accepted his role of mentor. It was a role Luther secretly enjoyed, even though he didn't like to display that joy. He was used to being a teacher to witches throughout the centuries. But this group gave him a different sense of responsibility. This was especially the case once he spent time with them at their mother's bedside, watching her die.

The sisters' excitement about being witches was intoxicating. He enjoyed watching their control grow as they became young women. Sebastian, meanwhile, reminded him of his own son from a life five hundred years in the past. They were the only people, along with Madeline, that made Luther truly feel alive again. Why else would he make the ultimate sacrifice in order to remove the need for all their training?

Luther wanted them all to be safe, including Isis. That girl had potential that outweighed even the sisters' combined might, yet Luther sensed no corruption in her soul. She would benefit from their training without the impending threat of Valeria looming over their heads. Now they could find their own paths in the world as witches. Luther was determined to do everything possible to keep Valeria in this world.

Luther took a deep breath. He didn't need the air

but he could still taste it. The air was exactly like Earth's. A handful of dirt and grass revealed the ground to be soft and moist, like wet sand from the beach. Luther would think the planet dead, except for the brown cactus nearby. It was very much alive, soaking in the moisture from the air. It must not have needed light, because there wasn't much coming from the sky.

At first, Luther thought it was this planet's nightfall. The sky, however, revealed no moon, no stars. It wasn't a cloud covering like any he had ever seen on Earth, but rather a gray casing without any lines, holes, or an end in sight. Was the sky always like this? Or, could it have been because of the time, or the season? Luther had no idea. The one person who would know stood a few feet away, gathering her senses, and shooting daggers at him through pitch-black eyes.

"Luther, what have you done?" she roared. Sharp fangs protruded from either side of her upper jaw.

"What I must," Luther responded.

He leapt to his feet at the sight of Valeria hunching over like a rabid animal ready to pounce. He allowed his own fangs to show, letting her know he was ready for this fight. If the fight had to be, at least they were on equal ground since this plane of existence did not cater to her Wiccan magic. It would simply be vampire versus vampire. Then again, she had found a way back, so maybe she had learned to tap into the power of this place as well. If she could, Luther would find out soon enough.

A loud snarl came from behind Valeria. It took her focus away from Luther. The gray-haired animal stood five feet tall on four legs. It looked like a hyena from Earth, except for the color and the extra-long snout with a black nose at the tip. The creature had fangs at a length that put Luther's or Valeria's to shame. It also had paws that looked far too big for its thin legs.

"Well, it has been a while," Valeria growled as she faced the animal with the same attack stance earlier aimed at Luther. "Good to be remembered."

The hard head of a second animal, similar to the first, rammed Luther's chest. The surprise knocked him off his feet. Luther never saw or heard the animal's charge. Either his instincts were rusty or the animals were like chameleons, able to blend into the grayish atmosphere. Luther went limp so they'd both roll from the momentum. It would have been a good instinctive strategy, if not for the cliff. Both Luther and the animal rolled until they ran out of ground.

As they fell straight down, the animal pressed its upper paws against Luther's shoulders. Its huge snout opened, exposing long and sharp teeth along with its fangs. Luther stretched out his arms and gripped the animal's immense throat. It kept this angry creature from biting off his face. As a vampire, Luther was sure he didn't smell like food. It meant the animal saw him as a threat, most likely due to Valeria spending hundreds of years hunting its kind for their blood. In essence, this species evolved over hundreds of years to survive her.

Luther shifted his weight, causing both the animal and himself to land on their sides on top of a huge gray boulder. Luther rolled off the boulder and onto his feet. The landing crushed his arm, but this wasn't the first time Luther had fallen a great distance. The pain in his arm would dissipate quickly. For the animal, however, this was not the case. It yelped upon landing on the boulder, rolled upright, and scurried away.

There was suddenly a shift in the wind. He spun around to find another of these animals charging his way. This time, he was ready. He leapfrogged over the charging creature. Its paws created streak marks in the dirt as it stopped short just before running directly into the huge stone. It was time for Luther to press his advantage.

He jumped on its back and wrapped his arm around its throat. The animal rose onto its hind legs, trying to shake Luther off. The animal's throat was solid—it was like squeezing a tree stump—but its struggle meant it definitely had a windpipe, which Luther had closed off. The animal dropped back down to all fours. It was a strong beast, but Luther had the better position and managed to keep his chokehold tight.

The animal tried the same move, rising to its hind legs. This time, as it came down, Luther let go, causing it to land hard on its front paws. Luther lunged forward, hooked the stunned animal in a headlock, and rammed it, skull-first into the boulder. Its lifeless body fell to the ground, leaving a red splotch on the boulder.

Luther's thoughts drifted to the many animals he hunted in the Nevada deserts. He took no particular joy in those kills, but they were necessary to satisfy his daily need of blood, a consequence of being part of the undead. The hunts had given him a level of instinct and experience built up over half a millennium, which had served him well. None of those animals were quite like the indigenous creatures on this world, or at least in this area of the Other World, but the same skills applied. This time, those skills allowed him to survive and prevail against an immediate danger. Soon, he would need to eat, which meant more confrontations with this species.

Thoughts of survival halted when a severed head of another from the same type of animal landed on the boulder. It splattered on impact, spraying Luther in the face with blood. He wiped the blood from his cheek with the back of his hand. He pressed it against his tongue. It had a tangy flavor but tasted similar to the red blood of every Earth mammal he'd ever tasted.

Valeria followed the animal's head off the cliff, landing feet first on the same boulder. Luther took a step back. Her black boots were now eye-level. He looked up at Valeria. Blood covered her mouth, cheeks, and balled-up fists. Her attacker became a feast, which meant Valeria was at full strength, and quite angry.

"Give me one reason I shouldn't kill you right now!" Valeria roared.

"If you do," Luther calmly answered, "you will once again be in this world alone."

The darkness in Valeria's eyes faded. She sucked in her fangs and leaped off the boulder, landing in front of Luther. She looked him up and down as if contemplating her next move. Luther stayed on guard, ready for a fight that could conceivably tear apart his new home world.

After a long groan, Valeria's fists unclenched. "We are lucky there were only a few of those animals in the area when we arrived. They are usually in far larger packs."

Valeria walked past Luther. "Come. I may as well show you around."

Chapter Twenty-Eight

Zack leaned back in the leather reclining chair in the witches' suite. It was the second time he was in their living room with the entire family of witches staring at him. Sebastian and Selena sat side by side in metal folding chairs in front of him. Sacha had her arm across Isis' back on the leather couch that matched his recliner. The couch faced the forty-six-inch flat-screen television on the wall to Zack's right. The suite was far larger than the one he shared with Uncle Herb back at the Felicity.

He didn't want to focus on the size of their suite, but he needed the distraction—it kept him from bursting into tears. He looked at Selena, hoping what she had just told him was a lie, a scam by witches trying to emotionally manipulate, then destroy a mortal human teenager. He knew damn well that wasn't the case.

"Let me understand this." Zack rubbed his forehead, trying to think past the throbbing in his brain. "My uncle gave his blood and his life to Luther."

Selena didn't respond. The room remained quiet, letting him absorb his own words.

"Whose idea was this?"

"It was his idea." Selena put her hand over Zack's. "He asked us if we could stop Valeria without Luther.

We...I told him the truth, that our odds were much better with Luther. I told him he didn't have to, that we'd find another way, but he knew we didn't have another way. Luther was about to die. We were going to return to Vegas without his input, and without his knowledge on opening the portal. We would probably have lost."

"How did it happen? I mean...how does it happen? How do you feed a vampire?"

"Herb found a sharp branch," Selena explained in a slow and calming tone. "He used it to puncture his carotid artery. He placed the hole in his neck against Luther's open mouth so the blood could seep in. Unfortunately, Luther was in such bad shape, he needed to absorb it all to become whole again."

"I...I just don't understand." Zack threw a glare toward Sacha. "I saw you heal Sebastian. You couldn't heal my uncle the same way? Or, even better, heal Luther before my uncle gave up his blood and his life!"

Sacha's head dropped. "Sweetie, we can't heal the dead. Believe me, I wish we could."

Zack shut his eyes tight. The explanation didn't make sense. Luther wasn't dead; he was only injured. Yes, it was a bad injury, but they could have healed him on that damn island the moment they had their powers back. He wanted to throw that fact in their faces. But Luther was a vampire. By the very definition, he had been dead for a long time.

"Did you know..." Zack grumbled. "When you sent me back with Sebastian...did you know what he wanted to do?"

"We didn't know," Selena replied. "But I suspect Herb had already decided at that point. That may be why he chose to stay with us and not go back with you."

Zack had been around magicians since he was six years old. They were usually clever liars—it was an occupational requirement. Over time, Zack could recognize a liar simply by looking into a person's eyes when they spoke. Selena's hazel-colored irises were as sincere as he'd ever seen. He could envision Uncle Herb convincing them of this plan. To Zack, his uncle was his parent in every way that mattered. It would take the most extreme circumstances for The Amazing Herb Galloway to consider leaving his nephew alone in the world. Stopping an all-powerful vampire who wanted to destroy humanity certainly qualified as extreme circumstances.

"Talk to us, Zack," Sebastian said. "What are you thinking?"

His focus dropped to his white sand-covered sneakers. "I'm thinking a bit selfishly right now. I'm glad the world is safe. I'm glad all of you are safe. But without Uncle Herb, my world has fallen apart. I don't know what happens to me now."

"Perhaps we do." Selena squeezed his hand.

"We have an idea," Sebastian added with his eyes pointed at Selena. "Actually, it was Herb's idea, and his final wish."

Zack's head shot up. "What idea?"

Isis and Sacha were now looking his way from the couch. Apparently, everyone knew his uncle's idea except for him.

"We'd like you to stay with us," Sebastian answered. "We could use your expertise to help us revamp our show."

Zack paused. His eyebrows stretched into a straight line. When they told him his uncle had sacrificed himself for their cause, he suspected they'd offer him a bed. But help them revamp the number one show in Las Vegas? It didn't make sense.

"What do you need me for? You're powerful witches. What can I add to your performance?"

"We want the show to come off more authentic," Sebastian answered. "We need to appear as real magicians and not give our audiences a reason to suspect otherwise. To make this happen, we could use a real magician's touch. That advice came from your uncle. Actually, Luther said it before as well. We trust your knowledge and your discretion to hand you that role."

"Are you looking to give up the witchcraft and become actual magicians?" Zack asked.

"Absolutely not," Sebastian scoffed. "The whole point of performing our show is to keep the use of our powers fresh. Besides that, we also need to blend in. We can't have the public figuring out we are witches using actual magic on that stage. Such knowledge could potentially cause a worldwide panic."

"That's where you can come in, Zack," Selena said. "This is exactly what your uncle wanted for us—a magician to offer expertise so we can protect our secret. Who better than his own student in magic?"

Zack had to admit it was a good plan. It also sounded like one that would come from the mind of The Amazing Herb Galloway. When it came to stage performances, he was like a chess master, always thinking several moves ahead.

"So, you want me to make your shows a bit

suckier?" Zack blurted to no one in particular. He was really just thinking out loud. If he had given two seconds of thought before opening his mouth, he'd have come up with a better way to say it.

"Yes, that's essentially what we are asking you to do." Sebastian's head turned. He eyed his family. "Somewhere along the way, we became so infatuated with the cheers and the excitement of our audiences, we forgot the whole reason we're up on that stage in the first place."

Zack understood that well. There was no greater rush than a sold-out audience cheering your every move.

"So, what do you say, Zack?" Sacha asked from the couch, with a bit of impatience in her tone. "Do you want to be one of The Witches of Vegas?"

Next to Sacha, Isis gazed at Zack. She made a slight nod, hinting to him the answer she hoped to hear. It was an intriguing offer, and he sure didn't have any better options. Without Uncle Herb, there was no other family he could look to for a home. Still, The Witches of Vegas were supposed to be the enemy. They were the bad guys, except everything about them seemed trustworthy. Hell, in the end, his uncle did trust them. He actually asked them to take care of his nephew after sacrificing his life for them. It was all so much to take in. Zack shut his eyes tight, trying to stop the room from spinning.

"Zack, are you okay?" Sebastian asked.

"I don't know. I think…" Zack hunched forward, dropping his head into his hands. "I think I need a minute to figure all this out."

"Of course," Selena said. "Take your time, sort it

all out in your head."

Sebastian was the first to stand. "In the meantime, I have a hunch we're going to get called into a meeting with our esteemed hotel manager. We should figure out our story when that happens."

"I think that can wait until morning. We've all been through enough today." Selena wrapped her fingers around the back of Zack's neck. "Remember, we are here for you, whatever you want to do."

Zack nodded, his way of saying thank you.

"Hey!" he called, never looking up. "Uncle Herb, did he have any final words?"

"Yeah, he did," Sacha answered. "He said to make sure you finish school."

Okay, now he knew they weren't making any of this up. Even on the brink of death, that would be Herb Galloway's greatest concern.

Several footsteps tapped the hard wood floor before the door closed. He looked up, expecting an empty room. The older witches were gone, but Isis hadn't moved from her seat. She threw him a nervous stare. "Is it okay that I'm still here?" she asked.

"Yeah, it's cool," Zack replied.

Isis stood from the couch, walked over, and sat in the chair Selena had occupied. Zack's gaze focused on her hand that cupped his knee. Her touch made him quiver inside.

"Zack, I'm so sorry about your uncle." The sniffle in her voice let him know that she meant it. "I know he was a real good person. He even tried to save me from Valeria."

"He was a great person. I can't believe he's dead, just like that." Zack held a hand in front of his face and snapped his fingers.

"No, not just like that," Isis said. "He gave his life to save ours. To save the whole world."

"To save me."

"Yeah, to save you."

Zack looked into Isis' deep brown eyes. He didn't want pity, and he was sure Isis wasn't offering any. Despite all the suffering Valeria had put her through, Isis had genuine and selfless remorse for Zack and his sudden loss. It said a lot about her character, especially considering both Zack and Uncle Herb—particularly Zack—played a huge role in her capture. Man, had she done the same to him, could he be so grudgeless?

"Isis, I never did apologize for my part in all this. I know it was wrong—"

"It's okay, I get it," Isis interrupted him. "We came into your world and we used our powers to destroy it."

Zack couldn't argue the point. "Still, I came to you under false pretenses. After we met, I knew I didn't want to hurt you. I wanted to call the whole thing off. But I couldn't stop thinking about you. I should have stopped it when you came to the show. I should have warned you, or just told you to leave. But I wanted to be around you. I couldn't help myself because…well, you know."

"Yeah," she responded through a nervous laugh. "We were under a love spell. I don't think either of us was thinking clearly."

"Are we still under the spell? Because I look at you and I feel like I still am."

Isis' eyes widened. Her cheeks turned red like tomatoes. "I don't think so. Hypnosis spells usually stop working once you know you're under."

"Oh, I guess that makes sense." Damn, now he wished he'd have kept his feelings to himself. Actually, Zack didn't know much about witches or how their powers worked. At least his feelings were his own and no longer the result of a lunatic witch's spell. At the moment, they didn't feel much different.

"Well," Zack said, "I'm sorry we played a part in your kidnapping."

She shrugged. "We're sure Valeria would have found a way even without you. But we wouldn't have beaten her on our own. I'd probably be dead and she'd be tearing up the planet if not for The Amazing Herb Galloway"—Isis sucked in her lips—"and 'the baddest witch in Vegas'."

"You heard that, huh?" Zack's face grimaced. "I thought you were out of it at the time."

"I heard it. It was actually kind of cool. You should use it as your stage name."

"Yeah, right." Wow, she was still able to bring a smile to Zack's face. He straightened his back. "So, listen, since we're not under any spells and both in our right minds, maybe we can have a do over? Get to know each other, but this time, start off by being honest? How does that sound?"

"Being honest?" Isis looked to the air in thought. "Yeah, we could try that." She stuck her palm out for a handshake. "Hi, I'm Isis. I'm a witch who pretends to be a magician who plays a witch on stage."

Zack snorted, then took her hand and gave it a playful shake. "I'm Zack. I'm a magician who was just offered a job to help witches look like magicians pretending to be witches."

"Are you taking the job?" She folded her hands in

her lap. She leaned forward. "I'd really like you to take the job."

"Then I guess I have a good reason."

"Good." Their eyes met, as did their shy grins.

Chapter Twenty-Nine

Twelve hours had passed since the battle with Valeria on the strip. Local newspapers had differing views. It was Isis who went to the hotel's newsstand and grabbed a copy of each one. Some called it a bold but unnecessary character performance. Others claimed it blatantly put bystanders at risk just so magicians could show off and advertise their show. The important takeaway—they all saw it as a scripted promotion for The Witches of Vegas' magic show. The world was safe and so was their secret.

Just as Sebastian predicted, they were summoned by Jerry Blanco, the hotel general manager, to the office for an early morning conference. The short, bald headed GM sat behind his oversized desk, laying his cigar against the gold-plated ashtray. Next to the ashtray was an extra-large pink coffee mug with the phrase "I'm The Boss, That's Why" printed in black bubble letters. Isis liked the mug, although she always questioned why such a rugged man had a pink coffee mug on his desk.

Jerry tapped one of his hairy fingers against the wood surface. It was one of the few areas on the desk that wasn't covered with papers. "What are you people doing to me?" He looked directly at Sebastian.

Sebastian and Selena sat in the two leather chairs in

front of the desk. Isis stood in the back of the office with her hands behind her back. She guessed Sebastian wanted her there so Mister Blanco would be less likely to jump into one of his profanity-filled tirades. It had worked since she was ten. The last time they needed her in of these meetings, it was over a drunken argument between Sacha and one of the casino managers. The dispute happened because of a late-night hook-up that apparently meant more to the disgruntled young manager than it did to Sacha. The manager resigned the next day. It led to a long, awkward meeting where Sacha had to promise to never again sleep with any Sapphire Resort employees.

"It was all for publicity, Mister Blanco," Sebastian said. "We want to keep the people coming to see the show just as much as you do."

Jerry reached into his top desk drawer, pulled out a newspaper, and tossed it on the desk. It was the one put out in the front lobby complimentary to the guests. The headline read, "Witches of Vegas flaunt it in front of the Felicity."

"Do you see the problem here?" Jerry looked back and forth, from Sebastian to Selena. He then shook his head and sighed. "You don't see it, do you?"

"What is the problem?" Selena asked.

Jerry took a puff of his cigar. He pointed it at Selena from between his fingers as he spoke. "The Witches of Vegas just put on a performance in front of the theater that houses our only competition. That's competition you're already creaming in paid attendance. Before that, Galloway's show was hanging by a thread. Today, the Felicity is outright canceling him. That's not a coincidence."

"No, it's not a coincidence, but it's also not a consequence," Sebastian replied. "The Felicity was looking to cancel his show, anyway."

"Maybe it's because of what you did, maybe it's not." Jerry dropped the cigar back into the ashtray. "But because of the timing, the local press is going to perceive it as a bullying tactic on your part. That's bad press, which can hurt us, especially once Galloway resurfaces in another property along the strip. I've seen that sort of thing happen before."

"Mister Blanco, can we let you in on a little secret?"

Harry rolled his eyes. "You people seem to have a lot of secrets. What's the big revelation this time?"

Sebastian leaned in. "What if I told you that Herb Galloway was in on the publicity stunt from the beginning? They were looking to cancel him anyway, so he used us to force their decision. It was with Herb's blessing that we put on our show in front of his theater."

Jerry gave the witches a blank stare. "Now, let me tell *you* something," he said, sounding a little bit pissed off. "The Vegas strip is a big place, but it ain't a big place. I've known Herb Galloway for a lot of years. Hell, I was the Front Office manager of the Felicity back when his show debuted." He pointed his forefinger at Sebastian. "I'm not about to believe for one second that Herb Galloway would sabotage his own show, for any reason, unless I heard it directly from his mouth."

"We don't have him here, Mister Blanco," Sebastian replied, "but we have the next best thing. Isis, bring in the newest member of The Witches of Vegas."

Isis opened the office door. Zack waltzed in. "Hey, Jerry, long time, no see," he said with a smile.

Jerry stood from his desk, eyeing Zack up and down. "Zack? God damn, it's been a while. How old are you now?"

"I'm fifteen."

"Man, you were nine or ten the last time I saw you. What are you doing here?"

"It looks like I'm bringing my talents to your theater."

Jerry looked down at Sebastian and Selena, then back up at Zack. "Help me understand, you're leaving your uncle's side and joining this show?"

"It was Uncle Herb's idea." Zack stepped past Isis and walked up to the desk between the two occupied chairs. "He wanted to make a clean break from the show before the Felicity board of directors shamed him out. He wanted to leave on his own terms."

Sebastian stood from his chair. He motioned Zack to take a seat, which he did. Once seated, Zack's gaze dropped to the floor. Based on the concerned expression on Jerry Blanco's face, he noticed it, too.

"Hey, kid," Jerry said. "Is Herbie all right?"

"There are, um, some health issues," Zack answered, "but I promise you, I wouldn't be here without my uncle's say-so."

"Moving forward, Zack will be consulting for our show," Selena said. "We will be looking to implement some of his uncle's best stuff."

"And he is fine with all of this?"

"He is," Zack said. "In fact, he worked out all the details that brought me here."

"We're going to need a few things," Sebastian said.

"Why the fu—" Jerry's eyes darted to Isis, who quietly walked up to the back of Zack's chair. "Why the heck am I not surprised that you need something?" Jerry asked, facetiously. "Let me guess, you need another room for the kid?"

"No, we're covered there." Sebastian answered, "He's going to take the mini-suite next to our suite."

Jerry's head tilted back. "Don't tell me he's sharing it with the vampire guy."

"Luther will no longer be performing with us."

"Oh, really? Well, I can't say I'm too upset by that," Jerry said. "Truth be told, he spooked a lot of our guests, especially when he hung out in the lobby in full make-up. So, what happened, he's taking that vampire act on the road?"

"In a manner of speaking," Sebastian answered. "What we will need is a one-month hiatus to rework our show. In that time, I am sure the negative press will have passed and we will be bigger and better than ever."

"A month." Jerry wiped the sweat off his brow with the back of his hand. "That's a lot of refunds we're going to have to dish out."

Isis placed her hands on Zack's shoulders and rubbed. Her thumbs pressed against hard knots under the skin. Isis could only imagine how stressful this was for him. He had to put his sorrow aside and discuss his uncle as if the man were still alive. Isis was sure that if it was any member of her family, she couldn't have done it and not burst into tears. Hell, it almost was Sebastian, her dad, last night. Isis could barely hold herself together after he came so close to a violent death right in front of her eyes.

"You know you can trust us," Sebastian said. "This will all work out to your benefit."

Sebastian locked eyes with Jerry and offered a bright white smile. Isis noticed the slight yellowish glow in his gaze. He didn't have the power to change someone's thoughts, but he could influence their trust in him. It was a power he used on the audiences, but rarely used in a one on one situation. There were times he made an exception whenever he felt it was absolutely necessary.

Jerry, however, had proved himself in many of these meetings a man with an incredibly strong will. He sat back down and tapped the desk. "I can give you two and a half weeks. Maybe a few days after that depending on how the schedule falls."

"Okay, we'll take it." Sebastian reached across the desk, offering a handshake. A huge gulp traveled down Isis' throat.

Jerry shook Sebastian's hand. "Take your break and we'll see your new show then. Needless to say, it better be just as good if not better."

"Thank you, Mister Blanco," Sebastian said.

"You won't be disappointed." Selena stood.

Zack followed her lead and stood from his seat. Isis stepped out of the office with the others following her.

"Hey, Zack!" Jerry called, coaxing him to turn back. "Give your uncle my regards. Let him know I wish him the best in his retirement."

"I will, Jerry, thank you." Zack stepped out of the office and pulled the door shut. His smile faded.

Isis took his right hand and wrapped both of her own hands around it.

"How did it go?" asked Sacha, who had been

waiting in the hallway.

"We're good," Sebastian answered. "We have three weeks. Maybe a little less."

"Three weeks. That's exactly what we wanted."

Sebastian nodded. "It should be enough time to get a bit of rest and implement the changes."

"I should head over to the Felicity," Zack said. "I guess it's time to clear out our hotel room, and the stage."

"Zack, if you're not up for this, it's okay," Selena said in a calm and soothing tone. "We can take care of it."

"No, I need to handle it. We've been on that stage almost my entire life. No one else should be sifting through our stuff."

"Of course," Selena said.

"You're right, Zack. It should be you, but you don't have to go alone." Sacha stepped forward. "Why don't I tag along?"

"I appreciate it," Zack replied, "but I think I need to go through everything myself."

"Then go through everything yourself. I'll keep a safe distance." Sacha gave him a wink. "Just think of me as transport."

"I guess I could use a ride, or however you're getting us there." Zack had a slight grin on his face. For Isis, it was contagious. She remembered telling Zack how Sacha was the coolest aunt on Earth. She was proving that statement right.

"Gather whatever would be appropriate for a showcase," Sebastian said. "We're going to set one up outside our theater so everyone who attends the show will know the magic of The Amazing Herb Galloway."

"Wow, that would be great," Zack said. "I know he'd appreciate that. I do, too."

"It's the least we can do," Selena said. "Unfortunately, we can't ever reveal your uncle's greatest contribution to the world."

"I know."

Sebastian placed his hands on Zack's shoulders. "You're part of my coven now, Zack Galloway. That also makes you part of my family and part of our lives. I promise you will be treated accordingly." The statement made Isis smile. Her biggest concern was whether or not Sebastian would truly accept Zack, who had zero connection, into their coven. So far, it seemed her concerns weren't necessary.

Before Zack could respond, Sacha slid next to Zack and put an arm across his back. She gave a playful push against Sebastian's chest, forcing him to take a step back. "All right, enough with the man-bonding mushy stuff. How about we get going?"

"All right, let's do it." Zack sounded a lot more chipper than he had once they stepped into the hallway.

Isis wrapped her arms around his waist and gave him a hug. Once she stepped away, both Zack and Sacha disappeared.

Isis suddenly found both her "adopted" parents staring at her. "What? Did I do something wrong?" she asked, hoping it wasn't over her embrace of Zack.

"How are you feeling?" Sebastian's tone was filled with concern.

"I'm healed," she replied. "No more pain, no more bruises. Just one stubborn scratch on my neck, but it's no big deal." She tapped the left side of her esophagus. "Besides that, I'm all good."

"We don't mean physically." Sebastian draped his arm around the back of Isis' neck. He pulled her in close. "How are you holding up?"

Isis closed her eyes as her head melted into Sebastian's chest. A tingling of embarrassment swept through her body. "I guess I'm still a little shaky. I didn't sleep much last night. When I did, I kept seeing her in my dreams."

"Oh, poor baby." Selena ran her fingers through a lock of Isis' hair. "You know you could have come into our room if you didn't want to be alone."

"We weren't sleeping much either last night," Sebastian added.

"I know, but I figure I'm not a little kid anymore, so I dealt with it. This is the second time in my life I got beaten up and then almost set on fire. I guess I just have that kind of face, right?" Isis looked up with a grin. Neither of her parental figures laughed. Okay, maybe the joke wasn't all that amusing.

Isis took both their hands and gave them a squeeze. "I'll be okay," she said in hopes they wouldn't push the issue any further. In truth, Isis did get a couple of hours of sleep, but while lying next to Zack in his queen-sized bed. She knocked on his door around three a.m., sensing that he was awake as well. Nothing happened between them except for deep conversation, then sleep. Isis felt quite comfortable lying next to Zack while using his shoulder as a pillow. The whole time, he was a perfect gentleman. Still, best not to mention it to her overprotective parents.

"What about you, Selena?" Sebastian asked. "You've been so worried about us since we got back to the hotel, we never checked to see that you're okay."

"I almost lost both of you last night." Selena tapped Sebastian's chest. "I'm far from okay with that. But I'm glad we finally faced the threat and survived. Maybe now our futures can be our own."

"Can I ask you guys a question?" Isis said. It was time to get it off her chest.

"Anything," Selena answered.

"Valeria told me that you took me in because my connection to the power is strong and you needed me to beat her." Isis stepped away so she could look them both in the face. "Is that the truth? I don't care if it is the reason, but I'd like to know."

"It wasn't the reason," Sebastian snapped. "Not at all."

"We took you in because you needed a family," Selena explained. "Yes, it was your strong connection to the power that made us aware of you in the first place. But at the time, we had no idea you were only nine years old. You discovered your powers at such a young age, which is so uncommon, and you had no one else. So, we decided to raise you and train you properly. Once we had you, it wasn't long before we fell in love with you."

"Well, I guess I can be loveable." Isis stretched her lips into a huge smile. She looked back and forth at two faces that cared about her a great deal. She felt the same about them. She really did like their answer. "With so much going on, I never said thank you for saving my life."

"It took all of us to beat Valeria," Sebastian responded. "We all did our part, Isis, including you."

"I have to say, it was pretty clever using the 'lighter than air' spell on her when you did," Selena said with a smile. "We taught you to use it on yourself, we never thought to teach you to use it on another person. That was great thinking outside the box."

"Well, I can't take full credit, it was Zack's idea. But I don't mean now. I mean for everything. For saving me back then, for taking me in. Making me part of your family." A tear rolled down Isis' cheek. "For giving me this great life. Thank you."

Selena rubbed the back of her thumb along Isis' cheek, wiping away the tear. "That's our pleasure, sweetie." Isis leaned her head into Selena's palm. She then reached in and gave her mom a hug. Selena kissed her on the top of the head.

"To repeat myself," Sebastian added, "we all did our part, including you."

"And Luther," Isis said.

"And Luther." Sebastian's shoulders slumped. It reflected the sadness they all displayed last night while holding a candle lighting ceremony for their vampire mentor. Isis didn't feel the same sadness. Not because she wouldn't miss him—she would—but because she was certain they'd see him again. Luther, and Valeria, too.

Isis stepped back so they could both see her face. She wanted them to know that she meant what she was about to say. "Maybe it's time we did more with my training."

Husband and wife exchanged a relieved glance. "That's exactly what we were discussing this morning," Sebastian replied. "Luther was right when he said we coddled you a bit much when it came to your teachings. I take full responsibility for that."

"It was both our faults," Selena added.

"I feel it was mostly mine," Sebastian continued. "Even as you got older and more comfortable controlling the power, I still couldn't stop seeing that shell shocked little girl who, for the first week, couldn't stop shaking. I remember after a few sleepless nights, we had to put a spell on you just so your body could get the rest it needed."

"You worried the hell out of us back then, sweetie," Selena said.

"Well, I had a lot to take in." Isis grinned. "Witches, vampires...the first time we met, I thought I was about to get stepped on by a giant red dragon."

"Granted." Sebastian returned the smile. "The point is our instinct to protect you and keep you safe, even in your training, left you unprepared when the real need for your powers came about. It almost got you killed. It's time we focus on helping you reach your potential, and we're glad you're in agreement. In fact, we should get started right away."

"I'm ready!" Isis skipped ahead as Sebastian and Selena took hands and followed her down the hallway. She spun around. "Whatever you're going to teach me, can I do it on the stage? I really want to do more on the stage."

Sebastian nodded. "We'll work it all into the show."

Chapter Thirty

Zack found himself in the Galloway Theater, perhaps for the final time. It was probably just as well, since it now had a different feel. To him, it used to be the most glamorous and exciting place in the entire universe. Growing up on the stage in front of a cheering audience made him feel like the luckiest guy around. All his insecurities stayed behind, even when he had the cool kids from school in the audience. Here, Zack was the coolest high school student in the room.

This time, the entire auditorium had a different vibe. At the dressing room entrance, he could only see Isis tied to that chair after Valeria manipulated his emotions to put her in that position. The seats reminded him how Valeria hovered above them without any sort of wire or harness, just the power to destroy their lives. The stage still had drops of Bambi's blood where Valeria sucked her dry. What the theater reminded Zack of most was the man who raised him after his parents were killed in a senseless tragedy. And now, that man was gone forever, just like them.

"Oh, God!" Zack dropped to his knees and sobbed. He wanted to hold in those emotions, but he just couldn't anymore.

"Zack, talk to me." Sacha leaned next to him.

"I'm freaking out!" Zack covered his eyes so Sacha

wouldn't see him tear up.

"Yes, this I can see." He could hear the smirk in her voice. "Do you want to talk about it?"

"I don't know where to begin. Everything is insane now!" he shouted. "A couple of days ago, I learned witches and vampires are real. What else actually exists out there? Are werewolves a thing?"

"I don't know. If they are, I've never met one."

"I lived on this stage, I performed, people cheered. Life made sense. Now, my uncle is dead, and I'm going to be living with a family who has actual supernatural powers that defy everything I've ever known as a magician." Zack pulled his hand off his face and slammed it on the floor. The impact made his knuckles sting. "I'm fifteen! I'm failing algebra in high school. That's what I should be worried about, not the fate of the whole goddamned world!"

"For what it's worth," Sacha said, "I was pretty good at algebra. In fact, math was my best subject. I could tutor you while Sebastian and my sis are tutoring Isis on how to float in the air without falling on her ass."

Zack looked at Sacha with raised eyebrows. Her nonchalance on the subject confused him. "Does my tenth-grade algebra grade even matter anymore? What if Valeria finds a way to come back? What then?"

"Then we'll deal with it, but it doesn't mean we stop living while we wait." Sacha ran her fingers through Zack's blond hair. "The world hasn't changed, Zack. For you, it's just gotten a little bit bigger."

"I…I don't know what I should do."

Sacha wrapped her hands around his elbow and stood up, guiding him back to his feet. "I'm not much of an inspirational speaker, that's Sebastian's gig. But let me ask you this." Sacha took a few steps forward, taking Zack with her. She pointed to the larger than life poster above the stage. "What would *he* want you to do?"

The younger and vibrant Amazing Herb Galloway looked down and smiled on the empty theater. Zack always believed its eyes were directed at him. Of course, that was how the picture was designed, so whoever looked up at it, no matter where in the theater they stood or sat, it would always seem like the eyes were aimed their way.

"Uncle Herb always believed in seeing the bigger picture. Hell, he gave his life for it." As Zack spoke, his watery eyes never wavered from the face on the poster. "He said he wanted me to stay with you. I'm sure it was so I could help you keep the world, and all of you, safe in any way I can. That means helping you protect your identities."

"Then it sounds like we have a show to put together."

"Yes, we do," Zack said with a renewed vigor. "You know, Sacha, when it comes to pep talks, you're far more inspiring than Sebastian."

Sacha laughed. "Let's not let him hear you say that, okay? That might cause him to mope around for days."

A snort shot out of Zack's throat. He didn't want to laugh about anything, not so soon after his uncle's death. But, he could totally visualize Sebastian moping.

Zack once again looked up at his uncle's poster. Sacha draped her arm across his shoulders. "I think we should take that, too," she said. "Do you agree?"

"Definitely." Zack trotted up the stage steps, "Hey,

speaking of Sebastian, can I ask you something about him?"

"Shoot."

Sacha followed him up the steps and through the back curtain where several magic props stood beneath a shelf that had smaller props. From the shelf, Zack removed a red cloth bag attached to a wooden handle. It was called a change bag, and it was his uncle's oldest magic trick. With it, he also grabbed a twelve-inch yellow hankie.

"I really do like Isis." Zack placed the yellow hankie into the bag. "I'm pretty sure she likes me, too."

"Well, duh," Sacha replied. "I thought your question was about Sebastian."

"It is. Do you think he'll be okay with us being together like that?"

"Hmm." Sacha folded her arms and tipped her head in thought. "It's hard to say. Isis liking a boy and dating, that's brand new territory. I'd suggest taking it slow, give everyone a chance to get used to the idea."

Zack reached into the bag and pulled the hankie out. It was now blue. "And if Isis doesn't want to take it slow?"

"Oh, they may kill her, and you." Sacha took the hankie from Zack's hand and turned it over, examining both sides. She seemed genuinely impressed as she looked in the bag to realize it was empty. "I mean that figuratively, of course."

"Good to know they won't literally kill either of us."

"We hope not." Sacha threw Zack a smirk. "Besides, Sebastian shouldn't be your biggest concern."

"You mean Selena? I get the sense she's the real

leader of your coven and she just lets Sebastian think it's him."

"You're quite intuitive, Zack. That's mostly the case. But I'm referring to Isis herself."

Sacha's answer made Zack do a double take. "What do you mean?"

"Isis is a powerful witch who is still learning to keep it all under control. She's also an emotional teenage girl and our power is tied into our emotions. That's why we homeschool her, it may not be safe for her to get overly upset or excited in a building filled with thousands of people. At least not at this point in her training."

"I get it," Zack said. "High school can be real upsetting at times."

"So can dating when it gets serious."

"Right. So, take it slow and easy."

Sacha gave him a serious nod. "At least until she can wake up from a bad dream without accidentally setting the room on fire."

"Does that really happen?" Or was she messing with him in order to protect her niece?

"Well, it has happened, more than once. It's why there's a fire extinguisher next to her bed."

"Wow." If only he knew this before Isis crawled into bed with him last night and fell asleep.

Sacha followed Zack around the backstage area. He eyed the props on the shelves. They couldn't all go with him. It was hard to make the decision, especially while his thoughts were focused on other subjects. Zack suddenly stopped in his tracks and looked back at Sacha. "How many other witches and vampires are out there?"

"I've never met a vampire other than Luther," Sacha answered. "I remember we spent some time with a family of witches back when I was around four years old. My memory of them is kind of vague. Selena's memory of that time might be clearer, but I recall my mom saying they left for Western Europe where there was a village filled with people like us. Since then, we hadn't run into any others, not until Isis." She looked back at Zack with a scrunched nose and a curved smile. "Any other questions, Zack?"

"Only about a billion."

"Well, you will certainly have time to ask them all, but maybe not today—"

"What about black cats?" Zack interrupted. "I thought witches always had black cats for some reason."

"Okay, I guess today," Sacha muttered. "Like any other witch, I like black cats, but I was told at a young age that I dare never live with one or my future would become unbearable."

"Wow, who told you that? Like a psychic or another witch?"

"An allergist, Zack," Sacha replied. "I'm highly allergic to cat fur."

"Really? Witches have allergies? You can't just, like, magic an allergy away—" Zack dropped his head and chuckled. "I'm asking too many questions, aren't I?"

"Just a few too many, yeah," Sacha laughed. "I promise, now that you're living with us, you will learn everything soon enough. I'm sure you'll become an expert on all things Wiccan—"

The knob turned. Zack and Sacha's attention

diverted to the stage's side door. Apparently, they were about to receive an unexpected guest. Zack tensed as the door swung open. His body relaxed when he saw the gym tank-top on the man walking in. "Kris," Zack said with a sigh of relief.

"Zack, so you are here," he said with genuine surprise.

"Yeah, I'm collecting some of our things, we're moving them to another location," Zack replied.

"I heard they cancelled you. That really blows." Kris looked him up and down. He had confusion written all over his face. "I was in the lobby for a while signing guests up for gym sessions. I didn't see you pass by."

"Um, I did pass you. I would have said hello but you were busy. I didn't want to bother you."

"Not as busy as I would have liked." Kris sighed and shrugged. "Most of the guests were more interested in asking where they could find the buffet. And people wonder why we have an obesity problem out there."

Sacha stepped between the two and cleared her throat. "Are you going to introduce me to your friend, Zack?" She turned to Kris and held out her hand. "I'm Sacha Quinn." She looked up into his eyes.

"I'm Kris," he said, slightly flustered. "I never forget a face and I've seen yours before. Have we met?"

"I don't believe we have," she answered through wide eyes and a huge smile.

"Wait, I recognize your name, Sacha Quinn." His mouth jutted open. "You're one of The Witches of Vegas magicians, aren't you?" His head spun toward Zack. "What is she doing here?"

"I'm joining their show," Zack said. "It's been in the works for a while."

"Your uncle knows about this?" He asked with a sideways glance.

"Of course," Zack assured him. "He arranged it."

"He did?" Kris stared up at the ceiling for several moments, his eyes slanted with confusion. Zack was sure he could see the wheels turning in the trainer's head.

Finally, Kris waved a finger at Sacha and laughed. "So that's why you did your show outside the Felicity? Man, now it makes sense." His head shook back and forth. "You magicians are always playing some angle. This time, even I fell for it."

Sacha laughed as well, although hers had a nervous quiver. "Yes, that's what magicians like to do."

"Hey, do you guys need a hand?" Kris asked.

"No, thank you," Zack replied. "I think we can handle it."

"Do you ever work at the Sapphire?" Sacha asked.

"No, I train full-time here at the Felicity's gym."

"In that case, we could definitely use an extra pair of strong hands." Sacha rubbed her fingers along Kris' massive bicep. "Might as well put those huge muscles to good use, right?"

"I'd be happy to," Kris replied. "You have a van outside?"

"Nope, it's just us here." Sacha's answer made Zack's head snap her way.

"Then, how are you moving everything?" Kris asked.

"Um, the van is coming later," Zack lied.

"Oh, okay. Gotcha."

Zack led them backstage, ready to pack everything up and take both his and his uncle's favorite items to their brand new home.

Chapter Thirty-One

For Isis, the next week went by in a blur. The morning after their "vacation" began, Selena and Sacha teleported the group to the island where Herb Galloway received a private, but proper burial. The decision was made to bury him in the exact spot he gave his life to save Zack, the witches, and the world. Sebastian declared Herb a member of their coven as Sacha laid the five crystals along his grave with a spell of protection so his body could never be disturbed. Zack was then left alone at the grave to say goodbye. He stared down at the grave for several minutes, never saying a word.

Once they returned, the group allowed themselves a full week for rest and recovery. In that time, Isis and Zack grew close. He offered to teach her some simple card and sleight of hand tricks. At first, Isis was willing to learn as a way to help Zack take his mind off of his uncle's death. She found that she enjoyed learning the tricks. Impressing her family, and a few hotel guests in the lobby, without using her powers was really cool.

Once the week had passed, it was time to revamp the show. The theater closed off and changes were made. That included placing Herb's poster high up on a wall for all to see. Zack had lots of ideas to not only prevent exposure, but for showmanship. Thin wires that blended into the background were hung in strategic areas throughout the theater. Tables and boxes were outfitted with dark cloths lined with pockets ideal for hiding objects. They also added a trap door in the middle of the stage that blended into the floor. It was similar to the one in the Galloway Theater. Of course, the witches didn't need any of these modifications; they were only there to throw magicians' keen eyes off the scent.

Zack also recommended one more great idea.

A newly installed ceiling camera pointed downward at a rectangular table with a green felt covering. The table sat centered between the front row and the stage. These were set up for the show's brand new opening act.

"As you can see, there are four piles of four cards, each with an ace facing up," Zack said into the mic attached to his collar. It made his voice boom from the speakers. A dozen members of the sold-out audience surrounded him and the table from three sides. They looked on with great interest. "I will now turn the aces over on each pile, showing their plain blue backs."

Zack wore a pressed short-sleeved white shirt with a black top hat and a matching cape. The new look worked, or so Isis thought as she watched him perform from the end of the stage. She leaned herself forward against the stair railing so she could get a good look. The ends of her smile nearly touched each ear. It stunned her that Zack was willing to give up the vest. Even more surprising was his willingness to spend over four hours with her shopping for new clothes. Of course, he insisted it was a one-time deal.

"Now, let me flip each pile over. Let's see if

something amazing just happened." Zack turned the first pile of four cards: an eight of clubs, eight of spades, queen of diamonds and a six of spades. "The first ace has magically disappeared."

Isis turned her head from Zack to the overhead shot of the table on the stage's big screen. It allowed everyone in the auditorium, no matter where they sat or stood, to see Zack's amazing card manipulations. Zack flipped over a second pile of cards revealing a ten of diamonds, a four of hearts, a two of clubs, and a ten of spades. "This pile's ace has disappeared as well," Zack explained to the audience.

Isis' attention was broken when an arm crossed the back of her shoulders. "You curled the ends of your hair," Sebastian shouted so Isis could hear him over the crowd noise.

"Mom did it," she responded. "She did an awesome job, I love it."

"She used her Wiccan powers?"

"No, a curling iron. Sacha brought one into the dressing room."

"It works." Sebastian's eyes shifted toward Zack and his performance. "I have to admit, he is very good," Sebastian whispered into Isis' ear.

"And?" Isis asked through a smirk.

Sebastian let out a deep sigh. "And he was right. It was a good idea to have an opener. It warms up the crowd." Sebastian's admittance filled Isis with pride. She decided to forgo the "I told you so," although he totally deserved to hear it. It had taken several persuasive conversations before Sebastian agreed to Zack's idea of serving as an opening act.

Isis and Sebastian watched the screen, which

showed a close-up of Zack's hand flipping over a third pile. Like the first two, it had four random cards, none of which was the ace that originally sat on top of the pile. While Zack performed, Isis wrapped her arms around Sebastian's waist and pressed her head against his chest. She locked her fingers and squeezed tight. The flashback of her dad almost bleeding to death from a bullet in his chest had finally stopped invading her nightly dreams.

Zack picked up the final pile of facedown cards. "Those aces all have pointy hats, just like witches," he announced. "And, also like witches, these aces can teleport themselves." Zack flipped over the last pile of four cards and spread them across the table. They were the four aces. The audience cheered and applauded.

Isis looked up at Sebastian who was nodding his approval. "Zack asked me to dinner after the show," she said to him. "Is that okay?"

"We always go to dinner following the afternoon shows," Sebastian replied. "Of course, he can join us."

"Oh, um, I think he meant just him and me."

Sebastian's gaze dropped to Isis' face. "You mean like a brother and sister kind of thing?"

"Eww, no!" Isis' arms dropped to her side. "Definitely not like brother and sister."

"Ah, so, this is a date." Sebastian eyed Zack like a piece of art. "I guess I can deal with that. He is the kind of boy I'd want for you. He's smart, has a good heart, and he's a little bit afraid of me. A perfect combination."

Isis rolled her eyes. "He's not afraid of you."

"He should be. I could turn him to stone, and then place him in the hotel lobby as a statue."

"Please don't turn my boyfriend into a statue." Of course, she knew he was kidding. At least, she hoped he was kidding.

"Boyfriend." Sebastian's eyebrows rose. "Is it that already?"

"I think so. We haven't said it, not out loud. But..." Isis looked up at Sebastian, widening her eyes as much as she could. Her lips stretched into a smile. "Just don't turn him into a statue, okay?"

"We'll see." Sebastian raised a thumb in the air, a signal for Zack to finish his set. Zack returned the signal with a "thumbs-up" of his own.

"Okay, folks," Zack said to his audience, "my time is done. If you enjoyed what I've just shown you, then take your seats and get ready to be amazed even more. The witches are about to take the stage." Zack gathered his cards and stepped back to the audience's appreciative applause. The sound of scurrying filled the theater as the people around the table returned to their seats.

"Are you ready?" Sebastian asked Isis, who replied with a nod.

Isis grabbed his wrist before he could walk up the steps leading to the stage. "Dad, can I ask you something?"

"Of course, what's up?"

"Zack said the reason you were able to get off that island, the reason we were able to save the world, it was all because he had a phone." She looked up at Sebastian. "Is that true?"

"I suppose there is some truth to that," Sebastian answered as he motioned her to follow him up. "His phone proved very useful."

"Maybe I should have one?"

"You want a phone?" Sebastian pulled the curtain's end open. "You're a powerful witch who can access the world. You're learning to project thoughts into another person's head. What do you need a phone for?"

"Everyone my age has a phone." Isis stepped through the curtain that Sebastian held open. "If Zack's phone saved our lives, wouldn't it be a good thing if I had one, too?"

"Let's talk about it another time, okay?"

"Yeah, okay." She was pretty sure that was a huge "no."

Sebastian followed Isis through the curtain. He snatched the microphone from its stand and took his place center stage and up front. Selena and Sacha stepped on each side of him as Isis moved to her spot mid-stage behind Sebastian.

The theater went dark. The curtain opened and a spotlight hit them in the faces. The crowd cheered with anticipation. Sebastian took a step forward and spoke into the microphone. "Ladies and gentlemen, first, let's have one more hand for our opening act. He is the nephew of Las Vegas' own Amazing Herb Galloway, and, he is the baddest witch in Vegas, Zack Galloway!"

The audience applauded. Zack rolled his eyes at Isis, who flashed him a mischievous smile. She couldn't wait to see his reaction once she got Sebastian to introduce him that way. Ever the showman, Zack turned back to the audience, removed his hat and took a big bow.

"And now, ladies and gentlemen," Sebastian announced, "prepare yourselves for an experience! After a quick vacation, it is now time for the return to the stage of...THE WITCHES OF VEGAS!"

Enchanting music played as the crowd exploded in cheers. Isis stretched her arms out. Her feet left the ground as she levitated high above the stage. She no longer needed the chant to make this happen.

Time for the show to begin...

Epilogue

Three months later

The three o'clock school bell rang. Zack exited the building along with most of the other students. Normally, he'd be among the crowd moving briskly along the school's front walkway that led to the Vegas streets. That would begin his long walk back to the Sapphire Resort. There, he would meet the witches in the theater for their afternoon practice. This time, however, he let everyone else pass as he waited in front of the school's double doors. Today was a special day for a number of reasons, and not just because it was Friday.

Zack waited while much of the crowd dispersed in several directions. Finally, he saw the one person waiting for him to finish his day. Isis waved to him.

Zack met her halfway down the walkway. "I wasn't sure you'd come."

"Really? Why is that?" she asked.

"I know you don't like to venture too far from the hotel by yourself."

"Well, I have been getting out a lot more recently," Isis said through a smile.

"That is true." Zack and Isis had explored most of the strip over the last few months, usually Friday and

Saturday nights after their show. It was Zack's favorite part of each week. He enjoyed seeing Vegas through the eyes of Isis, who was experiencing all the attractions for the first time.

"Besides, today is a special occasion." Isis gave him a hug. "Happy birthday."

"Thank you." Zack threw his arms across Isis' back.

"So, how does it feel to be a whole year older than me?"

Zack laughed. "That's only for nine more weeks, then we'll be the same age again."

"Are you ready for your birthday present?"

"Sure," Zack answered, although he had no idea what to expect. As far as he could tell, she had nothing on her. "Are you going to teleport it here?"

"No, I'm going to teleport us there." Isis took each of his hands. "I've been practicing for over a month just so I could do this for you."

The curiosity was now gnawing at Zack. She had been practicing teleportation quite a bit. For a while, the family had her teleporting all over their suite and the theater. Eventually, she was teleporting from one location to the other. For the last week, her practices took place while he was in school. At the time, he felt left out, but now, Zack felt touched in finding out it was all for him.

Isis had always teleported either with one of the other witches or under their direct supervision. He looked back and forth, seeing lots of his fellow schoolmates. But no Sebastian, Selena, or Sacha.

"The family isn't here?" he asked.

"No, it's just us going. But they are monitoring

us."

"Does that mean they'll be looking in on us the entire time?"

"No, they just want to make sure I don't accidentally teleport us into a volcano or something."

Zack loosened his hands. His excitement just took a slight dip. "Try not to do that, okay?"

"Don't worry, if it doesn't work, we'll most likely just go nowhere."

"Where are we supposed to go?"

"It's a surprise."

Zack didn't like the idea of Isis teleporting them out in the open. It was, after all, his job to help the witches protect their secret and this didn't strike him as the best way to do that. Looking around, however, he noticed the other students were either heavily engaged in conversation or staring into their phones. Zack and Isis weren't on anyone's radar. Apparently, even after saving the world, he was still invisible in school. There were advantages to that.

"Let's do it," he said.

"Okay, close your eyes. I'm now going to focus on the location."

Zack shut his eyes tight. Isis took two deep breaths, then mumbled, "teleport."

Within seconds, he no longer heard engines roaring from the moving vehicles on the streets. That sound was replaced by waves splashing against a shore. The hard cement of the school's walkway now felt soft and mushy. His feet sank into what he realized had to be sand, the same sand that blew into his face. The smell of seaweed was strong enough to make his nostrils itch.

Isis turned his body around. "You can open your

eyes now."

Zack found himself back on that tiny island Valeria tried to convince them was the Other World. He was standing in front of his uncle's grave. The sun shined off the five crystals, revealing their locations within the sand.

Zack looked at Isis. "Why are we here?"

"You said you wished you could talk to your uncle again," Isis said to him as her long brown hair blew in the wind. "That's why I wanted to bring you here on your birthday, so you can."

Zack did make that wish, but he meant directly, not to the grave. He understood that was an impossible wish to fulfill. He never saw the point in talking to a corpse buried six feet under the ground. Hell, he never even spoke at his parents' graves. But, as always, Isis' heart was in the right place and she did take them all this way.

Ah, what the hell? A lot had happened since Uncle Herb's death and Zack wanted to get it all off his chest. This was as good of a way as any to do just that.

"Okay," he said, "how does this work? I just go over and start talking?"

"Stand within the crystals. Sacha's spell will let his spirit hear you, if he's listening."

"I remember Sacha saying her spell wouldn't remain while she's thousands of miles away. She also told me contacting spirits was beyond any witch's power."

"That's all true. It's symbolic." Isis placed a hand against Zack's back, giving him a slight push so he'd walk forward. "You never know, maybe he is listening. Do you want me to give you some privacy?"

"No, I think I'd feel more comfortable with you here."

Zack stepped past the crystal, then stared down at the area of sand where his uncle's body was buried. If only he knew about this beforehand, Zack could have put together what he wanted to say. Speaking off the top of his head was never his greatest strength, at least according to his uncle. Might as well start with hello.

"Hello, Uncle Herb, it's been a while." He glanced at Isis, then back to the gravesite. "I'm really sorry for that, but this isn't the easiest place to visit." Damn, this really did feel weird looking down at the sand and speaking to it. He had to remind himself that his uncle was somewhere underneath.

"My new life with the Witches of Vegas has been good. They treat me well and with respect. I help put their shows together, making sure they're not pulling any miracles that can't be explained by some concept from our craft. I also open their shows with my table magic, just like I did for us. This time, my table isn't outside in the Vegas heat. It's inside the theater. There's also no tip jar, I'm performing strictly for the magic and to entertain the audience."

"He's really good, too," Isis said.

"I really can't complain, they treat me as one of their own," Zack continued. "Sebastian says he can't think of me as a son, but only because I'm dating his daughter. I guess that's understandable. Both he and Selena did say they look forward to someday calling me their son-in-law." Zack peeked at Isis. "I look forward to that, as well."

Isis' lips stretched into a huge smile. Zack reached for her hand and gave it a squeeze. He gave her a gentle yank so she'd stand at his side. Isis obliged.

Zack turned back to the grave. "My only complaint is that they make me attend school every single day. It means I don't get to open for their afternoon weekday shows." He let out a chuckle. "I'm not thrilled about that, but I'm sure you would approve."

"Well, it was his final wish," Isis pointed out while placing a hand against his chest.

Zack nodded his understanding. "School is actually going well for once. I'm not hanging out with anyone there, but it's not like I did before, right? It's been a lot easier now that Glen no longer gives me a hard time. A month walking around with two black eyes and his nose bandaged humbled the big guy a little bit. I am doing better in my classes, too. It turns out Sacha is very good at math. She's been tutoring me in algebra and brought me up to a B average."

Isis' eyebrows rose. "B?" she asked.

Zack sighed. "Okay, it's more of a C but I'm close to a B and it's still better than the D's and F's I used to get in math, right?"

"Ooh, don't forget your other news!" Isis said.

"Yeah, yeah, the other news." Zack looked up and shook his head back and forth. "They've convinced me to participate in an extracurricular activity. I'll be performing magic in the upcoming school talent show. Honestly, I don't see the point. Sebastian agrees with me, but Selena thinks it would be good for my social development or whatever."

"It's going to be awesome," Isis shouted. "We'll all be there to see your performance."

"No pressure, right?" Zack pulled on his shirt collar. "Since I agreed to do this, I plan on using some of your old tricks as a tribute to you, The Amazing Herb Galloway."

Zack let his hand slip from Isis'. He then dropped to his knees and leaned his palms against the sand. "I want you to know I miss you, Uncle Herb, and I always will. But the sacrifice you made keeps the world spinning and it made everything just a bit safer. You saved us all, because that's what was best for the bigger picture."

He peered back and forth at the clear ocean water hitting the shore all around him. "And for what it's worth, you do have the coolest burial site on the entire planet." Zack stood up. His gaze never wavered from the area of sand that covered his uncle's body. "Goodbye, Uncle Herb. I'll visit again, I promise."

As both Isis and Zack turned from the grave, the wind picked up. His hair ruffled from the breeze. Isis quickly covered her head with her hands. In the whisper of the wind, a voice echoed in Zack's ears. It said, "Happy birthday."

The wind suddenly died down. Zack spun back to the grave. His head shifted to Isis. Sebastian had started her lessons on how to create illusions. It wasn't a power she excelled at yet, but she could have created the voice.

"Was that you?" he asked her.

"Was what me?" Isis replied.

"You didn't hear the voice?" Zack exclaimed.

Isis' face scrunched. "What voice?"

Could he have imagined it? He really wanted to hear Uncle Herb speak to him one last time, so it was possible his brain played a trick on him. It could have also been the effect of the enchanted crystals. The witches were no longer controlling them, not from two thousand miles away, but could there have been remnants of their power that remained behind? There was still so much about his new family's world Zack didn't understand.

He had no idea what just happened, or if it really did happen, but the message Zack received was clear. The emotion he felt when he heard the voice sent a distinct message. Uncle Herb was proud of him.

"We should get back," Isis said. "I told my folks that we'd be on time for dinner. They ordered a chocolate fudge cake to celebrate your birthday."

"The one from the restaurant?" Zack's mouth popped open when Isis nodded. "That's my favorite. How'd they know?"

Isis wrapped her arms around his waist. "Well, we are very powerful witches. We have ways of finding out anything."

Zack paused. A chill suddenly ran down his back. "They don't read my mind, do they? Selena promised none of you would ever do that."

Isis' eyes rolled. "You order a slice every time we eat there, genius." Her lips formed a smirk. "Even the waiters know it's your favorite."

"Right. Gotcha." Great, now he felt like a total idiot.

At least his irrational panic once again brought out Isis' radiant smile. Zack loved that smile, especially when it was aimed at him. In fact, there was very little he didn't like about her. Amazing that a witch was the most normal girl Zack had ever known.

Isis' head popped up. The smile became replaced with concern. "Oh, hey, when they bring out the cake, you need to act surprised. I wasn't supposed to tell you about it."

"Why did you?"

"Because we said we'd always be honest with each other. I'm keeping that promise." Isis looked up into his face. "Seriously, you really need to look surprised."

Zack scrunched his nose, widened his eyes as much as he could and stretched his mouth wide. He threw his hands over his chest, feigning cardiac arrest.

Isis hunched over, giggling.

"What, too much?" he asked through a cheesy grin.

"Yeah, way too much," Isis laughed.

"Hey," Zack said, "thanks for taking me here. I think I needed that conversation a lot more than I realized."

"I know, and I'm glad." Isis wrapped her fingers against the back of Zack's neck. "One more thing before we leave."

"What's that?"

She leaned in and kissed him. Their lips pressed together for several seconds as the sounds of the ocean surrounded them. The last time they shared such a long and passionate kiss they were under Valeria's love spell. This time, the passion didn't come from a love spell, well, at least not one conjured by a witch.

Isis pulled her head back. They stared deeply into each other's eyes. "I'm betting we shouldn't tell them about this either, right?" Zack asked.

"I think they've figured us out. But maybe we shouldn't bring it up." Isis' head dipped downward. Her cheeks had turned red. "At least for now."

"Okay. Are you ready to take us back?"

"Yeah, that's a good idea." Isis took Zack by the

hands and leaned her body against his. Her eyes closed as she took a deep breath. "Go back," she chanted.

The beach blurred, then faded away.

A word about the author...

Mark Rosendorf is a high school guidance counselor in the New York City Department of Education's Special Education district. He is also a former professional magician. Mark shares his knowledge of magic with his students as part of the school's Performing Arts program. He uses stage magic to help teach teamwork and build confidence in his students.

Mark is also credited with published novels in various genres including The Rasner Effect series. He eventually decided on an early retirement from writing. When asked why, Mark's usual answer was because he lost his favorite pen.

Then, one night, at two a.m., a new and unique story shot into his brain like a lightning bolt, screaming for him to write it. Suddenly, despite the decision to never write again, Mark found himself spending several nights taking notes on the characters and their stories. That is how *The Witches of Vegas* was born and is now on these pages.

This is Mark's first young adult novel.

Isis, Zack, and the Witches of Vegas' adventures will continue…

http://markrosendorf.com

Thank you for purchasing
this publication of The Wild Rose Press, Inc.

For questions or more information
contact us at
info@thewildrosepress.com.

The Wild Rose Press, Inc.
www.thewildrosepress.com